IT'S MORE THAN JUST MILES FROM THE BRONX TO HOLLYWOOD . . .

"We're not accusing you of anything, you understand," the Chicano sergeant explained.

Lowenkopf understood. "I didn't kill him."

The blond sergeant's contempt was boundless.

"That's rich. A tin sergeant shows up from the East and we're supposed to take his word over a director's. Do you know what being a feature-film director means in this town?"

"Diplomatic immunity?"

Acclaim for Richard Fliegel's Allerton Avenue mysteries:

The Art of Death

"The pace is rapid, the premise and characters amusing, and the backdrop . . . colorful. . . . A witty and unconventional plot."

—*Publishers Weekly*

and

The Organ-Grinder's Monkey

Available from POCKET BOOKS

Books by Richard Fliegel

The Art of Death
The Next to Die
The Organ-Grinder's Monkey

Published by POCKET BOOKS

Most Pocket Books are available at special quantity discounts for bulk purchases for sales promotions, premiums or fund raising. Special books or book excerpts can also be created to fit specific needs.

For details write the office of the Vice President of Special Markets, Pocket Books, 1230 Avenue of the Americas, New York, New York 10020.

THE NEXT TO DIE

Richard Fliegel

POCKET BOOKS

New York   London   Toronto   Sydney   Tokyo

POCKET BOOKS, a division of Simon & Schuster Inc.
1230 Avenue of the Americas, New York, NY 10020

ISBN 0-671-68849-9

First Pocket Books printing November 1989

10 9 8 7 6 5 4 3 2 1

for Lois

1

Afterwards, when he thought about it, Shelly Lowenkopf always remembered Nino's Deli on White Plains Road. The door was glass with a wooden frame and stenciled letters peeling off—it rattled with every subway car lurching by on the elevated tracks overhead. When he opened it, three cowbells clunked dully together, the salty smell of mozzarella and salami rose to greet him, and the radiator clattered, fogging the door and windows.

Outside, brown leather gloves brushed snow from the grille of his Volkswagen squareback and groped under the hood for the latch.

Shelly had stopped as usual to buy lunch on his way to the precinct house. As the girl behind the counter slid the fat sausage from its freezer display case, sliced it, weighed it, and wrapped it in white paper, a man in a fur coat elbowed his hip. "The provolone looks fresh. Gimme a good thick slice."

Lowenkopf was waiting for a Rheingold. His glasses steamed slowly from the wire rims towards the center. The girl glanced at him and unwrapped the provolone.

The man in fur admired his reflection in Lowenkopf's glasses. He leaned forward. "Nino's got the freshest cheese, and the cheesiest counter girls."

Lowenkopf hated men who pushed their way to the front of lines and expected to have their jokes appreciated there. He longed to punch his face. Or arrest him. "She's not so bad," Lowenkopf said.

Outside, the hood of his VW was forced open. Snow struck the engine block and melted. A rusty pair of snippers clipped the cable binding battery to starter, and a guaranteed Delco was hoisted from Lowenkopf's car.

The girl spun a can of Rheingold across the counter, her eyes glued to the man in fur, who winked at her. She blew him a kiss, which he accepted with the cheese as his due, leering as he exited. Lowenkopf stuffed the sandwich and beer into his briefcase, paid Nino with a fiver, and walked out into the crisp cold.

The briefcase, brown alligator leather initialed "S.L." beneath the handle, was empty except for his lunch. It had been a gift from his sister Isabelle and he carried it everywhere. As he crunched through the dingy snow at the curbside, he saw the kid in a red flannel shirt leaning against the open hood of his Volkswagen with a battery under one arm.

The kid tugged at his glove and folded up a cuff of white-rabbit-fur lining. What the hell was he waiting for? The kid spotted Lowenkopf's black rubbers over black shoes, crouched behind the parked cars, and then loped off down the street. Shouting "Stop! Police!" Lowenkopf started after him. Dropping his briefcase on the curb, he tugged his .45 from its waistband holster and fired into the air just as the boy slipped through a breach in the fence of the Housing Authority playground.

Lowenkopf followed grimly, placing each foot carefully on the smooth ice. Two winters before, Greeley had broken his hip on ice. Lowenkopf remembered his partner's painful recovery and now watched his own flat footsteps. By the time his hand felt the brick playground house, the red shirt had passed the main gate and rounded the corner, disappearing into the Projects.

Doggedly Lowenkopf went in after him. The sidewalk divided into two arcs of wide, flat steps which climbed a frozen hill; the snow to the right was unbroken and Lowenkopf took the left fork in bounds, until it ended in a small triangle of green wooden benches and a flagpole. Two figures in jeans and peacoats untangled as he landed ungracefully beside them, and a toddler in crimson snowpants sat down heavily on the concrete flagpole pedestal. Lowenkopf squeezed his foot into the link fence and rested his knees on the crossbar. The red shirt backed into an apartment building across a stretch of snow broken by frozen brown earth.

There were two exits he would have to watch—the front lobby and a side door that emptied the back stairs into the street. He wedged the side door shut with a piece of railing chain and entered the lobby. Two overhead bulbs were out and the elevator light glowed dimly red. He smelled onions. An old man with a brilliant shock of white hair waited for the elevator. Lowenkopf opened the door to the front stairwell and crept up the first flight. On the second floor he slammed the staircase door and rattled the knob, counted to four, and then ran to the back stairs, looking down the first flight at his side-door trap. No one was in it, but Lowenkopf heard the hum-and-dragging-chain of the descending elevator. He pushed the button and caught the car—empty. Wedging a matchbook cover into the Hold button, he returned to the front staircase and commenced climbing.

On the third floor, a woman with an empty plastic garbage pail spotted his gun and ducked into the compactor room. He checked the back stairs. A soft patter shuffled up from below. Pressed against a wall between the third and fourth floors, Lowenkopf held his breath. The old man from the lobby turned the corner and stopped short, staring in the muzzle of the .45.

Calmly he set down his shopping bag and put his hands behind his head. His hair was pure white and shining—waxed. When he spoke, his voice echoed in the stairwell. "What is this, huh? A stickup?"

Lowenkopf lowered his gun and showed his badge. "Police."

The old man registered no surprise. "The manager's out again. One day she'll find me in the stairs, dead from a heart attack. *Then* she'll fix this crummy elevator." He hoisted his shopping bag.

Lowenkopf touched his arm. "There's a thief upstairs."

The old man listened for a moment, then continued to climb. "He must be on the roof already, trying to get across to the next building. They're connected on top."

Lowenkopf sprang up the last three flights. The black tar rooftop was covered with snow, melted where the heat of the building had warped it a mottled brown. Icicles hung from a ledge that ran completely around and connected to the roof of the adjoining building. There was a small brick vestibule on the next roof, from which he heard a thud of leather on steel. Making a wide circle, he saw the red flannel shirt back away from the jammed vestibule door to the brink of the roof.

A complexion red with cold beneath a hairline the color of oats peered up at him. The face looked crooked, the left lid slanted over the left eye. Only the right eye widened as the lips curled back to reveal badly yellowed teeth. But no sound emerged.

"Set the battery on the ledge and hold out your hands," Lowenkopf wheezed as his own left hand groped for the wire cuffs in his pants pocket. His face was stinging from the cold. He wished Greeley were there. With an exaggerated gesture, the kid in the flannel shirt cleared the snow from a spot on the ledge, set the Delco down, and plopped down beside it. Then he swung his legs over the edge and sneered.

"Let's not do anything dramatic here—" Lowenkopf began.

The red shirt waved bye-bye.

"For crying out loud"—Shelly lowered his gun—"it's just a lousy battery!"

Smiling, the kid slid off. Lowenkopf heard a scrape and a clang and ran to the edge. A Chinese puzzle box of fire escapes dropped to the ground six stories below, where the red shirt lay sprawled on the pavement. Two peacoats behind a stroller stared up at him in horror, while the toddler riding before them scrutinized the spectacle on the ground. The snow beside the body slowly browned. Windows squeaked open; pale faces over print housedresses and undershirts twisted up at the roof. Lowenkopf gingerly lifted his battery and retreated from the ledge. He kicked the hinges on the door of the brick vestibule as he passed, and it came unstuck.

He called in to the precinct house from Nino's. The curb in front of the deli was empty. His briefcase was gone.

Lowenkopf was the kind of cop who had come to define himself in terms of his profession. He lived and ate alone and fell asleep in front of the TV. He called his pledges in to telethons near the end of the first hour, and responded to the nightly news with righteous indignation. His own sins— forgotten birthdays, unreturned calls—lengthened in his conscience as their circumstances retreated. He knew some- day he would have to answer to his son Thom for the life he had lived and he enjoyed imagining that encounter. He did what he should have done, but no one seemed to care— except his ex-wife, Ruth, who noticed and complained. He had always insisted she visit her mother twice a year, though that hale old widow had been bitterly disappointed by her daughter's marriage and frequently told her so. It was from just such a visit that Ruth failed one day to return to him. He wanted to treat people as they should be treated, to do the right thing. What that was grew daily more obscure.

His courage always rose to the occasion. He had faced down a psychopath waving a shotgun in an elevator, but handed over a quarter each time his windshield was washed by a kid at the Willis Avenue Bridge. He donated blood every year in case Thom ever needed some, though the sight of a needle made him queasy. The catnap afterwards, with a wad of cotton pressed in the crook of his arm, was the sweetest sleep he knew. He had a medal and a sergeant's badge to show for thirteen years on the force. The medal had been the high point of his career, awarded in a ceremony at the mayor's office six years earlier. The low point he expected any moment as he sat in Madagascar's glass-walled office.

Captain Madagascar was the kind of cop who knew a round peg would fit into a square hole if you pushed hard enough. Now he adjusted the cushion on the seat of his wooden chair and eyed Lowenkopf as the roundest peg in his precinct.

"Of course we appreciate the position you were in." The captain began as if the subject had already been broached which of course it hadn't. Madagascar's summons had greeted Lowenkopf on his arrival that morning at the Allerton Avenue police station in the Bronx, where he now sat on a wobbly chair while the Captain poured himself a cup of Spanish Fly tea and resettled his red velvet cushion. "There he was with the Delco in his hands in front of your car. The logic was unavoidable. But perhaps you can tell me, Sergeant, why anyone would jump off a roof rather than face arrest for the theft of a twenty-dollar item?"

"That battery cost me sixty-five, sir."

"Really? I wouldn't think you'd sink that kind of money in that wreck. Volkswagen, isn't it? Sixty-five dollars, then. Still no reason to jump, is it?"

"He might have been aiming for the fire escape and missed, Captain."

"He might have. But we don't know that, do we?"

"We don't know much, sir. Not even his name. He wasn't carrying a wallet and we have no record of his fingerprints."

"A first offender. Do we have a photograph?"

"It's not a pretty sight, sir. His face hit the pavement when he landed. All we've got is an I.D. bracelet with the name Waldo on it."

"Waldo? That's all?"

"Just Waldo, sir."

"His family will have to find out the hard way, then."

"I don't know any other way, Captain."

Madagascar did not look happy. Lowenkopf knew he liked neatness in a case above all, claiming he could smell a messy one anywhere in his precinct. "It's not that we doubt you, Sergeant. It's just that the boy is dead. A case like this always raises some unpleasantness in the neighborhood, if the death isn't seen as strictly necessary in the line of duty."

"It *was* unavoidable, sir."

"I'm sure it was, Sergeant, but it doesn't *look* that way. It would help, for example, to have your story corroborated by a partner."

This was more than an example, Lowenkopf knew, but he played it straight. "I was on my way to work, Captain."

Madagascar raised a massive hand. "I know. Where is Greeley now?"

Lowenkopf pointed through the glass to where his partner's blond head hunched over a tiny mirror on his desk.

Greeley was gluing sideburns onto his smooth, pale cheeks. His hair was not in its usual neat part, but stood up from his head each time the detective mussed it with his hands. Greeley's vest and jacket lay folded neatly over the back of his chair. His top button was open, and his tie hung down crookedly. Lowenkopf and Madagascar watched him unbutton his sleeves and squeeze his cuffs to crush them before rolling them carefully and unevenly towards his elbows.

"Looks like he's going out on the street, sir."

Madagascar rapped his knuckles on the glass to catch Greeley's eye, and, with a wiggle of finger, invited him inside. Before Greeley reached the office, Madagascar murmured, "What the hell are you two working on now?"

"The Williamsbridge case, Captain. Greeley's after a phoney mohel who's been cutting up the neighborhood."

"What the fuck's a 'mohel'?"

"A ritual circumciser."

"You mean a guy who cuts . . . ?"

"That's right. Everything's been coming out crooked."

The Captain grimaced.

Greeley entered with a slight nod at Lowenkopf and a brief apologetic bow to his superior. "Forgive my appearance, sir. Undercover, you know."

"Quite," said Madagascar. "Sit down."

Greeley sat and crossed his legs expertly. The brisk crease of his Brooks Brothers trousers had been crushed by his shoes. The captain paused in respect for the commitment such a sacrifice implied. He tugged at the sleeve of his own blue serge and even Lowenkopf smoothed his green corduroy lapel.

"Homer," Madagascar began, standing, pulling his pant legs free of his thighs, and resettling his cushion, "your partner here tells me you're hot on an undercover trail. Do you think you could spare him from that case for a couple of days?"

Greeley glanced at Shelly encouragingly. "If necessary, sir."

"Good. I'll get you some reliable backup." Madagascar twisted around. "What else do you have on the burner, Lowenkopf?"

"The Keppler trial is coming up, sir."

"Right. We'll need your testimony there. It does seem more important to put drug dealers behind bars than to chase stolen batteries, doesn't it? Of course, this was your own battery. But you're not in business for yourself, are you, Sergeant?"

"No, sir."

"It might be better if we kept you away from the Projects for a while. That episode on the roof will cling to you like dogshit. We can't afford a screw-up like that with Keppler."

"No way, Captain. I've got Keppler cold. I was under the table when he made the deal. I watched him come in and I've got every word he said on tape. I could've played checkers with the pattern on his socks."

Lowenkopf's passion was matched by Greeley's reserve, which seemed to deepen as Madagascar addressed him. "And where were you?"

"Getting a haircut, sir."

Lowenkopf was on his feet. "It wasn't a planned stakeout, Captain. The opportunity sort of arose on the spot. It was either climb under the tablecloth or miss the whole thing."

Madagascar harrumphed. He was a square-shaped man whose head might have been severed from a larger slab of granite, his face creased in the Ice Age. A precise brown mustache strained to fill the expanse between a narrow mouth and a nose that started straight but ended in a bulb. Only his eyes were exceptional, small and awkward most of the time, but when they looked up, all brown iris. They looked up at Shelly now. "I don't like that way of working, Sergeant. Hiding under the table. On a hunch."

"There wasn't a moment to lose, sir."

"Jumping to conclusions. Playing fast and loose."

"But I got him, sir. We got him."

"See that you do. I don't like my men working alone. You should talk things over with a partner you can trust before risking your life. Now you have no one to corroborate your story."

Lowenkopf found his seat. "No, Captain, we're covered on that. If my testimony isn't good enough, we've got Billy Ringo, one of the two runners Keppler used regularly, to back me up."

Greeley leaned forward. "I thought you had *both* runners."

Lowenkopf shrugged. "Teddie Pepper backed out. He's got no record, so I didn't have much to use against him. But Billy's safe in Riverdale, and he knows enough about Keppler to put him away even without my testimony. You're going to enjoy it this time, sir, believe me."

"Last time," Madagascar reminded him sourly, "your witness rolled over and played dead."

"This time *I'm* the witness. Look, Captain, I know I've messed up a little with the roof-jumper, but I'd like a chance to make good. It won't happen again."

"I'm going to make sure it doesn't," Madagascar said darkly. "That's why I called Homer in." He lifted a sheaf from the neat piles of paper on his desk. "You were involved in the Holzman arrest last year, weren't you, Lowenkopf?"

"Indirectly, sir. It was really Greeley's case."

"But you had something to do with it?"

"He did, sir," Greeley confirmed. "He was in at the very end."

"Good. The mayor's office has asked for a detective associated with the Holzman case to consult with a film company making a movie about it. They'll be shooting the outdoor scenes in New York, and the Mayor"—he drawled the title—"is anxious to accommodate them." The mayor, next to Lowenkopf, was Madagascar's least favorite public servant. He dropped the sheaf of paper in Lowenkopf's lap and turned his back. "Congratulations, Sergeant. You're leaving for Hollywood today."

Lowenkopf shook his head. "I've got to find out what happened on that rooftop, sir. Why not send Homer? Holzman was his bust."

"Because I have no fuckin' reason to get Greeley out of town for the weekend. No one has fallen off a roof with Greeley's fuckin' battery in his arms. You couldn't spare the time for a trip right now in any case, could you, Homer?"

Greeley spoke sincerely. "No, sir."

"I suspected not. But your schedule is less pressing, is it not, Lowenkopf? And that sorry incident this morning signed your name to the airline ticket."

"I'll go under protest, sir."

"Good. We'll see you next week."

Lowenkopf stood, but the vague wave with which Madagascar customarily dismissed him did not come. He glanced at Greeley, still erect in his seat. "Is there anything else, sir?"

"Just one thing, Lowenkopf. I spoke to the M.E. briefly when the body came in from the Housing Projects. He described marks on the throat that suggested the boy might have been choked before his . . . descent. I don't suppose you have any idea how they got there, do you?"

"I didn't see any marks."

"It will come out at the inquest, no doubt. We'll see you then. And, Sergeant—there's a lot of injustice on the west coast. Don't try to set it all straight."

2

Whenever Lowenkopf went to Pelham to see his ex-wife, he parked his Volkswagen around the corner from the house and walked back beneath the trees on the opposite side of the street. Ruth's new husband Clem had asked him, in the nicest possible way, not to park his old heap in front of their manicured lawn, while Ruth, grown suddenly obedient to her husband's wishes, had looked on and said nothing. It was then that Lowenkopf decided he had made the right move in allowing her to divorce him four years before.

The house was exactly the sort Ruth had always wanted. She had insisted upon it, in fact, though it had strained their finances painfully and lent its weight to the final rupture of their marriage. Within weeks of the divorce, Ruth found someone who could afford to keep her as she felt she deserved and moved him in to pick up the mortgage payments. Now, as Lowenkopf strolled beneath the twiggy branches, he at least had the consolation that the driveway from which he was excluded was no longer his own.

He stopped a few houses short of Ruth's and watched his son Thom play with a wet stick in a pile of snow at the edge of the driveway. Thom stood the stick upright, squeezed the snow tight at its base, and bombarded it with snowballs too loosely packed to hold their shape in the air. The stick withstood an avalanche rather than a bombing, and when the powder settled, still stood, shaky but upright. Thom walked over to it and admired its determination. Lowenkopf felt something warm stir inside him. This boy, he thought, is why I do what I do—for him I'll make the world as it should be. Thom raised one red boot and kicked the stick spitefully, stamping it into the snow. Then he went into the house.

As usual, Ruth was caustic when Lowenkopf rang the bell. "What the hell are you doing here? It's only Thursday, isn't it?" She was tastefully dressed for a stroll through the African bush, with long shorts and a sleeveless blouse that must have looked better on the mannequin. The pout in her lower lip over the years had gained control of her face below the nose and was pulling at her neck and eyes.

"It's Friday, Ruth. The Captain's sending me away for a few days. I just came to tell Thom I won't be able to make it this weekend."

"That'll come as a shock."

He still didn't like her as a blonde. Her figure was growing more and more pearish, but her eyes were still crinkly, steel blue. "Where's old Clem?"

"He's at work, where every man with a normal job is in the middle of the afternoon."

"Look, I've got a right to hug my son good-bye before I get on a plane that might not land three thousand miles away."

"Oh, nothing's going to happen to you." There was a note of old disappointment in her voice as she closed the door in his face.

Lowenkopf noticed his wedding band on his left hand as he rang the bell again. He told himself the ring was to keep unwanted attentions from interfering with his work, but here with Ruth and Thom he was most aware of its weight. They were still a family of sorts, though an odd one, he told himself as he rang and waited and rang again. When the door opened, Thom stood on the other side and Lowenkopf was as usual at a loss for where to begin.

He knew how he wanted to appear to his son: as a man

who knew the underside of life, who had rubbed his nose on the grizzled cheek of evil and had returned for the love such courage deserved. At the same time he was acutely aware of another impression he might give: of a man desperate for his son's approval, whose battle against injustice might seem silly to a boy whose life experience ended with the tree-lined blocks of his peaceful suburban neighborhood. Thom never *seemed* to find him silly, yet a doubt always lodged in Lowenkopf's chest whenever he said, "Hello, son."

"Hi," said Thom. He had big eyes that watched his father, waiting for something Lowenkopf knew he could never deliver.

"I'm not going to be able to make it tomorrow. I've got to fly to the Coast. An important case." Why did he try so hard to impress the boy?

Thom stuck his boot in the crack of the door. "That's okay."

In the living room behind his son, the TV was on. Lowenkopf realized he had interrupted him—just as any of his visits interrupted the boy's life. From the kitchen Ruth called, "If your father's still there, tell him you've got chores to do. Clem'll be home any minute."

Thom looked up, but before he could speak, Lowenkopf said, "I'll bring you back something." He stepped aside and the boy closed the door behind him.

Lowenkopf snapped the last leaf from a sculptured bush along the path from the door. One of Thom's roller skates lay rusting in a pool of ice water at the edge of the garage door. He picked it up and placed it upright in the driveway. He opened the mailbox at the curb, found a letter addressed to him marked FINAL NOTICE with a bank's logo in the upper-left corner and stuffed it into the pocket of his overcoat. Then he got into his car and drove to his apartment to pack.

Throwing his suitcase on the bed, he worked from the ground up. Five pairs of black ankle socks, two with holes beginning at the heels. Four pairs of boxer shorts, in blue, beige, green, and white with small red lions. Three sleeveless undershirts. Three cotton long-sleeved shirts. A woolly blue tie with a square tip. Charcoal slacks folded in half and a blue wool blazer lined in grape. What did they wear in

California this time of year? He found an old cardigan, gray with a red stripe across the elbow, and draped it across the blazer. A pair of swimming trunks wrapped in a towel slid in along the side. His black lizard belt found a place beneath the handle, and a toothbrush and razor in a Baggie fit in next to the belt. A pen and notepad? They had paper in Los Angeles. He took his gun from his holster and slipped it inside the blazer, zipped up the suitcase, and shook it twice.

The file on the Holzman case was on top of his dresser. Where was his briefcase? His jaw tightened as he remembered. The battery he understood, or the thirty dollars it could be sold for. But the briefcase was useless to anyone but himself, for whom it had so much value. The pointlessness of the theft, the random personal cruelty, gripped his stomach and clenched his teeth. Or it could have been anxiety about flying. There was a honk from downstairs—he closed the bathroom window, checked the gas stove, and went down.

Isabelle dropped him at the airport on her way to work. She had been hired as a night manager, but usually showed up at her coffee shop two or three hours early. She was a careful driver and preferred not to talk as she drove. Beside her on the plastic seat Lowenkopf read the numbered terminal signs at JFK. In the mirror outside the passenger door he examined his teeth, tilted it up and adjusted his glasses and wiry hair, coiled around the edges of his ears.

"Put the mirror back and watch the signs," his sister snapped.

She spared just enough time to drop him outside the terminal below the Departures sign. He kissed her on the cheek as she sat stiffly in the car. "I'm putting the insurance in your name, Izzy."

"I don't want the money." She turned away her cheek.

"You won't get it. Insurance companies never back a losing proposition, don't you know? If everyone on the plane buys a policy, it's guaranteed to stay in the air."

She didn't laugh.

"I never buy insurance," a florid man in a houndstooth suit informed Lowenkopf companionably as they waited for their boarding passes. "If I go, I want my wife to miss me as much as possible. She's not getting any benefits from me to spend in Acapulco with the milkman."

Lowenkopf grunted unencouragingly.

"I'll bet you don't fly much." The man gestured with his chin at the insurance card protruding from Lowenkopf's jacket pocket. "New fliers are the only ones who spring for that malarkey. That's how the companies make their money. Did you see that wreck in Louisville last week? Same kinda plane we're flying, too."

Lowenkopf requested a window seat but quickly regretted it. After takeoff his view disappeared behind clouds, while a stocky woman in a flowered dress locked him off the aisle. She tucked herself in with a blanket from the overhead storage compartment and commenced turning solitaires on a tray that folded down from the back of the seat in front of her. Lowenkopf closed his eyes but could only escape the snap of her cards by renting a pair of earphones. The movie on Channel One, a madcap police farce, proved less comical than watching his fellow passengers, so he switched to Coltrane and turned to the other seats. Across the aisle, two girls in plaid skirts gaped at the screen, its flickering light reflected on their chewing cheeks. An old man beside them watched without earphones, now and then laughing and poking his dozing wife's knees. With each poke she startled in her sleep. Behind her, a slender, feminine man snapped on his overhead light and unfolded a newspaper from a brown alligator-skin briefcase which lay open on his lap.

Lowenkopf strained to read the initials on the leather by the handle, but the woman in the flowered dress had fallen asleep on his arm. He raised and lowered the back of her seat to wake her, but she merely stirred in place, crossing her hammy thighs, blockading him off from the aisle. He couldn't get out without moving her leg. Her skirt crept up so the tip of her girdle showed gray. He was trapped—but so was the feminine man, thirty thousand feet above Milwaukee. Lowenkopf stretched in resignation and closed his eyes.

When he opened them, Los Angeles lay below like a picnic blanket spread with dots and bunches of colored lights. His watch showed nine o'clock—six, California time. The cabin was bright. The movie screen was hooked in its sleeve, the No Smoking signs were blinking, and the slender man was gone. Lowenkopf shot up in his seat. The fat woman had also disappeared. He stuck his head through the curtain that separated the first-class cabin from the rest of the plane, but a stewardess chased him out. He made his way down the narrow aisle to the rear of the plane, where five lavatory doors in a semicircle described themselves as Occupied. He resolved to wait them out. A Japanese businessman exited the first door and pushed his way back to his seat. The woman in the flowered dress was next; she glared at him stonily as she squeezed past. A stewardess stepped out of the third door. An adolescent boy the fourth. Lowenkopf planted his feet resolutely in front of the last door and stood with his arms on his hips. Greeley, he knew, would have looked magnificent in that stance. He felt silly. Two girls in school uniforms opened the door, drew back inside, and slipped by with wary eyes on Lowenkopf.

The steward who led him back to his seat didn't care if he was a police officer—the landing signs were flashing. The slender man's seat remained empty. Once the plane touched down, Lowenkopf pushed through the line recovering hats and umbrellas and was the third man off the aircraft, waiting at the rail as all of the people he had jostled eyed him vengefully on their way to the baggage-claim area. The crew disembarked last. The captain carried a flight bag emblazoned with the airline's logo, his copilot bore a satchel with a Gucci stripe, and a stewardess trailing behind them swung an alligator briefcase initialed near the handle "S.L."

The hand belonged to the stewardess who had emerged from the third lavatory door. She walked a little away from the others with a firm, flat step. If the slender man had seemed feminine, this stewardess was suspiciously masculine in her gait, hips, and calves. Lowenkopf noticed her chunky calves only after she had crossed half the long hallway to the terminal exit. The muscles in her shoulders jumped as she turned her head, met his ogle, and ran. As she disappeared behind a line of businessmen who closed ranks to watch her, Lowenkopf began to run, shouting.

Carla Hollie waited in the terminal lobby holding a hand-lettered sign in front of her, inspecting the faces of all the men hurrying from the arrival gates. She wore a blue

T-shirt with a deep scooped neck and Levi's. Every now and then one of the fortyish men would look her straight in the eye and head right for her, and not until he roguishly said, "Hello, Shelly," did she know enough to snub him. Where was he? A man with a florid face caught her eye, waving. "Hiya, Shell," he said. Her eyes, full of disdain, bore down on him. He smiled and touched his hat.

After all, she wasn't *that* pretty—her face was too pointy at the chin. She reread the lettered sign, wondered if there wasn't an E between the two L's and the Y, and waited for the mysterious Shelly Lowenkopf. The crowd of arriving passengers thinned and petered out. A captain and a bevy of stewardesses passed by. Carla raised her sign for the last time and was turning to leave when another man approached her, sprinting.

"I am not Shelly Lowenkopf," she insisted before he could work the line.

The man struggled to catch his breath. "That's all right. I am. Did you see a stewardess go by with chunky thighs and a briefcase?"

"I don't usually notice their legs."

"Right. Where did the others go? The stewardesses who just passed by?"

"In that door. But it's for authorized personnel only—"

He disappeared behind the door, which swung easily after him. An airport security guard posted at the metal detector bellowed and followed him. Carla hesitated, then went in after both of them. Inside was a lounge full of pilots with their jackets off and stewardesses who scowled inhospitably through a haze of cigarette smoke as Carla interrupted their dice game. The security guard blocked Lowenkopf's view and pointed at the door. Carla grabbed Lowenkopf's hand and pulled him out of the lounge. "Let's go find your luggage," she said. "Your stewardess is on her own time."

She dragged him towards the baggage claim. The security guard eyed them sourly. Suddenly Lowenkopf stopped short, as a pair of chunky calves disappeared behind the closing door of the ladies' washroom.

Breaking the grip of Carla's fingers, he went in after the calves. Carla was right behind him and Security right behind her. There was no one at the sinks, and the first two stalls were open. When Carla entered, she found Lowenkopf crouched down, peering under the third, which was occupied. She saw a pair of the airline's low-heeled blue shoes with pantyhose bagging around the ankles above them.

Ignoring her, Lowenkopf banged both fists on the floor. "Open up! Police! There's no place left to run. I want that briefcase!"

The blue shoes touched toes together.

He kicked the door just below the latch, and the metal bent. He kicked it again and yanked. The door flew open, and a shriek rushed out to greet him. Carla and the guard pressed forward. A woman in a flowered dress sat on the bowl, her flowers rolled to her waist with a gray girdle around her knees. Her fingers clutched rubber and her face would have turned milk to yogurt. Carla's head dropped. She ran her finger along the sinks as the security guard sank his powerful grip on Lowenkopf's arms.

"I don't mind you guys selling flowers in the lobby, but when you start pushin' your way in where you don't belong and kickin' in the stalls, that's something else. Can't you get it in your head? The lady don't want your magazine."

Lowenkopf shoved him away and lurched for the last remaining stall. "I'm a cop, you idiot!"

"I don't care if you're Jane Fonda. You're comin' with me." The guard led Lowenkopf out of the bathroom and down the hall, dragging him persuasively, while Carla shook her pretty head, grabbed her sign, and followed them.

The desk sergeant buzzed Madagascar on the intercom. "For you, sir. Line two. Long distance. Something to do with Lowenkopf."

"Already?"

"I'm afraid so, sir. He hasn't left the L.A. airport yet."

3

Carla drove a steel-gray Mercedes 450SL, a convertible with its top down. On the back seat Lowenkopf's jacket flapped over his briefcase as the car sped north on the San Diego Freeway towards Hollywood. The sleeves of his white shirt were rolled casually up his untanned forearms. The warm California wind rushed past the windshield. Carla's thigh shifted on the leather seat as she accelerated. "It's not mine," she explained, anticipating his admiration, "but I thought it'd make an introduction to the way we do things out here." It took him a moment to realize she meant the car. If she was trying to impress him, she was certainly succeeding.

She was the kind of girl who grows between the oranges in California, healthy to the point of caricature, with peach-blond hair and thin, athletic limbs—a Hollywood nymph for whom the world was created around 1956. Her nose was so straight, the set of her jaw so certain, for the first time in his life the word "flawless" occurred to Lowenkopf as applicable to a person.

He ran his hand along the padded leather dashboard. "I can see why you'd borrow it, but who would lend a car like this? There must be half a million Angelenos just waiting to dent this baby out of spite."

She frowned. "It belongs to our director, Warren Searle. And people don't do things like that in California."

"Things like what?"

"You know." She flicked on her blinker and a white Mustang in the left lane slowed to let her enter. "We leave each other plenty of space. On the road and in the john."

He sank back in the seat. "I don't make a habit of busting into ladies' bathrooms."

She shrugged her slender shoulders. "Could be an interesting way of meeting people, I guess. I'm not judging it. It's just lucky you cops stick together, that's all."

Lowenkopf winced. He had waited resentfully for thirty minutes on a molded plastic bench while Sergeant Oquita of the LAPD called Madagascar in New York. Oquita chewed on his mustache with the phone at his ear and handed back Lowenkopf's badge. "I suggest, Sergeant Lowenkopf, that you give up your busman's holiday and visit Disneyland with the lady. They have a new video exhibit. Lots of fun."

"I'm not here on holiday," Lowenkopf had insisted. "Ms. Hollie works for Soapy Films, who have brought me in as a technical adviser on their new movie."

"I know that kind of work." Oquita nodded. "But why must these film companies go to the expense of bringing in New York's Finest when Los Angeles has so many of her own police to consult?"

Now Lowenkopf watched the scoop neck of Carla's T-shirt shift as she changed gears and wondered at his good fortune. She concentrated on the traffic with a seriousness that made him think of his sister Isabelle driving back to Manhattan alone.

"We're going to have to explain why we're so late. The production crew will love the story. But frankly it's not the best introduction you could have managed for Warren."

"Isn't that what you're here for? To make introductions?"

"I'm here to keep you out from underfoot, and out of trouble too if I can . . . which looks like it's going to be tougher than I thought. I mean—an old lady in a flowered dress? You can do better than that."

"You think so?"

"Why not? You're not a bad-looking guy. Like a teddy bear with glasses. There are certainly enough pretty girls to choose from out here."

"I can see that."

She smiled. "Wait till you see the studio. Just crawling with long-legged blondes."

"Is that who you work for? The studio?"

"No. This picture belongs to Warren's own company, Soapy Films. He dug up the money for it himself somewhere. I work for Warren."

"Do you like doing whatever you do for him when you don't have to baby-sit consultants?"

"Actually, I like baby-sitting. My mother must have

whispered something in my ear while I slept to make me a good mother someday."

"I thought every girl who hits Hollywood wants those floodlights turned on her."

"Every *woman*. Of course, I want that, too. But I'm taking the indirect approach. It's like getting into the surf at the beach—some people just dive in while others like to cool their toes in the waves awhile before taking the plunge. This way, while I wait for my chance, I get to see movies being made. Instead of drinks."

Lowenkopf nodded, watching a yellow curl dance against her cheek. He tried to remember what had brought him to her. He thought of a body facedown in the snow and covered his eyes with his hand.

"Are you all right, Mr. Lowenkopf?"

He withdrew his hand. "Why don't you call me Shelly? I'm not that much older than you, am I?"

Perhaps three years in Hollywood had taught her better than to answer that question directly. "Won't your wife mind?"

"Haven't got one anymore. When my hair started falling out, so did we."

He wasn't playing for sympathy, but he watched her check his finger and find the ring. "Your hair isn't falling out."

"Isn't it?" He ran his hands through his hair as he had seen Greeley do that morning in the precinct house and glanced at his reflection in the side mirror—wire rims and wiry hair, coiled like the inside of a radio.

She smiled. "How long will you be with us, Shelly?"

"I have to be in New York next week to testify before a grand jury. Big case." He thought she looked impressed.

"We'll be there too, next week, shooting exteriors." She slid a bit to the left and let the wind take her curls, blowing them back from her face. From her glance and the tilt of her head, the move might have been for his sake.

He patted the top of his hair. "Nice breeze."

She thought so.

They passed the Holiday Inn at Sunset and entered the Santa Monica Mountains, riding the freeway as it curved between the rises. Twin trails of lights along Sepulveda Boulevard tumbled into the Valley alongside them. It was almost eight-thirty when the Mercedes saw the red-yellow-and-white check of the San Fernando Valley floor, smoothed to the far peaks now invisible against the night sky. The lights twinkled in storybook fashion. Lowenkopf felt like Dumbo the Flying Elephant zooming into the Magic Kingdom.

Carla followed the Ventura east toward the Hollywood Freeway and exited near Univocal. They drove through the gates and up a steep hill.

"I thought you said a studio isn't producing this film."

"We're renting space. Warren's credit as a moviemaker went bust after his last three pictures lost a fortune, so he had to look outside for financial backing. But it's cheaper to shoot whatever we can here."

She pointed out the sights as they passed. Long, low soundstages, where interiors and special effects were shot, looked like opaque greenhouses in the dark. The Mercedes crested another sharp hill and started down into the streets of the back-lot sets.

Shelly tried to take all this romance for granted. "I thought Warren Searle directed a big hit lately. The one with the lady cop who was also a ballet dancer."

"That was four years ago. *The Taper Caper.* He's made three pictures since and they've all done dismally. His latest hasn't been out four months and it's already playing airplanes. *The Lace Case.* Ever see it?"

"They played it on my flight."

"Did you like it?"

"I switched to a music channel after the first few minutes."

"So did the rest of the country. That's why Warren is so invested in this one. *The Next to Die* is a real departure for him—an actual drama based on real cops in New York City, the realest place in the world. He wants everything to be authentic. That's why you're here. As insurance. I don't know how Warren scraped up the money for this one, but it's his last chance. If this picture goes down, so does he."

"You sound like an old friend."

"I wish I were. Warren's very loyal to old friends. His casting director goes way back, and the studio exec he works with was his roommate at Brown. Moviemaking is hardly a

27

family business, but Warren's managed to keep his people together. It would be a shame if Soapy Films were forced out of business."

"Is that in the cards?"

"Yes—if *The Next to Die* isn't finished. A lot of things can happen to a movie between the time the writer hole-punches his manuscript and the pictures flicker on the screen."

"Have there been problems on the set?"

"The usual stuff. Personalities rubbing against each other. There's a lot of money invested in each actor at this point, and everyone likes to feel appreciated. But Warren's just fantastic with them. This is my first feature with him, and I'm amazed at how he untangles things."

"Untangles who?"

She laughed musically. "You really *are* a cop, aren't you? Untangles everyone. You'll see."

From their vantage point on the hill, Lowenkopf could see over the false fronts of the back-lot sets to the studios beyond and the skein of strip developments and real-estate bonanzas which comprise what is called the Valley. Carla continued to point out the sights in a breezy patter. To the left lay Encino, once Clark Gable's ranch, now a grid of real estate as urban as any swath of Los Angeles. To the right, Burbank Airport, a low bunker surrounded by tiny aircraft and a huge parking lot. He watched a private jet descend, its landing wheels stretching forward and touching ground just as the Mercedes turned down a steep incline and entered the streets of New York City.

It was a replica of Madison Avenue in New York, around Fifty-fourth. Tall glass entranceways and sheer stone corner blocks grew from the pavement, fire hydrants and sidewalk gratings dotted the concrete, twisted copper utility taps stuck out from the buildings' bricks. It took Lowenkopf a minute to identify what was missing: the jetsam of particulars, street signs and shop signs and litter at the curb, the bits and pieces of themselves people leave when they close up for the night. It seemed shrunken, too, a New York for midgets, although he wasn't sure if it were the actual dimensions or the lack of unintended things that made the scene feel miniature. The Mercedes turned a corner. He saw light and a group of people clustered around a doorway.

This street was shabbier than the one they had left. Carla pulled up beside a white Porsche and cut the engine. Fifteen to twenty people made a diorama in the New York gutter, holding their places while fiddling with cameras, costumes, cables. Banks of bright lights were on, harshly focused on a few steps that led to a dilapidated doorway. A stocky man with a fixed jaw leaned against the doorpost. He wore a brief leather jacket and a deep scowl. He shook his head to fluff his hair—scarlet, wavy, and a bit wild. The door behind his shoulder was off its hinges and needed paint. Its upper half was glass, shattered but still in place; beyond, the jagged shadow of a staircase climbed to oblivion. Over his right shoulder, a crooked venetian blind hung in a filthy window, through which a bedroom's dresser mirror reflected the hallway bulb. To the left of the steps, a page of newspaper clung to a chipped iron railing. Another flight of stairs led from the railing to a submerged window framing a skinny black cat.

The red-haired man at the doorpost walked back and forth a few times with an odd, loping gait, then stamped his boot. Six heads turned to the sound. The largest, an upsidedown pear with wispy blond hair, belonged to a pudgy man in a brown crewneck sweater, its sleeves pushed halfway up his forearms. He held up a pink palm and murmured something. The boy he had been talking to, a black mass of hair over a UCLA sweatshirt, gestured for a carpenter, who banged a nail into the steps of the set.

This seemed to satisfy the red-haired actor. He gazed out over the cameramen's cameras and soundwoman's shotgun microphone, the heavy barrels of stark white light tilting down from metal trees, the neat arrangements of costumes and props, and large wooden spools of every sort of wire, stored in and spilling out of wagons and vans and cars and trucks, in and around which swarmed people taping cables and tugging hair and clipping clipboards and folding and unfolding folding chairs, with headphones on their heads and coffee in their hands, squatting in the street, sitting at the curb, standing on crates and cranes and soft crepe soles, in jeans and T-shirts, cashmere suits, cardigans with buttoned shirts, sweats, shorts, denim skirts, lingerie, and bandages—as if they weren't there.

Lowenkopf touched Carla's shoulder and jerked his thumb toward the steps. "Who's that guy supposed to be?"

She smiled sardonically. "That's your partner, Greeley."

"He's too short. Greeley's almost as tall as I am. And he's dressed wrong. That guy looks like a punk. Greeley wears a tie and jacket, usually herringbone or tweed."

"Nobody wants to see a New York cop in a herringbone suit. Someone like that always lives next door. New York detectives have to be dark and surly, with lots of teeth. Or hotheads. This one's a hothead."

"But Greeley's cool as ice," Lowenkopf insisted. "And he's blond. That ought to play in the movies. Where'd you get this guy?"

The first genuine look of surprise crossed Carla's face. "Don't you know who that is? That's Johnny Weems. Warren was lucky to get him."

"Why?"

"He's the hot hunk right now. We're shooting him in a short doorway, so he'll seem tall enough. That's his Porsche we're parked next to."

Lowenkopf glanced at the gleaming white car.

"I thought you said Searle wanted everything to be authentic."

"Do you think Greeley would be willing to dye his hair red?"

Lowenkopf started to climb out of the car. He felt her hand on his knee. "Don't get restless. They're about to start shooting. We'll sit in the car till the take's over."

Weems-Greeley slumped against the doorpost, scowling at no one in particular. Lowenkopf felt exactly as he had when *The Lace Case* started on the airplane. But this time he couldn't change the channel. "Who's that in the brown sweater?"

"Warren."

Searle was holding his palm before the actor playing Greeley, who stared over it sullenly. Lowenkopf followed the stare across the assemblage to a woman in a green nightie talking to a man in a rumpled gray suit. She showed her teeth and stepped aside just enough for Lowenkopf to glimpse the face of the man she was talking to—the same face that had peered into an alligator briefcase on the plane.

"That's my stewardess," Lowenkopf whispered urgently to Carla as he scrambled over the door of the Mercedes for a closer look.

Carla made a grab for him. "Not again? Oh, Christ—!"

But he was already after his man. The woman in the nightie noticed Weems's stare and dropped her toothy smile. As she did, her glance momentarily fell on Lowenkopf. He felt instantly enervated, as if the will had suddenly run out of him, drained by that brief exposure to her luminous green eyes. The man in the gray suit blinked at him and moved on, uninterested, until his gaze rested on Searle and Weems.

"All we need is a look here, Johnny," Searle was explaining gently. "The taxi's moving this way, rolling to a stop. You're here, watching it pull up. You want to know—and the audience wants to know—who's in it? Can you do that for me?"

Weems hung his head down and thought about that. "I'm sorry," he said, and he looked it, "but I need something more. Couldn't you get a cab in here for me to watch?"

Searle consulted his wristwatch, a diver's model built to withstand the pressure at the ocean floor. "I don't think we can," he said. "I'll tell you what. We'll have Miss Korn"— beckoning to the woman in the negligee—"glide past just the way a taxi would. Do you think you can do that for us?"

She thought she could. "It's Kern."

"Of course." Searle led her to her mark.

Lowenkopf edged through the crew toward the man in the gray suit. The shaggy UCLA alumnus quivered as Lowenkopf squeezed by. Lowenkopf assumed a casual air and prayed that would carry him through, but the UCLA man started after him. The man in the gray suit had joined Searle at the steps. Lowenkopf quickened his pace and drew near just as the man said, "Warren, we're into meal penalty time now."

"Thank you, Eliot, for reminding me of that," Searle said. His voice was expressionless. He raised two fingers, collecting the attention of the cast and crew. "All right now, let's try it. Let's see if we can get it in just one more take."

A man in a ragged cardigan yelled, "Quiet on the set!"

That stopped Lowenkopf in his tracks and his UCLA

tracker a few tracks behind. Lowenkopf could feel the scrutiny on his back. The man in gray glanced past him again, turning his critical gaze on the girl in the green nightie as she prepared for her move. Searle raised his hand, waited a beat, then lowered it, pointing at her.

She glided.

For an instant Johnny watched her, then turned to Searle. "She's moving too fast," he complained bitterly.

Searle waved at the woman wearily. "Please, Miss Korn. Slow down."

The man in gray turned his head towards Searle, a look of concern on his face. Lowenkopf had a chance for a good close study—of the face he was certain he had seen on the plane.

Searle raised his hand. The company held its breath. The woman concentrated, inhaled, composed her shoulders, and glided.

Johnny watched her.

"That was great!" Searle's hand fell like a wounded bird, the signal to cut the cameras. The company exhaled. "Fantastic." There was a spattering of applause.

The woman looked at Johnny. He turned to the crew, who continued to clap for him appreciatively. He bent his head, receiving their homage. The man in gray started to move away and Lowenkopf darted forward to seize his arm.

"What did you do with my briefcase?" he hissed in the man's ear.

"Pardon me?"

"The alligator briefcase with the letters S and L by the handle. I saw it on your lap on the plane. Where is it?" The man tried to yank his arm free, but Lowenkopf tightened his grip.

The man stared at Lowenkopf and called softly for Searle.

The boy in the UCLA sweatsuit came to his rescue. "Anything wrong, Mr. Hansen?"

Hansen tipped his head towards Lowenkopf. "Who is this?"

The boy took Lowenkopf's arm at the elbow and tried to pry it loose. "Who are you?"

The woman in the nightie stood nearby, listening.

For some reason he could not define, Lowenkopf addressed himself to her. "Shelly Lowenkopf, detective sergeant, New York Police Department. Investigating the theft of an important briefcase. This man"—wagging a finger at Hansen—"had it on his lap this afternoon, aboard a plane from New York. I saw it myself in his possession this very day."

Did he imagine an interest in her marvelous eyes? She stood out from the scene, sharp and clear. In a vague blur of movement behind her, Searle approached, followed apologetically by Carla. Lowenkopf registered a vague sense of danger, as if cast and crew were regrouping to repel an invader. They were still more curious than menacing, but Lowenkopf scented a threat of acute public embarrassment. He clung to his accusation and to Hansen's sleeve.

"I don't know what he's talking about," Hansen told the boy from UCLA, who had been unable to pry Lowenkopf loose without damaging Hansen's cashmere. "I haven't been on a plane today. All these people can attest to it. Warren, please resolve this."

Searle looked fatigued. He peered at Lowenkopf's face and extended his hand. "Hello, I'm Warren Searle. Can I help you in any way?"

Carla stood behind Searle and looked over his shoulder at Shelly. She did not seem anxious to claim him. She took a tentative step towards the director. "Warren, I don't think you've had a chance yet to meet Detective Shelly Lowenkopf."

Searle didn't seem to hear her and continued to show Lowenkopf an expression of polite expectation. Suddenly her words registered. "The New York cop? What on earth does he want from Eliot?"

She opened her mouth, had nothing to say, shrugged.

"I want my briefcase," Lowenkopf told him flatly.

"Eliot, do you have this man's briefcase?"

Hansen stared at Lowenkopf as if at an undiscovered species of vermin. "I've never seen this lunatic before in my life." He tried once more to yank his arm free, but Lowenkopf held on.

"I saw you this afternoon on a plane from New York."

Searle spoke evenly, opening Lowenkopf's grip on Hansen's sleeve. "Eliot Hansen has been working with me all afternoon—all day, in fact, from seven this morning. He was not on your plane. Whoever had your briefcase on his lap has probably still got it, and might strike again if he isn't apprehended. We'll donate Carla to that effort. Carla, why don't you help Detective Lowenkopf find his briefcase? Look around the airport and on the flights back to New York."

He carried Lowenkopf's hand from its place on Hansen's sleeve to a new spot on Carla's shoulder.

Carla gnawed her lip. Hansen started back to Johnny Weems, who looked bored by the encounter. The UCLA man stuck close to Searle, and Hansen followed them, brushing an invisible speck from his cashmere sleeve.

Taking Lowenkopf firmly by the wrist, Carla led him directly to the Mercedes, opened his door, opened her own, and got in. Rummaging through the glove compartment, she found a kerchief and tied back her hair. Without looking up, she said, "Aren't you coming?"

He didn't know. He watched her as she inspected her face in the rearview mirror, tore the kerchief from her hair, and turned to toss it into the back seat. Lowenkopf's battered suitcase was still there, with his jacket hanging over it. One sleeve of the jacket was hanging on the floor. She leaned over and picked it up.

There, on the floor beneath the suitcase, lay a brown alligator-skin briefcase.

She didn't tell him until they were back on the freeway.

"It was him!" Lowenkopf hoisted his briefcase over the seat and clutched it to his chest as if it might evaporate. "Hansen was on that plane. So much for your director's alibi. Turn this thing around and let's get him."

"Not a chance." She accelerated to pass an old Corvette.

"I'm a cop, dammit. Doesn't that mean anything to anyone out here?"

"No," she said. "As a matter of fact. You almost cost me my job back there. Believe it or not, Warren thinks I exert some influence over you. One of the things I'm supposed to do is keep you from arresting the studio execs."

"Is that who Hansen is?"

"That's right."

"Then why would he steal my briefcase?"

"Maybe he didn't steal your briefcase—did that ever occur to you? Maybe you brought your briefcase from the plane, dropped it in the back seat, and forgot about it. Maybe I carried it and forgot it—I could have. There is the remote chance that Hansen was where fifty members of the cast and crew saw him this afternoon. So maybe you should think it through some more before going back and latching on to his arm again."

Lowenkopf remembered the feel of the crowd and eased back into the leather seat. "All right. For now. Take me to Oquita and I'll let Hansen go until tomorrow."

She hit the gas. "You got it. Anywhere you want except the studio."

Lowenkopf inspected the briefcase in his lap, checking each of the eight corners for wires. He ran his finger along the seam. All of the stitching felt equally worn. There were no obvious tripping devices, and no one had cut and resewn the leather. He shifted to put his body protectively between the case and Carla, put his ear to the handle, then sat up and threw the latch, drawing his hands back immediately at the click. Nothing exploded. Cautiously he raised the lid, a few inches at a time, until the case lay open before him.

Carla fastidiously wrinkled her nose. "What is that?"

It was empty except for a paper bag with a large brown spot on one side. He opened the bag and sniffed.

"Salami," Oquita reported with a smile when the briefcase came back from the lab an hour later. They sat in a room with many desks, at which much paperwork was being done. "We found nobody's prints but your own, my suspicious friend. Nothing taken and nothing unexplained. Except, of course, the source of the salami sandwich."

Lowenkopf muttered something that could not be heard above the clatter of typewriters.

"What was that, amigo?"

"Nino's. It's a deli on White Plains Road."

"White Plains Road? Well then, that is that. I'll tell you, sometimes I go for weeks without once noticing this"—he slapped the silver buckle on his belt—"and then one day I look down and there it is. Perhaps your briefcase is like that—so close it disappears, like your lap when you stand up." He stood. "You see?"

Lowenkopf peered into the briefcase. "I had a beer in here."

Oquita smiled. "Somebody drank it then, eh? Maybe even forgot he did. I have in my desk a pass"—fetching it out—"that lets you into Disneyland for free. All the rides. Here, take it. After all the detecting you've done today, it's time you enjoyed yourself."

Lowenkopf's fingers kept their rhythm on the edge of Oquita's desk. In the center was a newspaper open to the horoscopes, held in place by a glass ashtray. Instead of the pass, Lowenkopf took from the ashtray a baseball signed *Fernando*.

Sighing, Oquita put the pass back in his drawer.

Lowenkopf felt a twinge of sympathy. He knew how he would respond to a story like his own. "When I came in just now," he said, "did you know me when you saw me?"

"Of course," Oquita reassured him. "I met you not three hours ago. I'm a policeman. It's my business to remember faces."

"It's my business too. To remember faces and to question coincidences. You question coincidences out here, don't you?"

"Certainly. But three hours ago you were brought to me for busting into a stall in the ladies' room at LAX. Now you are back with a stolen-property complaint. That is a coincidence, isn't it?"

"Is it? I see a face on a plane and a few hours later I see the same face on a movie lot. A crewful of witnesses insist there must be two men with the same face. That is a coincidence. But that's not all. The man on the plane has a briefcase just like one stolen from me in New York—another coincidence! That stolen briefcase just happens to reappear in the same place I see the double of the man on the plane. Isn't that more than coincidence?"

"Perhaps not."

"Perhaps so. If someone wanted to send me an invitation to investigate, they couldn't have invented a better one."

Oquita's manner was warm and encouraging. He opened his large hands. "But what is there to investigate, Sergeant? Nothing has happened."

Lowenkopf leaned forward. "What do you know about Eliot Hansen?"

Oquita nodded deeply and said, "Nothing at all. He is a lawful man, vice-president at a studio. He has no criminal record. I ran him through the computer while the lab examined your briefcase. He is part-owner of a crab place on the beach. His name appears on the liquor license. He has never been in an automobile accident."

Lowenkopf smacked his lips. "I like crab. What's the name of that place?"

"The Oyster Pit. But I can recommend a better dinner in the Marina if you like crab. Take the lady to the Black Whale."

Lowenkopf flipped open a pad from his jacket pocket and wrote something down.

Oquita lowered his voice. "Take my advice. You have a very beautiful young woman with you. Why not give her the attention she deserves? Believe me, she'll appreciate it."

There was a sharp tap of shoes on tile and both of them looked up to watch Carla cross the room. So did every other officer in the room. The typewriters fell silent. Carla's glance did not stray, but the forward thrust of her erect carriage rewarded their attention. She moved to Oquita's desk, sat on the edge, and crossed her long legs.

She exhaled. "What now?"

"Dinner," he answered, a bit loud. Then, softer, "Sergeant Oquita has been telling me about a great place for crab."

"All right." She stood up. "But why don't we stop at my apartment first, for a drink? I'd love to get out of these clothes."

Lowenkopf tried to avoid Oquita's eyes, but the sergeant never looked up. His attention was fixed on the baseball in his ashtray. He lifted it very gently and wiped it between his palms. But a thin smile was pressed between his lips.

Carla's apartment in Santa Monica was twenty-three blocks from the beach and darker than Lowenkopf had expected. Along an alley on the ground floor, all of her windows and a sliding glass door were covered with heavy drapes, the color of teeth, that did their best to imitate hotel-room decor. A sparse shag carpet, once white, thinly concealed the concrete floor beneath it. It was evidently not a place she called home.

"You know what they say," she joked as she led him to a small dining table and three strict, vaguely Danish chairs. "It's a great location."

Overhead, a metal fixture that looked like a wagon wheel served as a chandelier. Each of four spokes supported a plastic white candle edged in gold-painted plastic melted wax, surmounted by flaming electric bulbs, one of which was out. There were no paintings or wall hangings of any kind, though the walls were shaded a faint salmon color that brought out the gray patches in the carpet and brown water stains in the drapes.

Here Lowenkopf was commanded to wait. Near the table was a counter, higher than his waist, on which he saw a tape recorder with a cassette in it. Beneath the recorder were a few loose pages, which he managed not to read for four long minutes. When he did, he discovered they were pages from a script that ran like a transcript of one of his cases—a drug deal consummated in the fewest possible words, much like the one he had recorded of Keppler's from beneath the restaurant table. The dialogue rang true to him. When Carla emerged from a door that must have led to the bedroom and bath, Lowenkopf guiltily dropped the pages on the counter.

She seemed taken aback, but quickly recovered. She wore a blue sweater loose at the collar but nowhere else, moving with her as she scooped up the pages. "What do you think? This is Warren's latest handiwork, a scene we'll be shooting in New York next week. He likes me to read them into a tape recorder so he can hear them said aloud before he fixes them into the script. Listen." She snapped down one of the levers on the recorder, and Lowenkopf heard a fragment of the dialogue he had read. Her reading was not terrific.

"Is that you? I'm impressed."

She laughed and then frowned. "Then you're a rotten judge of acting. That was awful. This could be such a good opportunity for Warren to hear me read, but I just can't get it right."

"This is hard-boiled stuff. You've just got to be a little more tight-lipped, that's all."

She hesitated. "You know how these lines really sound, don't you? I mean, out there." Her thumb jerked over her shoulder toward the ocean. "When they're said by the genuine article."

"I've heard things like it, I guess."

"I'll bet you have." She moved beside him, holding the pages in front of her. Her young face was earnest and close to his. "Look, the hardest thing for me is reading both roles, really. It doesn't let me get into either one. Why don't you read one role and let me read the other? That way Warren will get to hear how this dialogue really ought to sound, from you, and I'll get a chance to let him hear what I can do. What do you say?"

"I can't act," Lowenkopf protested.

She held out one edge of the page for him to grasp, and closed his fingers on it. The page trembled. "You don't have to. Just read them as you've heard them said. I'll do the acting." She lowered her voice in what he recognized as a seductive ploy. But it didn't matter. "It would be a big help to me. Really."

Lowenkopf started to read—hoarsely, without conviction, aware only of the warmth of her arm and the scent of her perfume. All she seemed to want was that he say the words. She gave what looked to him like a heartfelt performance, purring when she should have purred, hitting all the right notes. Each of her words struck the cords of his abdomen. The minutes passed. When the tape on the cassette had wound a few centimeters thinner on one pole and thicker on the other, Carla looked up, smiled, and snapped off the recorder. Lowenkopf wanted to hear her speak again, in the husky, brisk manner she had found for her character. When she did speak, in her usual sweet voice, he could not tell if she were a director's assistant who had pretended to be a drug dealer or a drug dealer who was now pretending to work for Warren Searle.

"I'll give this to Warren tomorrow," she said. "Let's eat."

They drove to the Oyster Pit. Their car was parked by a muscular blond boy, and another just like him led them down the length of the patio to a round metal table, painted white, with a hole in its center for an umbrella that wasn't in it. Their table overlooked the parking lot. Curved street-lamps splashed pink lights on the Porsches, Mercedeses, and Bentleys. Beyond the cars, black sand stretched to the water's edge, where a curl of waves rolled in a carpet of tar flecked with white.

They ordered and were immediately served. Two plates piled with crab legs were set in front of them and a white plastic pail in between.

Carla broke her crab legs by hand and sucked out the meat with her teeth. Lowenkopf painstakingly used his fork. They both wore lobster bibs bearing a red oyster with the word "The" over it and "Pit" below. Between them the plastic pail filled higher and higher with shells.

A busboy brought them glasses of water floating lemon wedges. He bent at the waist near Lowenkopf's left shoulder and pressed his palms together. "Is everything fine?"

Lowenkopf grunted with his mouth full. Carla opened hers, couldn't speak, and nodded. The busboy beamed and moved off.

Lowenkopf lowered his voice. "Is it my imagination or are all of the waiters walking on their toes?"

Carla spit a bit of shell into the pail. "Where did you hear about this place?"

"Oquita mentioned it. Like it?"

She shrugged. "The Black Whale's better."

At the next table, a man with a walrus mustache swallowed oysters off the shell and wiped his fingers delicately on his overalls. Lowenkopf watched the maître d' mince by. "It looks like the manager's got his own affirmative-action campaign. Every one of these guys is gay."

"I wouldn't go that far," Carla murmured as a waiter in a crisp white shift approached their table. He smiled appreciatively at Carla, who answered his large white teeth with her own.

"How's the crab?"

"Great!" she sang.

Lowenkopf felt suddenly invisible.

"Mmmmm." The waiter moaned softly as she ate another leg. "You ought to come in Tuesday. Lobster night. The best."

She licked her lips. "I have a weakness for lobster. Big?"

"I said the best. Listen"—leaning over Lowenkopf—"I'm not working this Tuesday. Why not have dinner here with me? They always give me the juiciest tails in the kitchen."

She shook her head prettily. "I couldn't ask you to come in on a night off."

"No problem!" The waiter tried to scoop up Lowenkopf's plate, but Lowenkopf wasn't finished and hung on. "It's a lark for me. Maybe we'll go somewhere after. You like dancing?"

"Sometimes."

"Tuesday will definitely be outrageous. Wait'll you see me dance. Come on—you said you had a weakness for lobster. If you like big, I'll show you big."

She opened her mouth, but Lowenkopf dropped his fork, which smacked obtrusively against his plate and bounded to the floor. He slipped beneath the table to retrieve it.

His fingers met hers on the fork. "I'm sorry," she whispered, as if she meant it. Together they rose from under the table. Lowenkopf recovered his seat, fork in hand and daggers in his eyes.

The waiter whipped a pen from his pants pocket. He turned to Lowenkopf brightly. "Now—can I get you folks anything else?"

Lowenkopf picked up his knife. Carla put her hand over

his, shook her head, and smiled at the waiter, who shrugged his magnificent shoulders.

"Maybe some other time," he mumbled, moving out of their lives.

Carla sighed and returned to her crab legs with renewed passion.

Lowenkopf stuck his knife into the bread on a wooden board between them and couldn't get it out until he held down the board with one hand and jerked the knife with the other. It was a motion equal in intensity to but opposite in direction from the jab he would have liked to thrust into the waiter's back. His appetite was gone. Carla didn't seem to notice. A breeze blew over her shoulder and lifted the corner of her bib. He looked out over the ocean.

"What can I do?" she said, concentrating on the crab.

"You can tell me about Eliot Hansen."

"I've talked more about Hansen today than I want to for the rest of my life. Tell me about yourself."

He wasn't sure how to take that. "There isn't a lot to tell."

She nodded and swallowed. "Tell me about your life in New York."

"It isn't much of a life."

A wry smile curled her mouth. "It had better have something to it. Warren is betting his career on one of your exploits."

"That's Greeley," Lowenkopf corrected her. "Greeley is a whole 'nother story. He's the hero of the case your movie is based on. I'm just the guy who backs him up in the alley and fills out the paperwork while he's chasing down the bad guys."

"I don't believe that, Shelly. Though it's nice to listen to a guy who doesn't think he's Errol Flynn. Didn't you say you had to be in New York next week to testify before a grand jury? That must be something more than parking tickets."

Keppler's face flashed into Lowenkopf's mind. "Just some sleazy drug dealer."

"Tell me about him."

"You don't want to know."

"I do."

He shook his head. "No. I don't want to. He doesn't

belong here." He took a deep breath of salty air, just starting to cool, and avoided Keppler's name as if it would summon his ghost.

Carla didn't insist. She reached across the table, noticed her wet hands, and patted his hand with the back of her wrist. "All right, tell me something different, then. Just don't say there's nothing about you I'd find interesting. Who is Shelly Lowenkopf?"

Lowenkopf thought about his life. He imagined Thom in the driveway, Ruth sneering behind him, his Volkswagen parked in a tow-away zone down the street; he saw Isabelle filling his cup in her coffee shop, warning him, and wiping a smudge from his thumb with her sponge; he remembered Greeley recleaning his pistol, Madagascar squirming, his medal on its shelf in his apartment. He pictured his apartment, the windows overlooking a steep hill, accessible only to dogs, where leafless trees stuck out of the snow. And there was an image he resisted, a red shirt in the snow, that forced itself upon him, the snow browning, blotting out what pride he felt in Thomas or the medal. He shook his head, once, to clear the snow.

"I'm just a cop," he said. "The most striking thing about me is my alligator briefcase, stolen and then returned for no apparent motive. Does that make sense to you?"

His answer displeased her. "Can't you forget about that damned briefcase for tonight? Work is over and we're having dinner together. I don't have to be here with you. Can't you stop being a cop for just a little while?"

He'd heard that before. He took off his glasses and used the edge of his napkin to clean them. Then he folded them beside his plate. "All right. Let's talk about the movie. What's 'meal penalty time'?"

It was a shrewd question—factual, professional, a chance for her to show off what she knew. She answered breezily, "A union stipulation. Cast and crew have to eat every six hours or we have to pay everyone exorbitant salaries. Where did you pick that up?"

"Hansen mentioned it to Searle on the set."

Her eyes darkened. "I thought we weren't going to talk about Hansen any more tonight."

"I was trying not to. But this is new to me—it stuck in my mind. Give me at least some names to attach to the faces I met today. Who was the tall guy in the UCLA sweatshirt who tailed me around the set?"

This seemed to suit her better. "Be flattered. That's Alvin McDonald, assistant director. A real up-and-comer. He rarely notices anyone under associate producer."

"Are we talking about the same kid?"

"He's twenty-four. That may be a kid to you. This is his first picture with Warren. Gail Wranawski has a few nasty things to say about how he got the job—it seems he used to live with Warren's old a.d. But all that means for sure is that she didn't get it for him."

"Who's Gail Wranawski?"

"Casting director. I told you about her. She did makeup on Warren's film-school award-winner, and he hasn't done a picture without her since. Loyalty, remember? He once told Weems in front of me he'd fire him before Gail."

"Who?"

"Johnny Weems. Our red-haired Greeley. Warren's great discovery. Ask your daughter about him."

He shook his head. "Haven't got a daughter."

"Ask your wife."

There was a silhouette running along the beach over Carla's shoulder, a shape blurring with the tide as it broke in the middle of the shoreline and spread to either side. There was something familiar about the odd, loping stride. Lowenkopf watched the figure and remembered Ruth's cute comments about his own expanding waist. "I told you—I don't speak to her unless it's absolutely necessary."

"Uh-huh."

The figure on the beach slowed and looked over its shoulder as it moved into a patch of light. Lowenkopf put on his glasses. Too late. It disappeared in black sand. Carla was watching him playfully.

"What about the girl with the green eyes?" he asked casually.

She dropped her napkin over her plate in disgust. "I was wondering how long it was going to take you to work around to her. Not that you're interested in her, of course. She's a witness, I suppose, in the Great Briefcase Case—and you'll need addresses and phone numbers for all of them, no doubt."

"Don't be silly. My interest is purely professional."

"Would you please tell me what professional interest you can have at this point? Oquita told you—there's been no crime, no complaint, nobody to rescue. Look in your notebook if you don't believe me—there are no notes in it."

He felt for it in his pocket, and the briefcase at the foot of his chair. It was New York's influence in him, to check that it was still there, that it hadn't been spirited away again. And to keep investigating, wondering, even though he didn't know precisely what he was wondering about. "Are you going to tell me about her or not?"

"Green Eyes is Teri Kern—or Teri Korn, no one can ever remember which. That should tell you something about her. Warren used her in a small role in his last picture and for some unfathomable reason he is using her again. I don't know why—the picture was a flop and no one mentioned her for an Oscar. She has big green eyes. She's not married, if that matters to you, but don't get your hopes up, because she's got something going with Weems."

"She looked more interested in Hansen to me."

"Who isn't these days?"

She said it with just the right touch of misery to flatter Lowenkopf. He was about to answer when the running figure behind her burst suddenly into the pink light of the parking lot, reached into a jacket pocket, and unlocked a white Porsche. Lowenkopf noticed the hair color, made out the letters on the back of the jacket, and sprang to his feet.

Carla stood too. "I've got to make another phone call," she said.

The Porsche squealed out. Lowenkopf said, "Can it wait?" When she eyed him curiously, he continued, "Let's go for a walk instead."

She wrinkled up her nose, but when she slung her bag over her shoulder and motioned for him to lead the way, Lowenkopf knew she liked him more than she had said. And, he admitted to himself as he paid the check, there was something astir in his veins as well.

The shoreline was pitch black from a distance, roaring and hissing as a white line of foam faded and reappeared in a crash of water. The ocean was inky, the sky starless, the moon full, the tide ebbing. As they approached, he saw rocks embedded in the sand that formed the ocean floor during the day when the tide was in. Now a shallow rush of water moved among and between them, swallowing this or that rock from swell to swell. Carla watched the waves further out, galloping sideways along the beach, converging finally with the shore at some point to their right. With a great roar, each unfurled and spent its force. Lowenkopf listened to their warning like a shipwreck survivor cut off from everything he knew. Carla moved beside him with long, slow steps. She touched his arm. "Shelly, look." A small red sail slid so slowly across the water that its progress was imperceptible—but after a moment, there it was, ahead of where it had been. There was no standing still. The waves at his feet seemed to pull at the sand as they retreated into the darkness, and Shelly felt a similar pull at his emotions, a feeling that was suddenly stronger than he had guessed. Her fingers slid down his arm and settled in the crook of his elbow. "That's pretty, isn't it?" Her face turned to his, bright with moon.

He felt transformed, as if the black sky and brilliant moon had rolled away and left him holding a girl he did not know on a movie set. He understood that the woman in his arms was beautiful, desirable, that the moment was right for him to kiss her gently, then passionately, but it felt less an impulse than an obligation. For a moment he was Errol Flynn—a man in a spot with a job to do.

He bent and kissed her. She returned the pressure on his mouth, but when he moved to take her in his arms, she placed her hands between them and resisted.

"I don't think we should rush into anything," she said.

Her refusal, unexpectedly echoing his own, attracted him. "Why not?"

"Well, this, for one thing," she said, tapping his wedding band.

He slipped it from his finger. "I told you, I'm divorced."

"Then why do you still wear it?"

"I don't know. Nostalgia, I guess. I don't need it anymore."

She held it up. "You're sure?" It was a dare.

"Sure," he said uneasily.

With a fluid pitch she flung it into the tide, which broke in a sizzle around it.

"What did you do that for?" The spot where it had landed was swept clean by an undertow. For an instant he felt the pull of the current with nothing outside him to cling to—but when Carla moved beside him, he wrapped her in his arms, a driftwood gift from the sea god.

After a moment she broke from his grip. "That's more like it," she said, strolling forward among the rocks with a satisfied grin. A sense of dereliction spilled over him again.

The beach was suddenly bright. Stars flecked the ocean. There was a flickering of red and gold over a rise in the sand. Shelly's head ached from the kiss, the night air, and a healthy dose of jet lag. Carla was a few steps ahead of him in the sand, nearing midnight, while he was into the wee hours of his morning.

A finger of the moon in the water followed them along the surf. Something about the flickering ahead, the colors and constant changing rhythms, made him think of . . . fire. He started to run forward, yanking Carla with him.

"Shelly, wait. I can't." She stepped out of her shoes. "Where are we going so fast?"

He peered down the beach. "Something's wrong."

She stamped her delicately stockinged foot. "But we're off duty now, aren't we? For crying out loud, Shelly . . . can't you think of anything else you'd rather do than play policemen?"

A wave broke behind them and saved him from answering. The light flickered from over the sand, beckoning. He ached to follow it, to discover what the running man had run away from. But he was conscious of her, standing with her arms akimbo waiting for his reply. A beam of headlights swept the sand and went out.

"Shelly?" She coughed. "Do you smell something?"

The odor made his nose crinkle. It wasn't coming from the restaurant.

"What are they cooking down there?" she demanded. "Roast pig?"

Lowenkopf recognized the smell and it wasn't roast pig: the stink that came from blazes which erupted without warning, trapping apartment dwellers in their beds. "Go back to the car and wait for me. No—see if you can get Oquita on the phone first. Tell him to get down here fast."

Her gaze was fixed on the light over the sand, but there was nothing unsteady in her voice when she asked, "What is it?"

"I'm not sure, but Oquita will want to find out for himself." Uncertainly she moved towards the flickering light. He caught her arm. "Believe this"—he tapped his nose—"it knows whereof it speaks. Get going."

She went, bless her.

As he moved toward the fire, the stench grew stronger. He could make out a ring of stones surrounding a glowing pile of white ash and dark, crackling wood. Between the stones and the fire was a black space dotted with spots of white. Marshmallows. He stepped into the light and saw a man on the other side of the bonfire leaning into the pit.

Too far into the pit. Holding his nostrils, Lowenkopf moved closer. The man, or what was left of him, lay facedown in the fire, the remains of his cardigan shriveling on his back. It had been blue. His left arm and face were roasting in the coals. Lowenkopf had seen many corpses, but he had to fight to keep the stink from wrenching up the crabmeat in his stomach. Dragging the body out of the fire, he forced himself to examine the face, but there was nothing left to recognize. He rested what remained of the head and burnt left arm on one of the stones ringing the firepit, using a plastic bag of marshmallows for a pillow.

The back of the head was baked with blood. After a few moments' search, he found a piece of wood with a dark stain on it. The corpse had had his head bashed in by someone who had let his victim topple forward into the fire but hadn't stopped to throw the murder weapon in after it. The body was still hot. With his fingertips, Lowenkopf pulled a black leather wallet from its back pocket. Inside was one hundred and ten dollars in tens and twenties, a yellowed photo of Warren Searle, credit cards, and a driver's license in the name of Eliot Hansen. From the front pockets he recovered fourteen cents, a white silk handkerchief, six keys on a diamond keychain. There was a hundred-lire coin in the hip pocket, a good-luck piece worn smooth. The dead man wore soft leather sandals, gray silk pants, no shirt under the scorched cardigan. Lowenkopf circled the low flame and poked the ashes with a stick until he saw the dull gleam of a luminous watch dial. His chest ached from holding his breath. The sand retained no marks of any kind.

He joined Carla in the parking lot just as Oquita pulled up in a squad car. Another cop sat beside him, a bronzed blond with the collar of his sports jacket turned up.

Lowenkopf set his foot on the bumper and leaned against the hood of the squad car. "You'll find a barbecue by the water. The main course is a Univocal studio executive named Eliot Hansen. You'll want to put out a call for Johnny Weems, too. He may have been at the picnic."

Carla sank in her seat, covering her ashen face.

The cop unfolded from the passenger door. "You New York cops move a little fast, you know that? For us laid-back west-coast types. Take it a bit slower, why don't you?"

Lowenkopf nodded agreeably. "There's a dead man in the sand," he said, enunciating crisply. "Over there. Do you want to take a look? Or do we need some more time to chew it over?"

The blond swaggered over. "If there's any chewing to be done, I'm gonna do it." His thumb prodded Shelly's chest above the open shirt buttons. "And you're gonna be the chewing gum."

Oquita slipped out on the driver's side and jangled his ring of keys. "Sergeant Snyder, I think it would be a good idea to get the evidence kit from the trunk." He dropped the keys in his palm and shoved him towards the back. "What makes you point a finger at Johnny Weems?"

"I saw him."

Carla, who was just sitting up, sank into the Mercedes' front seat again. Lowenkopf reached in and pulled her up. "Are you sure it was him?" she whispered. It sounded like a prayer.

"I saw Weems—or someone dressed to look like him—run down the beach, climb into a white Porsche, and drive off."

"Here?" Snyder squinted cynically.

"He came down from the fire this way and then stepped out over there. Under the light."

Snyder dug both hands in his back pocket and let fly a cutting, "Right."

Oquita brushed his mustache fastidiously with both hands. "And when he stepped into the light—what exactly did you see, Sergeant Lowenkopf?"

"I saw a red-haired man in a jacket—a shiny one. I could read the lettering on the back. It said, 'The Next to Die.'"

"And what do you take that to mean? A warning?"

Lowenkopf waited for Carla. She dragged out the words one by one. "That's the name of Warren Searle's new picture."

Lowenkopf prodded her. "Just going into production. Who would have one of those jackets now?"

Another pause. "Only the cast and crew."

"I saw him drive off in a white Porsche. Didn't you tell me that Porsche we parked next to today was Weems's?"

She blinked at him twice. "Johnny's got a lot of cars. One of them is a Porsche. But there are a million Porsches in Hollywood."

Oquita was listening, his eyes averted. "This is certainly true. Did you get the license number?"

"I couldn't see it from the patio. And I had no reason to note it at the time."

Oquita nodded. "Then you didn't actually see his face?"

Snyder let out a bark which Lowenkopf interpreted as a laugh.

"I saw everything else. Come on—what have you got to lose? Put out a call, pick him up, find out where he's been the last hour or so. If I'm wrong, no harm done. If I'm not, you've broken the record for west-coast homicide arrests."

Snyder snickered in disbelief. "No harm done, huh? Get *him.*" He turned for confirmation to Carla. "Johnny Weems is a *movie star.*"

Lowenkopf made his case to Oquita. "And maybe a

murderer. What is this, a company town? Don't you guys bust killers who work for the studios?"

"We bust everybody," Snyder insisted, "but another idea just occurred to me. Isn't Hansen the guy you put the arm on today for stealing your lunch?"

"My briefcase."

Snyder ignored his correction. "Three hours later, we arrive at the scene of the crime and what do we find? You, less than one hundred yards from Hansen's corpse, eager to finger one of the biggest names in Hollywood. Do you know what Weems's pictures gross?"

They all assumed it was a rhetorical question, but Snyder, born of a theatrical family, waited a beat before continuing.

"No. I didn't think so. Well, I'll tell you something. There was only one person from that movie lot on the scene when I got here. You know who that person was? *You.*"

Lowenkopf turned to Oquita, who was shaking his head sadly. The Chicano policeman looked at his partner, made a V with his fingers, and said, "Two."

Carla waved listlessly from the Mercedes.

Snyder ignored her. "What the hell are you doing here, Lowenkopf?"

"We came here to eat."

"Come off it! You expect me to believe you just happened to pick a place a hundred yards from where your briefcase suspect was murdered? With thousands of restaurants to choose from? One or two of them better than New York."

Lowenkopf grabbed Oquita's shoulder.

"You sent me here."

Oquita inspected the hand on his shoulder. "I suggested the Black Whale."

"But you know how I came to be here. Think—if I were planning to murder Hansen, would I alert you beforehand? Would I send for you now? I'd keep my mouth shut and hope they'd put Surfer Boy here on my trail."

Oquita shrugged and wiped a bit of grease off his mouth. He had evidently been dining when he was summoned.

Snyder stuck out his jaw. "Who do you mean, Surfer Boy?"

Lowenkopf rolled his fist.

Oquita threw up his hands in surrender. "Okay, okay. I'll talk to Johnny Weems. If I don't trust a policeman's eyes, whose will I trust? But if you don't mind, we'll stop by your hotel tomorrow morning, Detective. After we've finished up here. No harm in checking all the suspects, eh?"

5

Lowenkopf was hot: his arms, pulled back around the diagonal bark of a eucalyptus tree, were bound at the wrist; yellow flames licked the soles of his feet. There was a loud buzzing in his ears. Suddenly it ceased and his whole body shook, as Carla's purring saw bit into the far side of the tree at the height of his waist. It was powered by a car battery. As he watched her, she faded, until only her grim smile of determination lingered. In front of him stood Thom, watching painfully. *You know, Dad,* he said, *you would be a great cop if you could just avoid jumping to the wrong conclusions.* Lowenkopf would have ended as a burnt slice of toast, had he not forgotten to close the blinds.

But he had forgotten them, for which he could hardly be blamed. The night before, Carla had dropped him in front of his hotel without a word of rebuke, and the guilt was killing him. She rejected his offer of a nightcap by flinging his briefcase at him and screeching off. Once inside the hotel, his fatigue caught up with him. It was all he could manage to slide his shoes under the bedspread and let his eyelids fall. He could still hear the springs complain. Or the saw buzz. Or the phone ring. He picked up the receiver.

The dial tone sounded like the loser's note on a game show.

The buzzer rang again, softer than a dial tone and in a higher key. Lowenkopf dropped the phone in its cradle and shuffled out to the door of his suite. Oquita and Surfer Boy were waiting in the hallway. The blond put his mirrored glasses on and walked past Lowenkopf into the room.

"Nice place you got here." He stood by the window with his hands in his back pockets and rocked on his heels. "Not as nice as Johnny Weems's, of course."

Outside on the lawn, a eucalyptus tree trembled in the sunlight. Lowenkopf could not get used to the greenery. Avocado and rubber trees—plants he knew potted on his windowsill—were blown up bigger than life here, lost in a thicket of palm leaves and dazzling flowers. They made him feel, by contrast, smaller than actual size. Huge pink hibiscus and passionflowers stuck out obscenely from the bushes, protected from the casual picker, like all wildflowers, by California law.

Lowenkopf invited Oquita in. "You questioned Weems?"

"Yes." The Chicano entered with a nod to his host. "He tells us he was with Warren Searle last night. After the crew broke up, they called in to the commissary for some almond-butter-and-tomato sandwiches and spent the next few hours in Searle's office on the lot."

"Why?"

"Mr. Searle wouldn't say, and neither would Weems, but the boy who took their order remembers making the delivery. Searle accepted it himself at the door, and tipped the boy two dollars."

"What time was this?"

"Ten minutes before the murder." It was an opportunity for Snyder to sneer.

Lowenkopf glanced at him, returned to Oquita for confirmation. "Searle corroborates this?"

"Every word," Snyder insisted. "Weems is as clear as Perrier. The only question that remains is, since he was with Searle on the lot, why would anyone say they saw him at the Oyster Pit?"

Lowenkopf ignored him and opened white shuttered doors near the terrace to expose a small stove and refrigerator. A pot of coffee sat on a cold burner, which he turned on.

Snyder waited pregnantly for Lowenkopf's answer. When none came, he pressed on. "What time did you get to the Pit last night?"

"Just after eleven. The maître d' seated us immediately. My seat overlooked the parking lot and Carla—Ms. Hollie —faced me. We ate crab legs and went for a walk on the beach. We were together every minute of the time, so when am I supposed to have hit Hansen?"

Snyder didn't back off. "Not every minute. You sent the girl back to the restaurant to make a call. She never actually saw Hansen dead."

"She smelled him."

"She smelled roasting duck." He flipped open his notepad. "Or pig. Could have come from the restaurant. Maybe it was the marshmallows. How did you know he'd been killed?"

"I saw the back of his head and the bloody log—that's how. I'm a cop, remember?"

Snyder muttered, "That's what makes me sick."

"Of course, we're not accusing you of anything, you understand," Oquita explained in an effort to defuse Snyder's tone.

Lowenkopf understood. "I didn't kill Hansen for stealing my briefcase."

"We checked out that story too," Snyder interjected. "Know what we found? More hooey. Half the cast saw Hansen on the set all day yesterday. A cameraman, the best boy, script girl, and your girlfriend all placed him at the studio while your plane was in the air. And we haven't spoken to everyone yet."

"Then where's my motive?" Lowenkopf countered. "If Hansen wasn't on the plane, I couldn't have killed him for what he did on it."

"Ahh, but you *thought* he was." Snyder wagged a mani-cured fingernail in front of Lowenkopf's nose. "Plenty of people told us that! There may be some other motive we haven't discovered yet. But we will."

Oquita took a subtler tack. "When did you make your airline reservation?"

"Just yesterday. Why?"

"Hansen was in New York two weeks ago. I wondered if your reservation was made before or after that visit."

"What was he doing in the city?"

54

"Your city, you mean," Snyder corrected, moving beside Oquita to cement their solidarity. *"You tell us."*

Imperceptibly, Oquita stepped aside. "You didn't know?"

"No. But you're not finished with Johnny Weems, are you? Searle may be a nice guy, but he's got what's left of his career riding on Weems at this point. He'd come up with an alibi for Weems no matter where they both were. Did the counter boy see both of them or just Searle when he made that delivery? He's really the only solid alibi Weems has got, isn't he?"

Snyder's contempt was boundless. "That's rich. A tin sergeant shows up from the East seeing things on airplanes, and we're supposed to take his word over Warren Searle's. Mr. Searle is a feature-film director. Do you know what that means in this town?"

"Diplomatic immunity?"

Oquita put a hand on Lowenkopf's arm. "We do our job. But the papers do theirs too, eh? Did you actually see this . . . running figure pull into the parking lot?"

"I was watching Carla. Didn't the lot attendant see anyone?"

"He said there were many white Porsches there last night. He didn't notice their drivers."

"As if anyone wouldn't know Johnny Weems," Snyder mumbled.

Lowenkopf said sharply, "I didn't."

The blond policeman turned his palms to heaven, resting his case.

Oquita smoothed his mustache. "We will have to see what more we can discover. There are many parts to a man's life. Who knows what part confronted Hansen last night? But I don't think Searle is protecting Weems for business reasons. There are, of course, other reasons. In the meantime, we will let you know if we find something that concerns you, and you will let us know where you are."

"In other words," said Snyder, relishing this, "keep out of it."

Oquita took his partner by the arm and led him to the door. "In this way, we can keep all of the bases covered. That is all."

Lowenkopf stopped him at the door for one last question.

"Do they really serve almond-butter-and-tomato sandwiches at the commissary?"

"I'm afraid so," Oquita said.

The water had boiled out of the pot on the stove. Lowenkopf called room service for another pot, hung up, and dialed again. The phone rang twice before Carla answered. There was a deep silence when she recognized his voice.

Shelly was at his groveling best. "Don't hang up. Can I buy you breakfast to make up for last night? I feel terrible, leading you around like that."

"Don't stop there. What about accusing my boss of complicity in murder? That was a good one. But I'll get over it. I was about to call you myself."

"No kidding?"

"Warren asked me to." There was a professionalism in her tone he disliked. "I'll pick you up in fifteen minutes. In front."

"I haven't eaten yet."

"Don't. Eating is a business activity in Los Angeles. Warren's waiting for us. And Shelly"—the use of his personal name sounded oddly impersonal—"I won't be in the Mercedes. Those days are over."

He patted his belly in the bathroom mirror and sucked air through his teeth. She was boiled—he could understand that. But their moments on the beach stood out in his memory. They couldn't have faded so quickly for her, could they? In the back of his skull, he heard Ruth answer, "Sure they could."

He tested both taps at the tub, stepped out of his pants and shorts, and had one foot wet when room service rang with his coffee.

He stood blinking in the hotel's sunny driveway when a green Mazda with a dented door and white vinyl roof neatly patched over in cloth tape pulled up in front of him. Carla sat forward in the driver's seat, tilting the sun visor over her face.

"Get in. Quickly. Before somebody sees me."

He crouched to avoid hitting his head and fell into the seat. The springs cried painfully beneath him.

"This yours?"

"I'd rather be dead than driving it. My Bug wouldn't start. This belongs to the station."

"It looks economical."

He fancied she smiled in spite of herself. He rolled down the window and stuck his elbow out. The warm air rushed past him. His shoulder strap ended without a buckle, and his seat belt wouldn't unhook. There was no visor flap on the passenger side, so he used his hand to block the sun. The gears ground into third and they bounded off down a hill.

Her knee flexed as it tightened on the clutch. She wore a plaid skirt that matched her socks and a white blouse open two buttons at the throat. She looked lovely and he told her so.

She frowned. "We've had enough of that. We're here to talk business."

"What kind of business?"

"What business are you in?"

"I'm a cop."

"Are you ever! I won't ask you again to let it go for a night." She stopped with a jerk at the light. The car rolled forward, waiting for a truck to pass. Then she made a right turn, through the red light. "Don't get your gun out, Lowenkopf—a right turn is legal on a red light in this town."

It was going to be a long day.

It was in any case a long drive, through Hollywood and Beverly Hills on Sunset Boulevard, along the foothills of the Santa Monica Mountains to the Pacific Coast Highway, south between the ocean and the Palisades, turning onto local streets at the Santa Monica pier and following the beach to Ocean Park. The exhaust of the green Mazda spat at every light and stop sign, until Carla parked in a crowded lot next to a white building decorated with an enormous painted blue orchid.

Lowenkopf followed her out of the lot. "What are we doing here?"

"Working."

Inside, people of all descriptions waited for tables in the outdoor garden section, sipping coffee and crunching croissants on stools at high white tables, or wandering through shelves of baskets and woven place mats. The room was a fluorescent barn. A brisk take-out trade leaned against freezers featuring strawberry tarts ringed with banana slices and concave kiwi pies. Carla elbowed their way into the garden and led Lowenkopf to a table beneath a sycamore, where Warren Searle sat sipping a glass of white wine and poking at an omelet.

"The Florentine is much better," he complained as they dragged wrought-iron chairs to his table and joined him. "It must have been the Florentine I had last time."

Carla leaned over his left shoulder. "I'm almost certain you had the Florentine. Send it back and order the Florentine."

"I don't think I'll do that. We're running over budget as it is. And now this thing with Eliot." Searle pushed the plate away and settled over his wine. The waitress tried to lift his plate. "But perhaps Mr. Lowenkopf would care for it."

Lowenkopf squinted at the omelet. "I think I'll try the Florentine."

Carla ordered a croissant and a cup of Turkish coffee. The waitress abandoned Searle's meal without further struggle. He dragged it a bit closer to him and picked at the cheese stuffing.

Lowenkopf tried to sit casually back in his chair, but the painted white metal wouldn't give. "Did you, uh, send for me?"

"Yes," Searle said, nibbling at the tines of his fork. "Two policemen came to see me this morning. They told me about Eliot, although they didn't have to, really—I sensed something was wrong. Did you ever get that feeling, Mr. Lowenkopf, that something is wrong?"

Lowenkopf nodded. "Every day."

"It's not a common experience for me. I tried to reach Eliot last night, repeatedly, until about two in the morning."

"The police came to see you?"

"This morning. They asked me a few questions, about Johnny for the most part, and thanked me for my help. I sensed they suspect Johnny murdered Eliot."

"So do I."

"Then you're wrong." Searle shook his head paternally. "Johnny was with me yesterday, from the time we finished shooting until midnight. He was out of my sight seven times: once to make a phone call, once when I went to the head, and five times when he did. The fan magazines don't know he has a weak bladder, do they?" He smiled a thin smile at Carla, who returned it.

Lowenkopf didn't share their amusement. "If you don't mind my asking, Mr. Searle—what did you two talk about?"

Searle made a sour face. "We talked about titles—he wants to change the name of my film. And he had a list of people he wants dropped from the crew. I refused both demands and he let me know how he feels about me. As I'm sure you've gathered, Johnny's not the most charming person on the lot. But there's absolutely no doubt in my mind that he is in no way involved in Eliot's murder."

Lowenkopf scratched behind his ear. "Forgive me, Mr. Searle, if I seem crass for insisting, but with your whole film riding on him, the guilt or innocence of Johnny Weems is not entirely free of your own interests."

"Neither was Eliot Hansen, Sergeant Lowenkopf. Do you have a wife?"

"Ex-wife."

"Even more to the point. Would you supply an alibi for her murderer?"

Lowenkopf savored the idea for a moment.

"Neither would I for Eliot's. Eliot was my ex. I'll tell you the truth—Johnny is the kind of man who could have done something like this. But it just happens that he didn't, and I want the killer found."

The waitress brought Carla's coffee. Lowenkopf waited until she left. "So do the police. Why not tell them what you've told me?"

"I have. Exactly what I've told you. But I'm not especially impressed with the officers assigned to the case. *The Next to Die* is my fourth cops-and-robbers film, so I guess I can spot a good cop when I see one. The Mexican seemed to know a thing or two, but he hardly asked a question. His partner wanted a screen test. Carla mentioned that you have expressed some interest in the case, so I thought you might look into it a little for us."

"I'm way out of my jurisdiction here."

"I meant in a private way, of course. You have been assigned to consult with us, haven't you? This is where I need your counsel most desperately." Searle pointed his fork at Carla. "She can help you do whatever you need to do."

Carla glanced at him coolly. "Professionally."

Lowenkopf didn't want to seem too eager. "I'll look into this, if you like. But I don't need a deputy. Carla's not a cop. And I don't want to take her away from her work."

"It will be work," she assured him.

"And I can spare her from mine," Searle decided. "The police will be swarming all over the set and crew today. We'll see what happens tomorrow. Carla has all the names and addresses you'll need, so why don't you get started?"

Searle stood up with a last forlorn look at his tattered omelet.

Lowenkopf caught his sleeve. "There's one thing I'd still like to know. Why did you drag me all the way out here to tell me this? Couldn't we have met in Hollywood just as easily? Do you have a reason for keeping this secret between us?"

"No secret, Detective Lowenkopf. I live out here. On a Venetian canal, near Eliot. But you'll discover all that once you get under way. Give me a jingle when you find something." He swept his linen jacket from the back of his chair and hurried out of the garden.

Lowenkopf turned to Carla. "Is he going to pay the check?"

She frowned. "Does that pass for humor among police people?"

Lowenkopf folded his hands contritely on the table. "All right. I'm sorry I was a cop last night. What do I have to say to be friends again?"

She was silent, considering her spoon, then raised her eyes. "I don't do this very often, but here goes. You were working last night when you pretended you weren't. Fine. What I want to know is, was that part on the beach just work too?"

He shook his head twice. She looked very sexy just then, with bright red lipstick on her mouth, cup, and napkin. He leaned across the table towards her just as the waitress brought his breakfast. He stared at the plate a minute, where a puffed omelet swam in yellow sauce. "Is this the Florentine?"

She nodded.

"It's not what I had in mind."

Carla began to laugh.

The alley to Hansen's house was in a part of Venice that should have given up expensive tenants years before. Carla parked between a red convertible and a rusty fence in what had once been a gas station and led Lowenkopf around the shattered fragments of the convertible's windshield on the pavement. Lowenkopf thought it odd that wrecked automobiles were accepted without comment on the streets of Los Angeles, while the human detritus of New York—panhandling drunks, doorway sleepers—were so rarely in evidence here. On their drive, he had seen a bag lady pushing her belongings along the beach in a shopping cart. He thought of the women he knew in Manhattan who dragged their bundles from steampipe to park bench. Life really was easier here.

One of the four panes of glass in Hansen's front door had been broken. A jagged corner still clung to the frame. Lowenkopf ran his fingers over the plastic grass of the welcome mat and picked up shiny bits on his fingertips.

Carla squatted beside him and peered at his hand. "Glass?"

He singled out a grain on his thumb. "Sand."

The door was unlocked. They walked into a spacious living room with a floor of polished oak covered with a deep rug in beiges and grays. The same colors were used in Colombian cortinas hanging over the stones of a fireplace

61

climbing the north wall. In front of the fireplace was a sofa pit in white Haitian cotton, with twisted black iron lamps on clear glass tables at both ends. There were three watercolor prints on the walls, done on what looked like bark, with signatures Lowenkopf didn't recognize. The east wall was glass from floor to ceiling, with a sliding door leading to a redwood patio. A pine stair and banister ran up half a flight to the kitchen, where a uniform was investigating an open refrigerator. With a purple fig.

He slurped the insides of the fig and dropped the skin somewhere behind him. "Sorry, folks. Nobody's home. House is closed. Police business."

"We're here on official business." Lowenkopf held up his badge but kept his thumb over the front of it. "Working with Sergeant Oquita of the Thirty-ninth."

"I used to be at the Thirty-ninth." The uniform wiped his mouth on a linen napkin. "I don't remember you. How long you been there?"

"I'm not with the Thirty-ninth now, exactly."

The uniform waited.

"I'm out on assignment from New York."

The uniform took a closer look at Lowenkopf's badge, pushing his thumb out of the way. "So you are. On assignment, huh? I guess I'll just put in a call to New York to reassure them you're on the job." He lifted the receiver from a wall phone and cradled it against his ear.

Lowenkopf remembered Madagascar. "Is that really necessary?"

"You got some objection?"

"It's a long-distance call."

"This guy won't mind. You should see the way they live here. Jesus. My wife and I've been waiting to buy a little house in Simi Valley—an hour and a half to work. You should see this place. Four bedrooms upstairs and another room he didn't know what to do with. That window's two goddamn stories high. What's the number?"

Lowenkopf tapped his back pocket. "Damn! Must've left my New York phone book in my hotel room."

The uniform grinned. "Who you kidding?"

Carla took the phone from him and gently replaced it in its cradle. "Officer, I'm sure you've heard of Warren Searle, the film director? He asked us to stop by and make sure nothing had been misplaced. He thought we might be of some use to your investigation. I knew Eliot Hansen, and Mr. Searle thought you might need someone who knew him to check things over here."

The California cop addressed Lowenkopf. "You know Hansen too?"

"I knew him when I saw him."

Carla grimaced. "Mr. Lowenkopf has come along to assist me."

Lowenkopf did a double-take. "To assist *you?*"

She smiled reassuringly at the uniformed police officer. "I've got to go upstairs for a minute, to see what's missing from Eliot's wardrobe. Sergeant Oquita thought it would help. You can come up and keep an eye on me, if you feel you should."

He beamed back at her. "You can go up. To assist the investigation, like you said. But *he's* got to wait down here. And I'll stay here to make sure. I can't have every cop on a holiday trooping through the house. This ain't Disneyland."

"Oh, come on. Cop to cop. We'll just be a minute."

The uniform stood firm. "Then maybe you should wait outside."

They compromised on the sofa.

Carla bounded up the stairs and the officer returned to his post at the refrigerator. He glanced once or twice at Lowenkopf, who sat on the sofa dejectedly, unable to concentrate on the coffee table's magazines, staring at the ceiling as if trying to see through to where Carla had begun his investigation. The officer felt sorry for him. "Can I get you something while you wait? This guy Hansen had everything." He held up a large cold ham with a carving knife stuck in it.

"I just had breakfast."

The officer cut another slice for himself. "These out-of-town assignments really bust your butt, don't they?"

"Uh-huh."

The officer nodded, mouth full of ham.

Two stone bookcases filled most of the south wall, and Lowenkopf used the silence to examine the shelves. The selection was unexceptional—popular fiction, pop sociology, books on African and pre-Columbian art, cinema, a book-club smattering of science fiction, and several celebrity autobiographies. The dust on the front lip of each shelf had been brushed away, but Lowenkopf lifted a few books at random and found an unbroken line that had not been disturbed by the dustcloth. None of the books had been recently removed or replaced. There were no unfaded squares on the walls where pictures might have hung, and no spots of uneven wear on the floor. An unlit fire waited in the hearth. The door to the terrace was newly washed and slid easily on its track. A blue sailboat was moored at a dock protruding from the patio into a small canal. Both banks of the canal were lined with similar patios attached to similar houses, and a flotilla of similar boats rocked gently beside them. To the right, the channel passed beneath a curved stone bridge on which a cluster of red flowers grew.

Lowenkopf felt the uniformed cop approaching him from behind. They stood together a moment in the doorway, looking out. Lowenkopf whistled softly. "What is this, a private river?"

"Just about," the officer said. He was gnawing a turkey leg. "They built these canals years ago, when Venice was a real tourist attraction. Like the Italian Venice. Only now mostly junkies and Mexicans live here. Except for the beach, of course, and the first mile or two inland. These canal houses are worth a few C's apiece. Not that I'd want to live here, if I could afford it. Neighborhood's not safe enough for me."

"A few hundred apiece?"

"Four or five hundred thousand." The figure rolled off the officer's tongue. Across the water, two children ran from a house and bumped their way into a rowboat. He bit another huge chunk of turkey and added, "They live good lives, these people."

Lowenkopf pictured Thom on the middle bench of the rowboat. There was a soft bump and the boy at the oars looked up. Lowenkopf met the boy's brown eyes and felt an instant of contact with a world more substantial than his own. The boy turned away, and he was again closed out—stranger, intruder, cop. He stepped out onto the redwood patio and watched the water lap the planks beneath his feet. "Did Hansen throw many parties here?"

"We didn't find anything to show it, but they all do."

"Anything in the sink?"

"Two glasses. One tomato juice and the other Scotch."

"That's all?"

"Why not?"

"I'm a bachelor myself," Lowenkopf explained. "When I go out I might leave a few dishes to wash up later. Unless I know I'm not coming back."

"But you don't have a maid in here," the officer said. "We think he had a maid in here yesterday. A neighbor's seen one with a key of her own, and thought it might've been on a Friday. There's a look to a place that's just been cleaned, and this place has it. If there was a maid, we'll find her. But I doubt if she'll tell us anything. Between you and me, this place is a dead end."

His sentence was punctuated by a shriek from the second floor. Both men froze, then bolted up the stairs. Lowenkopf was a step behind the uniform, but he was the first to recognize the note of triumph in Carla's wail. They found her cross-legged on the bed with a screenplay in her hands, bouncing on the mattress.

"The case is over," she announced triumphantly, her face alight.

The officer took the screenplay from her. "I really wish you hadn't touched that, miss. It might be important evidence." He stood holding it indecisively as if it were hot.

Lowenkopf held out his hand and the officer passed it off with relief. On the light blue cardboard cover, between the first and second brass clips, was a label with the name *Orange England.*

"Not that. This." Carla tapped a slip of paper sticking out from the screenplay. "What do you do when you're reading something and the phone rings?"

Lowenkopf turned the screenplay facedown on the bed at the point marked by the slip of paper.

"That breaks the binding," the officer objected, rescuing it from the bed.

Carla concurred. "And Hansen was neat, too prissy for

that. You use a bookmark. If you haven't got one handy, you use any piece of paper that is."

Lowenkopf lifted the slip of paper, which had fallen on the bedspread. It was torn from a larger piece, and the message had been ripped in half. What still remained said, "—ound ten. I'll drop by the Pit. A." There was nothing on the back. "Who's A?"

The officer accepted the note from Lowenkopf and smoothed it on the bed. Then he tucked it uneasily inside the front cover.

Carla paused for effect. "Alvin McDonald, the a.d.— that's assistant director, if you've forgotten. Some of the crew call him 'the big A' because he sits in a sling chair with his feet up while they hang the lights."

Lowenkopf examined the paper over the officer's shoulder. "It's a small, neat handwriting. Know any lady A's?"

"I'm not sure. Teri Korn?"

They both stared at her in silence. Finally Lowenkopf asked, "Where's the A in Kern?"

She tapped her temple with her forefinger. "This is Hollywood, don't forget. People change their names. Teri could have been born an Arlene, Alice, Agnes. I know what some of them started with, but not everybody. I know who does, though. Gail Wranawski, the casting director. She hired everybody, and she's been with Warren forever. She'll know every Lipshitz on the set."

"Have you got her number?"

"Sure. But there's not much point in calling her, really. It's Alvin. I *know* it is."

They compromised and tried both McDonald and Wranawski. McDonald wasn't in, but Gail Wranawski answered her phone. Twenty minutes later they found her sitting on a crushed-velvet barstool in a condo on the cliffs of Santa Monica with a sweeping view of the mountains and the ocean. Carla had agreed to let Shelly ask the questions, a promise she appeared to regret as soon as they arrived. Gail Wranawski was a tall woman with starkly cropped brown hair, long cigarettes, and magnificent legs. She wore gray silk lounging pajamas and spike heels which dug into the red rug.

"Warren's an A in more ways than one," she told them easily, in a tone that suggested she knew the value of a good bit of gossip. "Averil Warren Searle. You didn't know that, did you? He doesn't use his first name because it's the same as his father's, a real-estate kingpin who developed half of Irvine, or some such place. But Warren didn't murder Eliot. Couldn't have done it. He's a doll. I'd take him home to mother, if he'd go. I've worked on every picture he's made, and I'll work on all the rest. He's a prince. A bit of a faygela, but a prince."

She sat in front of Lowenkopf but swiveled on her stool every few minutes to make sure Carla was watching too. Carla nodded politely and said, "I think it's Alvin. Don't you?"

Gail had other ideas. "Johnny Weems. Take my word on it. Weems is a prick. Searle made him a star in *Pas de Murder,* but two hits later he's impossible to bargain with. Touchy as shit."

Carla's mouth was open for a follow-up question when she noticed Lowenkopf's expression. She closed her mouth and settled on her barstool. Suppressing his eagerness, Lowenkopf asked, "Weems is an A?"

"Archibald Krueler. Scotch-German. A man who steals ashtrays from Holiday Inn. He could have done it."

"Searle says he didn't."

Gail considered. "Then I don't know who did. Maybe Eliot's boyfriends pulled him apart."

"Did he have a lot of them?"

"Thousands."

Lowenkopf flipped out his notebook and ball-point. "Who would they be?"

Gail pouted. "How would I know, darling? I can't keep track of everyone's love life. It's all I can do to keep track of my own." She swung her magnificent legs in front of Lowenkopf and wobbled to the kitchen, where she plopped ice in two glasses and swirled one at him. "What do you like?"

"Nothing. How did Searle meet Weems?"

Gail poured herself a generous Bloody Mary from a pitcher already mixed in the refrigerator, left the second glass on the counter, and returned to her barstool. Carla eyed the drink covetously as it passed. "I'm sorry," Gail said, "what did you ask?"

"How did Searle meet Johnny Weems?" Lowenkopf repeated.

She raised an eyebrow. "Eliot introduced them. Johnny was a friend of his from sushi class."

Prepared to laugh, Lowenkopf realized she didn't find it funny. "When were Hansen and Searle lovers?"

Gail swiveled towards Carla. "Someone's been waving that old flag, have they? Some news stays news long after it's accurate."

Carla didn't reply.

"They're not anymore?" Lowenkopf demanded. "Are you sure?"

Gail raised one hand as if swearing an oath. "Absolutely, darling. Well, who can be absolutely sure of anything? I mean, I know it ended, but it could have started up again secretly, couldn't it? So I won't say I'm absolutely certain. But I do know this—Warren Searle wouldn't hurt a louse. Even if he were its lover. Which, given Warren's tastes, is conceivable."

Lowenkopf checked his notepad. "What about Teri Kern?"

"What about her? That's her name, Teri Kern. Farmgirl from Kansas or Nebraska, someplace like that. Maybe Iowa . . . or what do you call the ones up north? Dakota. She brakes for animals."

"Who do you think stood to gain by killing Eliot Hansen?"

"Who knows? Eliot was putting together a new package, a costume drama, I think, about Mary and William of Orange—a good choice for this city, isn't it? Maybe somebody wanted in on it. Maybe somebody wanted out. This is a very complex town, Mr. Lowenkopf. Do you mind if I call you Shelly? It's a complicated, confusing, nasty little bungalow colony. Maybe somebody put the screws on Eliot and turned them a smidgen too tight."

"Who was involved with the new project?"

"Warren is the only one I know of for sure. But when

there's an open role in Hollywood, there's five or six thousand hopefuls ready to fill it who'll do whatever it takes to get the chance. And I mean *whatever* it takes, dear. Ask Carla here."

"Carla," corrected Lowenkopf.

"Of course. Not that I'm accusing her of anything, you understand. She's just not really right for Mary. Someone will show up." She gave Carla an encouraging smile over the rim of the Bloody Mary. "And something will come along for Carla, too."

Sure of it, Lowenkopf wasn't about to be sidetracked. "Who could have known that Hansen would be on the beach last night?"

"Everyone," Gail said. "Eliot was like most men who have never been married—set in his ways. He bought his share in that restaurant so he could have his clams just the way he liked them. Anyone who's ever had dinner with him has been dragged along that damned beach afterwards."

"But it was late, wasn't it? Did he always eat that late?"

"He ate when shooting was over. Anyone on the set could have guessed what time he'd be there. Anyone who's eaten with him."

"Who would that include?"

"Warren, of course. McDonald. Probably Weems while they were signing him—I didn't have anything to do with that. And I don't keep tabs on Eliot's intimate dinner parties, either."

She emptied her glass and refilled it at the refrigerator, holding up the pitcher for Lowenkopf again. He shook his head, but this time Carla spoke up. "Could I get one of those, please?"

Gail took down a plastic cup from a cabinet, spilled some Bloody Mary into it, and passed it to Carla. Then she poured a long shot of Scotch into the empty glass, dropped some ice in, and set it before Lowenkopf on the bar. "Just in case. What else can I tell you?"

Lowenkopf sniffed the Scotch. "Who's paying for this film?"

She smiled at him. "The checks say Lester Cravit."

"Who's he?"

"New York lawyer with garment-district money. All those lovely bald men who go into their sweatshops and sew, sew, sew every day have to have someplace to spend it, don't they? They give it to a lawyer, the lawyer puts it in a bank and issues checks in his own name. Illegal investments, political payoffs, anonymous contributions, show biz. I say a little blessing every night for the Lester Cravit Esquires of this world and another for the men whose money they're spending."

Lowenkopf sampled the Scotch. Smooth as burnished silver. "You're the casting director, aren't you? That means you hire the talent?"

"If you want to call them that. The big stars, of course, are often lined up before I come on board. But I make the new stars. Could have been a star myself if I had any boobs."

"Is there an A behind Wranawski?"

She smiled crookedly. "It isn't the sort of name people change their daddy's for, is it?"

"No. And I'm sure you can tell me what you did last night."

Her smile bent. "No, I can't. But I can tell you with who. Robert Culpepper. You'll have to get the details from him, dear, though I doubt that he'll give you any. Robert's a gallant, considerate man."

Even Lowenkopf had heard of Culpepper, the high-stakes producer of stage, screen, and cathode-ray tube whose musical about apartheid had swept last year's Tony awards. He was impressed. "He'll vouch for you?"

"Not if he's a gentlemen. But he'll tell you we were together. That is, when he gets back. He left for the east coast this morning."

"Did anyone else see you together?"

"We're not into anything like that, you evil man."

"I meant earlier in the evening."

"I don't know. Probably a bellhop somewhere." She yawned and shifted on her stool. "I know who you can ask—the doorman at the Beverly Wilshire. He knows me and saw us come in. Though it's a strange man who'll take the word of a doorman over Robert Culpepper's."

Lowenkopf thanked her and apologized for his suspicious

nature. She looked like she might be a sour drunk and he didn't want to stay to find out. Carla had run through a rainbow of scarlets and purples during the interview, and it was time to get her out before she blew. He guided her to the door.

"Clara," Gail called musically as they neared the threshold, "why don't you stop by my office tomorrow? Perhaps we can find something more creative for you to do."

Carla responded immediately. "What time?"

"Oh, some time after noon."

"One?"

"Sometime like that."

"I'll be there."

"Do try."

They hugged each other fondly.

Outside the door, Carla exploded. "I've been doing everything short of begging her to consider me for weeks. Now she suggests the idea as if it were divine inspiration."

"Glad to help," he said.

"Don't believe it. That performance was for your ears only. If I show up at her office, which I won't, she'll say, 'Did you have something in particular in mind?' If I say yes, she'll say, 'Oh, that wouldn't be right for you,' but if I say no, she'll say, 'Why don't you come back and see me when you do?'"

"That's Hollywood?"

"You're getting the idea."

The night watchman at the Beverly Wilshire corroborated Wranawski's story in every detail. She and Culpepper had arrived in Culpepper's limousine shortly after nine-thirty. The long black car and its laconic driver sat in the hotel's drive until well past one in the morning. Yes, he knew Mr. Culpepper's limo well, and he knew Ms. Wranawski. He had personally held the car door when they arrived and closed it after her when they departed. Culpepper had tipped him five dollars each way.

"You see?" demanded Carla over a cup of tepid herb tea in the hotel coffee shop. "What did I tell you? It's got to be Alvin McDonald. Gail might be a very strange person, but her alibi's as good as you can get in Los Angeles."

"Culpepper couldn't be in on it with her, could he?"

"Robert Culpepper? If he wanted Eliot dead, he'd have had him shot."

"You mean mob connections?"

"I mean he's hired half the cowboys in Hollywood one time or another. One of them good ole boys would do it for a favor."

"This is a weird town."

"And getting stranger by the minute." Carla tipped her head gracefully towards the door. An old woman in an ostrich coat shuffled backwards into the room. Carla stood. "I think I'll put in our call to Alvin again."

She retreated to the phone at the back of the coffee shop just as the woman approached, with thick black mascara and a kerchief around her hair. She hesitated, regarded Lowenkopf with trepidation, then broke into a teary grin, lips trembling and eyes grown suddenly red. "Albert?" she said. "Is it really you?"

Lowenkopf looked around, saw that she could be speaking only to him, and slid back along the booth's plastic bench. "No, it isn't," he said.

The woman sat down on the part of the bench his retreat had made available. "It's so good to see you again." She patted his hand with her own, which was remarkably dry and warm. Leaning forward, she whispered loudly, "Don't worry. I won't embarrass you again."

Lowenkopf was mortified. A couple at the next table regarded him sourly. "I never saw this woman before," he told them. The old woman chuckled and signaled imperiously for the waiter.

Carla watched him through the glass of the booth as the phone buzzed at her ear. She watched him suffer the woman's unsteady nostalgia and buy her a soup and a sandwich. He's really a decent guy, she thought to herself, with a twinge of something she didn't care to identify. He looked the way her father had a few years before, young enough still to want things, and old enough to doubt he'd get them. But Shelly was softer, as if the hard pride her father wore had been cracked off him, exposing a concern at once endearing and embarrassing. He seemed to care a lot about a lot of things, which was odd to her but not uninteresting. The stink of oranges had always clung to her father, but Lowenkopf, she guessed, had never *seen* an orchard. He was a frankly Eastern guy who considered himself savvy and had no idea at all where he'd landed.

On the fifth ring, McDonald answered the phone, and told her it was a bad time to come. "Lemme get this straight," he said. "You're working with the police? I thought Lowenkopf was New York fuzz."

"He is. We're looking into this ourselves."

"Then leave me out of it." He hung up on her.

They drove over anyway. McDonald lived in an apartment in Marina del Rey overlooking his boat, which was docked with hundreds of others in a boatyard built by the city of Los Angeles to ease the plight of young executives. A sleek white sailboat with two red sails was moored to a dock within fifty feet of his doorbell. McDonald and another man were sitting on the deck in blue canvas chairs, playing chess. The chessboard was on a barrel, at the base of which stood two bottles of gin, a bottle of vermouth, an ice bucket, and highballs. A radio played below, the sweet scratchy voice of Marianne Faithfull gone punk rock, singing a John Lennon song. The other man, smaller than McDonald and slender as a palm tree, slid his queen across the board with a sly murmur. McDonald laughed, looked up, and saw Carla with Lowenkopf.

"Shit."

The other man glanced up and returned to his move. He lifted his rook and pursed it delicately against his lip, considering the board. He had bleached white hair and wore no shirt over the chiseled muscles of his arms and chest. He regarded them again with a trace of irony in his face, his fine eyebrows arching over beautiful eyes.

Lowenkopf followed Carla down the dock. "Is everyone in Los Angeles gay?"

"Alvin isn't. He's pinched my ass too often for that. Why do you ask?"

By the time they reached the boat, McDonald was casting off. Two of the three ropes that held the sailboat to the dock were loose on the dock and he was struggling frantically with the third.

Lowenkopf slapped the fiberglass side. "Going somewhere?"

"Out." McDonald didn't look up. "I tole you it was a bad day." He called to his chess partner, "Help me wit' this thin', why doan you?"

The man at the board didn't budge. "I don't know how to tie those ropes."

"They're not ropes—they're lines. And I'm not tyin' it, I'm tryin' to untie it, go'dammit." His right hand was bandaged and the rope slipped. The rear of the boat drifted away from the dock. "If you doan gimme a hand, you're gonna be floatin' out there by yourself."

The man on deck picked up his glass and went below.

Lowenkopf caught the stern of the boat and reattached a line just as McDonald managed to work loose the prow. He stood uncomprehending, blinking at the reattached line for a moment. Then he seemed to collapse at the waist. "All right," he said. "What can I do for you fast?"

McDonald climbed onto his deck. Carla fleetly hopped up after him and gave Lowenkopf a hand. He wobbled for an instant on the edge and sat down against the boat's silver rail. "Where were you last night between ten and midnight?"

"Damned if I know. We hit the Charthouse 'round nine las' night—maybe nine-thirty—an' woke up at ten this mornin'. Wit' this." He held up his bandaged hand.

"Anybody see you there?"

"Lotsa people."

"Who?"

"I doan know who they were. Whoever was there. We aren't exactly Little Miss Keep-to-Herselfs."

While Lowenkopf questioned McDonald, Carla poked around the boat. It was expensive but not well kept, stylishly designed but poorly cleaned and managed. She kicked a sprawling line into some kind of pile and listened with one ear to the interview.

Lowenkopf asked, "Do you know who was at the bar and saw you?"

McDonald answered, "Who?"

"I don't know who," Lowenkopf said patiently. "Is there anyone you know of who'll admit to seeing you there between ten and midnight?"

"There's Charlie." McDonald pointed belowdeck.

"I mean you and Charlie."

"Can't we vouch for each other?"

"Can't you do better than that?"

"There's no better than Charlie. An' as far's he's concerned, there's no better'n me. Hey, Charlie!" he yelled into the doorway. "Come up an' tell 'em where we were las' night!"

Charlie's white head emerged, followed by the impressive physique, now in a striped sailor shirt. He held an imported beer. "We were at the Charthouse. Then here."

"On the boat?" McDonald asked him.

"Belowdeck."

"Tha's right," McDonald confirmed. "I remember that."

The bartender at the Charthouse placed them there, but not until after midnight. "It's busy as hell in here by then. People waiting for tables at the bar and over by the door. Some of them go for walks along the boats until their name's called. All I remember is, around midnight, Charlie got into an argument over a table. They mighta come in anytime up to an hour before." He shrugged. A waitress put in a call and the bartender went to fill it.

That left them pretty much where they had started. Carla sipped a daiquiri. "How are we going to remember all we learned today?"

Lowenkopf sampled her drink. "We must have learned *something* important."

"If only we knew what it was. I'll call Warren and pass on the good news. Maybe he'll give us another day if he sees I'm prompt and honest." She left him at the bar and marched to the phones by the rest rooms.

He ordered a beer and munched a few goldfish pretzels. Why was any man murdered? Usually it boiled down to only a few reasons. Money—but Hansen still had cash in his wallet. Jealousy—but whose? Searle wasn't satisfied that the police investigation would be thorough enough. That didn't sound to Lowenkopf like a murderer. Who had Hansen been seeing lately? Searle would know, but asking might be touchy. Did Hansen know something he shouldn't have? About whom? Lowenkopf always hated these cases, with motives hanging on some chance discovery. How do you find out what a dead man knew? He longed for a fact, an Occam's razor to limit the pool of suspects. It could have been anyone on the set, anyone at the Oyster Pit, anyone Hansen knew through his family, his grocer, his hairdresser, anyone. Maybe he hadn't even known his killer. It seemed unlikely that he would have turned his back on a stranger alone at night on the beach, but after all, this was California.

There were always two tracks to follow—motive and opportunity. No one he had met yet had unwittingly betrayed a compelling motive, and apparently none of them had the opportunity to swing the fatal firewood. The murder weapon itself was a dead end—no one had bought it, hidden it, or disposed of it in any way that might suggest a clue. It had been lying there conveniently close at hand, ready to be used. What *was* Hansen doing on the beach? Roasting marshmallows? Why not? Some men like jelly beans.

Why didn't the murderer dump the weapon in the fire? No one would have dusted a burning log for prints or checked for blood and hair until long after it had turned to ash. A premeditating murderer would have thought of it; therefore, the act had to be spontaneous. He had seen someone who looked like Johnny Weems running away from the scene. If it wasn't Weems, and the murder wasn't premeditated, why would anyone want to run around resembling a red-haired yahoo with a gold chain around his neck?

A pretty blonde sat on Carla's stool. Lowenkopf waited for her to turn and catch his eye. She never did. He watched the foam evaporate on his beer.

Weems could have done it. But if so, then Searle was lying to protect him. If Searle *was* lying, why had he asked Lowenkopf to assist the investigation? Who was A? He scratched the initial with his fingernail into the cocktail napkin and stared at it a moment, waiting for the rest of a name to crease the paper beside it, but it hung ambiguously before him like all of the other odd bits of information—if you could call it information—that had fallen their way that day. His instincts told him just one thing—McDonald and his friend Charlie couldn't commit a murder without leaving their signatures in the sand. Of that, at least, he was certain.

The bartender tapped his arm. Carla was signaling dramatically, waving her hand and pointing to the door. He couldn't make out what she was trying to communicate. She frowned and crossed to him, smiling automatically at the heads turning phototropically in her wake.

"Searle wasn't in, so I called Oquita, just to see if he had anything new. His lab found a palm print on a beer bottle at the firepit. Oquita's men have been at the studio all day, dusting for prints to compare with it. What do you think they found?"

She waited for him to guess. He shrugged.

She took his hands in hers. "It's what I've said all along. Alvin's chair was full of them. It's his print."

They ran back to the dock, but the red-and-white sailboat was gone.

7

Within the hour, McDonald's dock and apartment were awash in blues, cordoning off the area, scribbling down neighbors' statements, staring at the water from stations on the pier. Oquita strutted the wooden planks, obviously relishing the squeak of salty wood beneath his feet.

"At first we missed it completely," he informed Carla, practicing for the reporters. "We found only one print on the bottle, a left-handed print. Since the victim's left hand had been burned, our first thought was that it was his. But I wondered—just one print? I drink a beer in my right hand, but hold it in my left to twist off the cap. I spent all day at the movie studio, dusting everything until I found a palm that matched. You see? We are not so laid-back that we fall asleep on the job." He elbowed Lowenkopf's ribs fraternally.

Lowenkopf rubbed the spot. "You think McDonald killed Hansen?" It was getting hot and his clothes were too warm.

"I would ask him, but he isn't here to answer, is he? Wonder why he left in such a hurry?"

Snyder emerged from the apartment with a message for Oquita. Carla pulled Lowenkopf towards her car before the blond cop could gloat. He offered no resistance, either to her grip on his wrist or to her firm line of reasoning. "It's been a long day. Why don't we make it an early night? Searle's shooting tomorrow. We've got to be on the set by six."

She loaded him into the seat and slipped in behind the wheel. As the stick shift hit the gear, his seat belt buzzed. She leaned over and buckled him in. "What's the matter?"

He looked at her hands in his lap as if he wasn't sure what they were. "I don't feel much like moving now, that's all."

She patted his seat-belt buckle and withdrew her hands. "You'll feel better once you've had a chance to sleep on it. It's not easy admitting you're wrong. Especially to an amateur who was right."

She was as smug as Oquita with the way the investigation had worked out. But Shelly wasn't sure it had worked out. He took a deep breath, let it out slowly through his teeth, and said, "That wasn't McDonald I saw on the beach last night. He might be smart enough to wear a wig, but he couldn't ape that lopsided Johnny Weems lope. McDonald's no actor, is he?"

She leaned back to her steering wheel, annoyed. "It's Alvin, Shelly. Oquita's got his fingerprints, remember?"

"So McDonald was on the beach," Lowenkopf conceded slowly. "But that doesn't mean he killed Hansen. Searle I'd believe—a little reluctantly, I admit, having written him off as a suspect—but not McDonald. No way. Have you ever met a murderer, Carla? I've known a lot of them. Usually you can see it in them, once your radar goes up. McDonald keeps coming up clean."

But Carla was prepared to be logical. "Maybe that was just a jogger you saw on the beach. Did you ever think of that? They're all over the place these days. Alvin could have done it. The bartender doesn't remember seeing him until midnight. And his hand's bandaged."

"Cut, not burned," Lowenkopf insisted. "His palm was wrapped but his fingers were exposed. Did you ever burn your palm without your fingers?"

"I've never burned anything. Except my tongue."

Lowenkopf ignored the tongue she provocatively flashed for his inspection. "He cut that hand on a broken bottle. I'm sure of it. But I think I know how we can settle this. There are two last stops to check out. Just for my own peace of mind."

He looked so pitiable she burst out laughing. "I can see I won't have any peace until you do. Where first?"

"Someone should find out if that parking-lot attendant can't place McDonald—or anyone else—in the Porsche. Or anywhere near the beach. You think you can handle that?"

"You mean alone? Where are you going?"

"I want to talk to Johnny Weems."

She raised one eyebrow sarcastically. "Sure . . . I drop you at a movie star's house in the Hills and go merrily on my way to a parking lot at the beach. Whither thou goest, I goest also, buster." She turned the Mazda on two tires and headed for the freeway. Lowenkopf braced his shoe against the dashboard and closed his eyes.

The crash never came. Weems's vast Colonial sat three stories high on a hill overlooking the West Gate. Carla's tires made gravel fly in the driveway, until she settled in a little cloud of smoke beside some birds of paradise whose stooped blue-and-orange flowers jutted out from a cluster of rubber trees like scrawny storks at a bath.

The front door was ajar. Carla rang the doorbell twice. When no one answered, she led him into the hall, a dim chamber rather like the entrance to a church. To their left was a living room with fur couches; to their right, a passageway lined by a mirror on which Mickey Mouse and Minnie had been painted in a compromising position. In front of them, a black door opened on a stairway leading down. From beneath their feet came the sound of heavy machines rolling on a concrete floor. Lowenkopf began to descend the short flight to the basement.

He was immediately confronted by a wall of television

sets on double-decker rolling carts, thirty of them at least, arranged side by side in unbroken succession. All were on, but none showed a picture. Instead, the visual equivalent of random noise, a patternless flickering of thousands of independent dots of color, repeated endlessly on screen after screen, none of them tiring, none of them ever the same. For an instant, all of the noise resolved itself in an image thirty times over—the girl with green eyes he had seen on the set, curled on a vinyl chair, stretching a green sweatshirt. The girl on the screens seemed to look through him. She said flatly, "It's Carla. With someone else." Then she disappeared in a snowstorm of random noise.

Two of the rolling carts suddenly parted and Weems emerged. His hair was crammed into a farmer's Cat cap, and seemed orange-red in the light. The rapacious absorption in his eyes caused Carla to grasp Lowenkopf's arm. "Come in," Weems commanded, and disappeared between his machines.

They followed him into the space. On the other side of the wall of screens they found a small video studio. At one end was a raised platform that served as a stage, on which a couch had been placed, draped in paisley sheets. In front of the platform Teri Kern wiped her neck with the sleeve of her sweatshirt, her knees drawn up on a white vinyl lawn chair. Weems reappeared from behind another cart with a television set on its upper shelf and a videocassette recorder below. He had been screwing a coaxial cable into the back of the video machine. Now he loped nimbly down the length of the cord to a camera at its end. He adjusted the angle of that camera, focused the zoom lens of another, and turned the fifteen rolling carts around so they could watch the screens.

"Very good. You're just in time. Hold that right there." The last command was for Lowenkopf, who found two electric wires without casing thrust in his hands. Weems wrapped silver gaffer's tape around the connection and Lowenkopf's fingers. Reaching behind Lowenkopf's head, he snapped a switch and a battery of blinding quartz lights on telescoping stands glared down.

Carla shaded her eyes. "Just in time for what?"

Teri Kern crawled out of the lawn chair and slithered to a seat on the couch. Weems pushed a button on a control panel buried in a bushel of wires, and her face reappeared on ten screens. With a warm steady stare at Lowenkopf, she crossed her arms, seized the waist of her sweatshirt, and lifted it over her head. Her large breasts bounced free and pointed at Carla competitively.

Weems pushed another button, and ten more screens resolved blizzards into image, as Teri's brown nipples stared out. He turned a third camera on Carla. "Just in time to make a tape. Teri won't mind sharing the spotlight, will you, darling?" Darling didn't mind.

The last ten screens filled with an image of Carla backing to the stairs. "I think I've had enough show business for one day, Johnny. See you."

Lowenkopf caught her hand at the threshold. "I'd like to stay," he said. "If it's all right with you."

She tried to yank her hand free. "Go ahead."

"Here." He pressed his room key into her palm.

She glanced at the screens and smiled bitterly. "I wouldn't take too much for granted, Lowenkopf." But she dropped the key in her purse.

Weems pushed a lever and the two images of Teri collided on all the screens. He laughed mirthlessly as the wooden door overhead slammed behind Carla. "And she says she wants her chance." The double image on the monitors splintered into slivers of Teri Kern confronting each other abstractly.

Lowenkopf groped his way to the lawn chair. "This is fascinating stuff. But I was hoping you could spare a few minutes—"

"Watch this," Weems commanded. His hands hovered over the control panel like a maestro's approaching the piano, descending in a sudden, silent crash. A green inkblot shaped like a spread eagle was superimposed over the screen and Teri's warm flesh tones ran an unflattering shade of fuchsia. He tilted both cameras and zoomed in on her face. The next moment she disappeared entirely in a spasm of raster manipulations; jerky fragments of the screen's illuminated surface folded back upon themselves a dozen times over. Lowenkopf stole a glance at the stage as the girl neatly rolled her sweatpants down over her knees. She slipped him a crafty smile.

Weems waved his arms frenetically. "Move a little, will you, darling? Do something. Dance." As he fired instructions, he provided an example, dancing in a small circle with his fists above his head as if supplicating a deity to receive an offered sacrifice.

Onstage, Teri responded. She moved when Weems said "move" and danced when he said "dance," but her eyes remained on Lowenkopf, fixed and transfixing. A sensation of spotlights overcame him—he had felt it the morning before when her gaze first brushed him on the set.

"What are you looking at?" Weems demanded. Lowenkopf averted his eyes guiltily, then realized Weems was addressing the girl. Weems noticed Lowenkopf's expression and said, "Oh. Get out of her range, will you? Sit behind something."

Lowenkopf retreated to the console. "Is there anything I can do to speed this up?"

"Can you sing?"

He shook his head.

"Then just keep quiet. You can turn on the audio deck over there." A quarter-inch audio tape was primed and ready to go on a steel reel-to-reel machine. Lowenkopf touched a white button, which softly lighted under the pressure of his finger. The wheels began to turn and the sound of wheat bushels scraping against a concrete floor came flawlessly from two large speakers mounted on the wall above the lawn chair. With each repetition of the sound Weems jerked a dial, and the screen image jumped suddenly to the right, exploding in a crash of eagle feathers and purple slivers of Teri. Then a small flicker of yellow light licked the center of the picture, the music ended mid-brush, and the screens faded to black.

"Now, that's art!" Weems announced, closing the iris on each of the video cameras. "That's the first movement. Dry yourself off." He threw the girl a towel and wheeled on Lowenkopf. "Now you can tell me what you're doing here."

Lowenkopf felt in his pocket for his badge. "I—"

"I know who you are. You're the nobody from New York who's been telling the cops I clobbered Hansen with a chunk of firewood. I'd like to take the opportunity to thank you for that. It's been a real pleasure. Now, get the fuck out of here. I'm on my own time and Searle's got no claim to any part of it."

Lowenkopf tried to be slow to take offense. He looked around the room and counted ten. "Thinking of going into competition with him?"

Weems erupted with a single barking laugh. "This is art we're making here, not some cheesy cops-and-robbers picture. Not what you thought it was, is it? That's why you're a cop making thirty grand a year and I'm looking at her tits through a zoom lens." He pushed the rewind button on the video recorder and was off again, snapping off floodlights, closing barn doors, tugging at the connection he had taped over Lowenkopf's fingers.

Lowenkopf followed him to the end of his patience, but when Weems turned off the last monitor and headed for the stairs, Lowenkopf grabbed him by both arms and leaned him against the wall. "If you don't sit down long enough to give me one minute of your time, I'm going to break your crooked nose all over again."

Weems touched his nose lovingly and sat. "How do you know it was broken?"

"I've broken them before."

Teri watched them with interest. Lowenkopf avoided her eyes.

Weems rubbed his nostrils. "All right. One minute. I'm counting."

Lowenkopf lifted a footstool with his shoe and set it in front of Weems. He took out his notebook and wrote on his knee. "You knew Hansen before this film, didn't you?"

"Yes."

"From where?"

"He lined me up for Searle's final film-school project. They used to screw each other."

"When was the last time you saw him?"

"When you accused him of stealing your briefcase, you shit."

"What did you do after shooting the scene?"

"I had a little talk with Searle. The bastard treats me like the hungry kid he used in film school. I did *Pas de Murder* for a song. We had dinner together. You know what the sport orders? Sandwiches. That should tell you something about Searle."

"What did you talk about?"

"The weather."

"If I've only got one minute here, cut the crap." Lowenkopf flipped back to an earlier page in his notebook. "Why did Searle tell you he'd rather fire you than Gail Wranawski?"

"Who told you that? I don't know what kind of hold that broad has on him, but I wish I had a piece of it. It's not between the knees, because he's a fruit—you knew that, didn't you? I wouldn't want to give away any family secrets."

"I know. You just told me a minute ago, and he's told me himself. Get back to Gail Wranawski."

"She started as his makeup girl. Made me up that first picture. Now she decides who can play a corpse in his films and who can't. She goes around with some hotshot producer, but let me tell you something, copper, when it comes down to it, her ass is no bigger than mine."

"You asked him to fire her?"

"I *told* him to."

"Why?"

"Because she talks too much. Like you. Come to think of it, you have a lot in common. You're both losers."

"But he didn't. Why not?"

"Ask Searle. Your minute's up." Weems theatrically watched the seconds tick on a large gold dial strapped to the inside of his hairy wrist.

"One more question. When did you leave Searle?"

"Who knows? Sixty-three, sixty-four. Now, get out of here before I call the grown-up cops. Get him a cab." He threw the command at Teri and marched up the stairs.

Teri slid past Lowenkopf to the lawn chair and coiled around the telephone receiver. "Did you enjoy that little game you played with Johnny?"

"What do you mean?"

"He didn't seem to enjoy it much. Somebody must have, or you wouldn't have played. Ergo, it must have been you."

He was impressed by the cool lines of her logic, the only straight lines anywhere on her. "I must have enjoyed it, then."

She pulled up her legs to make room at the foot of the lawn chair. "Then it was worth it. I'll tell you something else. I enjoyed it too."

"I'm glad." He propped his foot on the chair's bottom edge and leaned on his knee. It left him posing awkwardly.

She enjoyed that too. As she dialed she stretched her legs until her ankle touched his. "Maybe you'll interrogate me sometime."

"Do you know anything worth interrogating you to get?" Even as he said it, he felt a cringe of shame at his collar. Or it could have been heat.

She slid forward. "Lots."

Her face was very close to his. He tried not to sound doubtful when he said, "Like what?"

"About Johnny."

His interest was suddenly sincere. "Do you know where he was last night?"

She smiled coquettishly.

"Where?"

She placed her free hand over his mouth and said into the receiver, "White Knight Cab? Could you send a car now, please?" As she gave the address her lips barely moved over the mouthpiece cradled at her neck. Her free shoulder peeped out whitely from her sweatshirt and a stark shadow underlined her collarbone. She hung up and put everything back into place. "I can't tell you for sure where he was, but I can tell you where he wasn't. He wasn't with Warren Searle last night."

"How do you know?"

She was offended. "I recognized the scent on his collar when he came in. It's too expensive for Searle."

"Can you prove it?"

She paused for effect. "Yes."

"How?"

She drew away from him and looked him over, taking stock. When the answer came, her tone was indifferent. "If he didn't eat with Searle, he must have eaten somewhere else. Johnny's always scrupulous with his dinner receipts. Taxes, you know. If he was out with a woman, he paid the bill. If he paid the bill, he's got the receipt for it somewhere. Usually he stuffs them in the side pocket of his jacket. I could bring it to your hotel room sometime."

Her logic was dazzling. Lowenkopf slipped into the limpid pools of her cool green eyes. "Why would you do that for me?"

She curled up on the left side of the chair, leaving the right side empty. "Maybe 'cuz I like you. Maybe because I don't like Johnny."

He waved at the video machines and couch covered in sheets. "Then why put up with this?"

"I put up with a lot of things I don't like. A girl has to start somewhere." Something in the way she said it made him think of Carla.

Weems's tromp on the stairs cut them short. His curly red head cleared the ceiling and his steely eyes glowered at Lowenkopf. One by one he clicked on all the television sets. Wordlessly Teri rose from the chair and resumed her place on the couch. Weems strolled over to her and, glaring at Lowenkopf, pointedly pushed back her hair.

Lowenkopf trampled as many cables as he could on his way out.

Weems watched him with satisfaction. "Nice stuff, huh?" Teri again filled all the screens. "But let me tell you—this is nothing, Lowenkopf. That camera in the corner can record a mosquito in the dark. Just imagine what we do with that."

The parking-lot attendant at the Oyster Pit recognized Weems's photo immediately, but didn't recall seeing the actor the night before. He didn't remember the white Porsche either, or rather, he remembered too many of them. "Give me a clue—Carerra? Targa? Nine-twelve? Nine-forty-two?" he said, and that was the end of that line of questioning. Still, the ocean was calming, the moon ran its finger over the waves, and the sky was luminous. A sailboat hung in the water a few hundred feet from the shore, its sails drooping. Lowenkopf wandered over to the shoreline, listening to the surf. With a start he realized he was within a hundred feet of the scene of the murder.

The lab crew had removed all the grisly details, but he imagined he could still taste something more than salt in the air. Stones and charred wood littered the sand. He tried to identify the spot where the body had fallen. There was a rock whose coloring seemed darker than its neighbors', drier, perhaps—Lowenkopf remembered the head that had smashed against it, and a chill touched the base of his neck. At some point on these cases he always imagined the life taken as a bird freed or forced from its cage. In Hansen's case, it had fled. Music was coming softly from somewhere nearby and he listened for a moment to Marianne Faithfull drawling John Lennon's lyrics. The chorus hung ghoulishly over the charred firepit.

He repeated the line and waited for the music to rise, and suddenly wondered how he knew it would. He had heard that song somewhere recently. Last night at the Oyster Pit? He looked back at the restaurant and could make out the terrace on which he and Carla had eaten. Their table was occupied by a woman in a pale summer dress and her blazered companion, happy, no doubt, to be together. Lowenkopf heard the chorus again. "They weren't playing music last night!" he said aloud, and spun around for the source of the music to the drooping red sails on the water. There was a movement on deck, the music stopped, and the blur, now a figure, disappeared. Something in the movements rang a bell and Lowenkopf suddenly placed the lyrics.

He stood in his shoes and socks and rumpled corduroy suit at the edge of the sand. Across a stretch of black waves, a crimson sail wagged at him, pitching now and then as the ocean swelled beneath it. Lowenkopf knew the limits of his own powers as a swimmer. But the red sail beckoned to him, enticing him by underscoring the gulf that lay between them. It was like watching through a window as a woman danced, the music reaching out for a partner. He had heard that song on McDonald's dock in the marina. There was no mistaking it. Or the winking red sail. McDonald was on that boat, and Charlie too. They had returned to the scene of the crime. By the time he could reach the Oyster Pit and convince Oquita to summon the Coast Guard, the red sails would disappear in the night. *If* he could convince Oquita, which, given his track record, was no sure bet. He had seen a red sail and heard a snatch of a song—that was all. But there they were, and here he was, separated only by a few thousand gallons of water.

Without taking his eyes off the boat, Lowenkopf kicked off his shoes and stripped down to his undershirt and shorts. He was determined not to let this opportunity slip by—he thought fleetingly of Searle, Oquita, Carla. He was a fair swimmer at best. Thom was better, but he wouldn't let Thom near the water with waves like this. There would be a tide, but it was a short way out and back. As soon as he was positive McDonald was aboard, he could swim back and phone Oquita. He nervously watched the pull of the tide on the foam as it receded, felt the frigid water touch the bottoms of his feet, and then ran like a madman into the surf.

The tide was moving out. He hadn't anticipated the strength of the undertow, which pulled him out soundlessly and effortlessly. When he reached the boat, he put both hands against its side and rested, winded. He heard only the lapping of the waves against the bow. More than once he clutched smooth fiberglass to avoid being sucked under or slapped against the hull. His bones felt like ice, and that more than anything else gave him the push he needed to climb up and scout the deck.

He had concluded it was empty when, on the far side, a shape that had been huddled over the edge stood up. "All right, I've got you now, come on out." McDonald's voice carried clearly in the night air. Lowenkopf dropped back in the water with a plop just as Charlie's muscular form flopped onto the deck in a black wet suit. Wet feet slapped the plastic deck and the pop-sizzle of a beer can made Lowenkopf instantly thirsty.

"Well?" McDonald.

There was the thin metal click of an old Zippo lighter. Charlie didn't like to be rushed. "Nothing. There's nothing left. This was a stupid, pointless exercise. We're pigeons here, waddling around waiting to be shot. If there was anything to tie us to this place, they have it now."

An ocean of black water rocked between Lowenkopf and the telephone in the Oyster Pit bar. He had learned enough. But the trip back to shore looked far more perilous from his new point of view. The current which had carried him out now strove to keep him.

McDonald crossed the deck and perched on the railing, inches above Lowenkopf's head. "So what do we do now?" He sounded dispirited.

"I'm going to do nothin'," Charlie said. "No one has made any formal charges against us, have they? Or is there something you haven't told me?"

"You know what I know." McDonald swore defensively.

"I hope a little more than that," Charlie muttered. "Tell me, when did you last manage to haul this crate to Catalina Island?"

"Two weeks ago."

"Then you know how to get us there again. Trim the sails, or whatever you have to do to make this move. I'm getting into something dry."

McDonald did not offer a protest. Metal scraped, a rope squeaked through a pulley, canvas flapped. Lowenkopf could not tell if Charlie had gone belowdeck—he hadn't heard him descend, but could discern only one pair of feet shuffling overhead. If they would just step back a yard or two, he'd take his chance. He imagined the inevitable splash.

Something slashed the water alongside Lowenkopf and disappeared behind the sailboat's stern. His heart thumped so loudly he thought they would hear it on deck. His eyes were glued to the stern. A wave caught him from the side and he slipped beneath the water but emerged, gasping, without shifting his gaze. For an endless minute, whatever it was did not reappear. Then suddenly a flash of white.

"Oo-ohhh . . ." No sooner was it out than Lowenkopf

regretted his alarm. The fin turned on its side—and into a paper plate. Had they heard him on deck? Like a turtle emerging from its shell, Lowenkopf raised his head and met McDonald's soft eyes peering down into his.

For an instant Lowenkopf returned the stare. Then McDonald cried, "Charlie!" and the spell shattered. Lowenkopf dove down under the waves and kicked back as hard as he could. The current dragged at him—stroke as he would, the beach maintained its distance. The undertow which had carried him out now kept Lowenkopf near the boat and the frightened men on it.

There was a splash in the water behind him, out of sync with his own rhythm. Lowenkopf kicked back along the surface, sending back a spray at whatever followed behind, but slowing his forward progress to a standstill. A few hundred feet now separated him from the sand and the telephone line to Oquita. He would have to fight for every inch. Somewhere in the inky liquid behind him stroked Charlie in his wet suit, a born Californian in his element.

Like a blanket around his limbs, a weariness came over Lowenkopf. He swallowed water, spit it out, went off his rhythm, and swallowed some more. His bones felt brittle with cold and his chest ached as he drew each breath. His feet skidded under him. He kicked a little and slapped the surface with his arms. The beach looked farther than the moon.

His mouth was full of water. He coughed and sputtered it out, lifting his head above the waves, gulping air, struggling to stay afloat, paddling wildly to keep the enormous weight on his shoulders from crushing him. Suddenly he felt a hand grip his ankle. He kicked back violently, slipping below, clawing his way to the surface. Charlie was somewhere nearby, but he didn't much care now. His shoulders knotted, throbbing. He dropped below, gulped water, raised himself, and sank again.

A hand locked on his knee, dragging him down just as his breath expired. He kicked against the hand, lunging towards the surface for air. The grip was inescapable. He swam towards it, setting one foot against the wrist and stamping with all his weight. His left leg broke free, but his right was caught in a vise. His lungs felt as if he were screaming. He thrashed to the surface for an instant, exhaled, but before he could breathe, was yanked down.

He floated in absolute silence, in the sealed vault of ocean. Above him, the surface hissed whitely. Everything that died in the sea waited below. A vision of Charlie's swollen cheeks swam past as Lowenkopf drifted in the belly of the sea.

He came to in a puddle of water on the white fiberglass deck of a sailboat. His cheek was propped on a blue mat, its polyester hairs pricking his lips. McDonald slumped in a canvas chair nearby, watching with clinical interest. But Lowenkopf was on the boat, alive. There must have been more interest somewhere.

"You're a hard man to rescue when you're drowning." Charlie's ironic tone might have sounded friendly from a friend. From Charlie it ran ominously.

Painfully Lowenkopf raised himself. "You boys are in a lot of trouble." He didn't sound as convincing as he'd hoped. Of the three of them, he thought, a neutral observer would find Charlie the most compelling—leaning against the mast, flicking cigarette ashes on the deck, while Lowenkopf drooped in a pool of water. He would have liked a chance to try his opening line again.

Charlie gave McDonald a smug glare. "I told you no one would believe us."

"Give me a chance," McDonald insisted. He moved his chair closer to Lowenkopf and spoke with the tone of enforced patience with which dogs are trained. "Mr. Lowenkopf"—a stage pause—"do I look like a murderer to you?"

Lowenkopf peered at him closely. "Yes."

McDonald let his soft soles fall on the damp deck between them. He leaned forward. "I mean it. If I was going to kill somebody, do you think I'd crack him over the head with a chunk of wood? As opposed to, say, a poisoned postage stamp?"

It appeared to be the aesthetics of the crime that disturbed him. But Lowenkopf ached and didn't give a damn. "You could. If it was handy."

Charlie cursed, crushing his cigarette against the mast.

"Give me a minute, will ya? You've got to give somebody a motivation they can work with."

"Real people don't behave like actors, Alvin."

"I know that. But he's just come out of the water. You can't expect him to reason like a rational human being." McDonald edged his chair closer. "Mr. Lowenkopf—or what should I say, Lieutenant?"

"Sergeant." From Charlie.

"Sergeant," McDonald continued, without losing a beat. "Think of it this way—what did I have to gain? Searle likes me. At least he did. Hansen liked me too. My career was going great guns. And now? Pssst. Dead in the water. I'm the last person they should suspect. I've got a negative motive." He looked at Charlie for confirmation.

"Sounds good to me," Charlie said. "Good enough to fry."

Lowenkopf spit something off the tip of his tongue.

McDonald tried again. "Hell, when this is over, I'm going to sue somebody. How would your captain like that?" Lowenkopf refused to picture it, but McDonald must have read something on his face, because he pressed his point. "I'll tell you something no one knows. Hansen was putting together a package with a job in it for me. Above the line. The story of Will and Mary—king and queen of England. He was going to put me in the director's chair. Now, am I going to mess up something like that?"

Lowenkopf shook his head to clear the water from his ears. "Carla was talking about that," he said. "She said Hansen was going to give it to Searle, as usual."

"Not this time," McDonald insisted fervently. "We had a talk and Hansen changed his mind. Why would I knock him off before he put it in writing?"

Lowenkopf stuck his pinkie in one ear and shook it. "That's a nice story. Why don't you try it on the jury? But there's one little problem. Your fingerprints were found at the scene of the crime, and they're the only fingerprints found there. What did Charlie do, hold him down while you hit him?"

"I played the ukulele," Charlie said.

McDonald looked desperately from one of them to the

other. "I was there, all right. I made that fire. You know that talk with Hansen I was telling you about? We had it on the beach. Charlie and I were having a barbecue by the Oyster Pit when Hansen came by."

"And I suppose he gave you the nod for a multimillion-dollar picture because your marshmallows were so good."

"Not *his* marshmallows," Charlie hissed, slapping his own rear end expressively. "Mine."

McDonald looked at Lowenkopf, his eyes boyishly innocent. "We had pictures," he explained, "of the two of them. Together."

It took Lowenkopf a moment to understand. "You were *blackmailing* Hansen?"

Charlie laughed. "We tried."

"Didn't he bite?"

"Oh, he bit," McDonald assured him. His face grew pink as a wave of indignation overcame him.

"Can you imagine anything dumber?" He was outraged by the untimeliness of the death, the personal bad luck. "Charlie and I want that killer more than anybody. But as long as you cops are looking for us, nobody's going to find him. That sonofabitch not only stuck us on the hook for murder, he put the kabosh on two years of deals. He can't get away with that in this town!"

It had McDonald's sort of reasoning going for it. Lowenkopf glanced back toward shore but could only make out the bright silhouette of the Oyster Pit. "Is that what you nearly drowned me to tell me?"

"You were drowning nicely on your own. What I think Alvin is trying to ask you is to get your Keystone cousins on the stick. We can't stay out here forever."

Lowenkopf moved to the railing and stretched the cramps from his arms. He peered over the side. The current looked strong.

Charlie regarded him peevishly. "We might just as well have tied a message to a stone and dropped it over the side. Who do you think we've got here—Johnny Weissmuller? Here"—he tossed Lowenkopf a lifejacket—"this ought to keep you afloat. I've had enough drama for one night at sea."

As Lowenkopf floated back to shore, buoyed by the life

preserver, kicking leisurely behind him, he had a little time to reflect. "Now, this isn't something I expected to do," he said to himself. In the night sky he found Orion and Cassiopeia, Madagascar and Carla. "It's true what they say—life *is* different in the West."

When his knees struck sand, Lowenkopf stood. From the gentle sea he rose, shivering. He was too wet and gritty to put on his clothes, so he bundled them under his arm and jogged to the Oyster Pit. The terrace was jammed with well-dressed people eating fat red lobsters. He slapped up the steps, rivulets of seawater dripping from his undershirt and boxer shorts.

Nobody gave him a second glance.

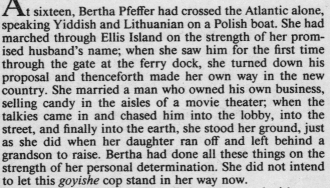

At sixteen, Bertha Pfeffer had crossed the Atlantic alone, speaking Yiddish and Lithuanian on a Polish boat. She had marched through Ellis Island on the strength of her promised husband's name; when she saw him for the first time through the gate at the ferry dock, she turned down his proposal and thenceforth made her own way in the new country. She married a man who owned his own business, selling candy in the aisles of a movie theater; when the talkies came in and chased him into the lobby, into the street, and finally into the earth, she stood her ground, just as she did when her daughter ran off and left behind a grandson to raise. Bertha had done all these things on the strength of her personal determination. She did not intend to let this *goyishe* cop stand in her way now.

"This is my grandson, Theo," she announced with great clarity as she placed a smudged Polaroid snapshot on Greeley's desk. "He's a good boy deep inside, but on the outside he's rotten. Three nights now he hasn't been home, so this is the first place I come to look for him."

In the photograph Greeley saw a scrubbed boy with neatly combed hair in a white shirt and a red cross-tie. On the back of the picture a date was penciled in a rough hand—18 July 1977. "Is this the most recent photo you can show me?"

"What? Yes, it's a little old—seven years, eight years—but that's what I have."

"Nine years."

"Nine years? All right, nine years. He still looks like that." She sat squarely in the hard wooden chair, satisfied she had done her part, waiting for Greeley to do his.

He found the form and rolled it in his typewriter. "The same last name as yours?"

"What then?"

On his third attempt he spelled the name correctly and took down what information the woman offered. Her grandson had left their apartment in the Housing Authority projects three days earlier and had not been home since. Yes, Theo had stayed out overnight before, but not three days. No, he had not taken anything with him: his clothes were still in his closet, his pictures of mostly naked women caressing long red cars still on his walls.

The woman silently admired Greeley's trim blond head. "Now you know everything. So what can you do for me?"

"Give me a chance, ma'am. We'll see." Greeley checked the arrest reports, then the coroner's report. No Theo Pfeffer had been logged in the last forty-eight hours. That was good news.

"Very nice," she agreed when he told her. "So where is he now?"

Greeley shuffled through the papers again. There was no answer in them. "Isn't there anything else you can tell me about him? A mark, a mole, something that might help identify him?"

All the wrinkles in her face screwed up in the lines that had etched them. "A mole? Where would he get a mole? What do you think I raised, a rodent?"

Greeley's gaze never wavered. "Has he ever been arrested before?"

"Before what?"

"Has he ever been arrested at all?"

"God forbid."

"Then why did you come here?"

"You're the police, aren't you? Where else should I go?"

Greeley hated to give up any case with less than complete success, but after twelve years on the force he knew when to cut his losses. Further investment of time would only make his inevitable failure on this one more acute. He stood up, walked around his desk, and leaned against it, hands in his pockets and a sympathetic smile on his lips. "Mrs. Pfeffer, I'm sorry, but New York is a big city. We're not going to be able to find your grandson unless you can tell me more about him."

He meant it to conclude the interview and she understood his intention. Touching the tight gray bun at the back of her head, she rose majestically, raising herself against the edge of his desk. Then, carrying rather than leaning on her cane, she made a last attempt to enlist his interest. "I can tell you plenty, Officer. His favorite meal is a piece of white chicken with a hamburger on a separate plate. When I need a light bulb changed or the toilet fixed, he's a good boy, but as far as his comings and goings, who knows? When you want a little excitement, he always knows a joke, but when you need a little peace—such noise! Buttons jangling, nameplate scratching the furniture, slamming drawers and stamping his big feet. Is that what you need to know?"

Greeley was half-leading, half-pushing her out, but her outburst made him hesitate, his delicate instincts sensing an opportunity. "What do you mean, a nameplate?"

"A nameplate . . . with a name on it. The kind they wear loose around the wrist. But this one didn't have his right name on it."

Greeley's spine tingled with a familiar chill. "What name did it have?"

"Wally. No . . ." She thought a second. "Waldo."

10

When Lowenkopf returned to his hotel, a number of odd things happened. "Call your office. They need you," the desk clerk told him in a bored monotone, crumpling the note as soon as he had read it and returning at once to a book propped open behind the counter. Lowenkopf leaned over to make out the title: *The Buccaneer's Daughter*. The clerk resettled the book a little further down the counter.

Lowenkopf retrieved the slip of notepaper, uncrumpled it, and read it again. "I don't have an office here."

The clerk looked up from his romance, irked at being disturbed. "Do you have one anywhere?"

"In New York."

"I'd call there then, don't you think?" With an incredulous shake of his head, the clerk returned to his ravished maidens.

Lowenkopf went to his room. Gail Wranawski was waiting for him in a chair outside his door. She stood when she saw him coming. "I hate to bother you this time of night, Sergeant Lowenkopf, but I didn't want you to come away with the wrong impression from our interview today. I didn't mean to suggest that Warren might be in cahoots with Johnny on this business about Eliot. Not at all."

Lowenkopf reached into his pocket but the room key wasn't there. He nudged the door softly. "I didn't get that impression from what you said."

"Good. I mean, Warren is definitely not your man."

"That was the general drift of your opinions, as I remember them," he assured her. There was a chambermaid in an overcoat waiting for the elevator who wouldn't look his way. He rattled the door more violently, but the maid stared intently at the elevator door.

"Good." Gail thought about it a moment longer. "Good."

"Right." He took the knob in both hands and shook the

door so loudly a man in pajamas burst forth from a room near the elevator and stared first at Lowenkopf, then the maid. Unable to escape his gaze, she glared back sourly and trudged toward Shelly. Behind her, the elevator opened and closed. She undid the lock with a snap and refused Shelly's single. Triumphantly he held the door for Gail. "Would you like to come in?"

"Not really," she said and hurried after the maid into the elevator.

He used the phone in his room to ring Greeley. "I suggest you catch the next plane home," his partner warned him. "Your canary has changed his tune."

"Billy Ringo?" The name suddenly seemed odd to Lowenkopf, a character in a novel he had begun but no longer cared to finish. For the first time it occurred to him it might be a cowboy name—somehow it had always reminded him of the drummer Beatle. He sank into a chair, his bones aching from his swim. "Is he changing his testimony?"

"He's refusing to testify at all." Greeley's tone was friendly, almost merry. "I think it's got something to do with an old woman who came into the precinct house today with a missing grandson whose description matches your corpse. Named Theo Pfeffer."

Lowenkopf said sullenly, "Who's he?"

Greeley's shrug was audible through the wires. "You figure it out. Billy'll discuss his decision only with you. I'm sorry to have to say it, partner"—without a trace of pity in his voice—"but the holiday is over."

Some holiday, Lowenkopf thought sourly, but when he opened the drapes, a fragrant cloister of eucalyptus changed his mind. The view from his window in Washington Heights, a few bald trees in the snow, seemed meager in comparison. He thought of the stores across Broadway—a greasy spoon, a beauty parlor, a kosher butcher which shared an awning with a travel agency whose windows were filled with faded posters of Puerto Rico. Lowenkopf unbuttoned his rumpled shirt and walked into his bathroom. He snapped on the light, screwed up his face in the mirror, and discovered an Arab in full desert regalia lying on his back in the bathtub.

The man sat up and looked around wildly. "What am I doing here?" he demanded indignantly.

Feeling faintly foolish but duty-bound, Lowenkopf whipped out his gun. "You tell me."

The Arab stepped gingerly over the side of the tub. He was shoeless. The socks sticking out from beneath his robe were lovely, a rich weave of purple and cream patterned like a checkerboard. He set both feet on the ground, concentrating on them. "If it's money you want, you've taken the wrong prisoner. My government cannot pay. Not until the price of oil goes up, at least."

Lowenkopf stared at him. "What are you talking about?"

"This is a kidnapping, is it not? A terrorist act of some kind? I should have anticipated something like this. Is it the carefully executed plan of some fiendish organization? Or are you acting alone?"

Lowenkopf was tired. "Shut up!"

The Arab hesitated a moment, then balanced on the edge of the tub. "I will not be silenced. Go ahead—shoot if you must. But you will never silence us!"

Lowenkopf raised his gun to the man's temple. The man at once clammed up. "That's better," Lowenkopf said. "Now, get the fuck out of here."

The Arab looked at him skeptically. "For nothing?"

Lowenkopf cocked the hammer. "Out."

The man hopped off the tub and ran for the door. "Bless you, sir, bless you. You will not be forgotten for your kindness, I assure you."

Lowenkopf held his gun on the man until the door clicked shut behind him. Then he lowered his arm and trudged to the door, peering out through the peephole. The gun weighed heavily in his hand. He released the hammer with his thumb and dropped it on a coffee table, then fell back into his chair and pulled off his shoes without unlacing them. He didn't want to think anymore—about Hansen or Charlie or Arabs in his bathtub. He wanted someone to be nice to him, to cluck sympathetically at the sympathetic parts or at least grunt in agreement. He dialed the precinct house in New York, but Greeley had gone for the day. He dialed Carla. No answer. She had accepted his key. Maybe she was on her way. He dialed room service, ordered a light dinner for two with a large bottle of champagne, and fell asleep in front of the television, waiting for her. When he woke, Bogart in a white lab coat was knocking a smaller man on the head from behind. When the knocking sound repeated but the screen switched to a commercial, Lowenkopf realized it was his door and answered it.

In the hallway Teri Kern bent over a cart piled with covered dishes and a bottle in a pail of ice. She wore a low green dress and jade earrings so long they tickled the hairs at the base of her neck. Her mouth was coral and her scent familiar. Her tongue flicked the lipstick at the side of her mouth. "I hope I'm not disturbing you."

"No . . . I was just going to call you." Behind him the blue light jumped and Bogart chuckled mirthlessly. Lowenkopf moved to turn off the set, and as he did, she followed him into the room, pushing the tray with the front of her thigh.

"I only said that I might come see you. I didn't expect a champagne dinner waiting. You were pretty sure of yourself."

It was exactly what Carla had said the last time he'd seen her, and a long way from the truth. He lifted the cover from one of the plates. Steaming clumps of cauliflower, pea pods, carrots, and broccoli were artistically arranged on the dish. Carla hadn't said she was a vegetarian, but he suspected she might be. Suddenly famished, he lifted a spear of carrot, was about to bite into it, but offered it first to Teri. "Would you like some?"

She picked up a champagne glass and dangled it between her fingers. "Thank you."

He popped the cork, filled her glass, and splashed a little into his own. She touched her glass to his and smiled, her lips poised for a word that did not come. When after a beat he had not approached, she turned her head and addressed the window.

"Were you really expecting me?"

The back of her dress was cut even lower than the front. Lowenkopf looked past her shoulder at the reflection in the windowpane behind her. "You said you would come," he answered diplomatically.

She studied him over her shoulder. "And you believed me?"

Her eyes were the color of virgin forests. Yes, he believed her. Why shouldn't he? He tried to remember what he was asked to believe.

She moved closer imperceptibly, as sunlight travels from leaf to leaf. "We've come a long way quickly, haven't we?"

He had.

She gave him her profile and tipped her glass. The long throat undulated smoothly as she swallowed. She handed him an empty glass with a coral crescent at its lip.

He refilled it.

She drained it again.

He took it from her but instead of refilling it, set it on the tray. "You should have something to eat with that," he cautioned instinctively, removing the linen from a few of the plates. In the center of the tray a black steel pot hung over a blue Sterno flame. He lifted the lid. A sweet smell of wine and bubbling cheese floated up.

Teri peered down into the pot. "There's wine in this, right?"

He ran his finger around the edge of the pot for a taste, but before it reached his mouth she drew his hand toward her own and licked the cheese from his finger with the delicate tip of her tongue. His finger was still burning when she gave it back to him.

"Okay," she said, "let's eat." With a gesture that signaled surrender, she pulled up a chair next to the tray and sat down in front of him.

There was a plate of bread cut into squares, a pair of fondue forks crossed over them. Teri tried to pierce a chunk of cauliflower, missed it, and struck the plate with a soft "tink." Lowenkopf slid a sliced pea pod on her fork for her. She held it up and nibbled the tip, rolling it for a few seconds between her lips. He fell in love and speared a square of bread for himself. She dropped her pea pod in the soft cheese and lifted it out. His bread followed after.

"Go ahead." He waved his fork in invitation.

She gobbled her pea pod whole. When she opened her mouth a moment later, a puff of steam escaped. "Now you."

Richard Fliegel

He tapped his fork once on the edge of the pot and his bread chunk fell in.

By the end of the meal, Lowenkopf had forgotten when they had met and why. The wine in the cheese was tart, and the champagne dry. He no longer wondered how she had found her way to his room; he no longer cared. She fed him clumps of cauliflower on her fork and slurped pea pods from his. They had fun together, Lowenkopf came to admire her habit of stirring her champagne with her tongue before she drank it, to excite the bubbles. Every bite she took made him happier. Her smiles spun into each other and her eyes were incredibly green.

"Do you want that receipt now? For Johnny's dinner last night?"

Something else he had entirely forgotten. "Do you have it with you?"

Two slender fingers tapped her purse. "Here." She undid the clasp and tugged a bent strip of cardboard out of an eyeglass case. Reaching over the table, she placed it ceremoniously in front of him. Lowenkopf smelled Joy as the cleft between her breasts grew fleetingly deeper. He knew it was a practiced move, but a new respect for practice was growing in him.

He read the name of the restaurant. "Where is this place?"

"Beverly Hills. About halfway between the studio and the beach."

"From the size of the bill, he must have fed a large party."

She glanced at the total. "That's a supper for two. One of them wasn't very hungry. Or watching her waist." She brought out a cigarette and held it up, awaiting a light.

There were no matches in his pants pocket. She tapped the beads of her bag and a pearl lighter with gold works slid out onto the tablecloth. Picking it up, he shielded the flame for her with his hand as Bogart might have done on a windy airstrip. She rested her hand on his to steady the flame, and when she looked up, did not remove it. Her fingers slipped into his palm and carried his hand to the table with an unmistakable squeeze.

He was afraid to move his fingers. The slightest answering pressure would betray Carla irrevocably. "So Johnny didn't eat with Searle after all. In the right hands, this slip of paper could go a long way." A second, less noble motive for his hand's stillness slowly dawned on him—any motion of his own hand might shake Teri's loose. His two motives joined to render his fingers absolutely immobile in hers.

"These look like the right hands," she whispered, modestly evading his gaze. There could be no further doubt—it had not been a spasm of her wrist. Lowenkopf felt himself on the threshold of an altogether new life, in which lovely girls with luminous green eyes led him from whirlpool to whirlpool in an endless swirl of lovemaking in hot tubs, swimming pools, and wave-swept beaches beneath California stars. He imagined Greeley visiting one day in a three-piece suit while a tan and muscular Shelly Lowenkopf reclined in the barest bikini trunks beside a poolful of Teri Kerns. He would pat Greeley on his sweaty, stained back, leave him on the lounge chair, and dive without a ripple among his scantily attired admirers.

The tingle in his palm was spreading. Teri's green eyes narrowed precipitately.

He managed a painful smile.

"You ought to lie down." Was there a note of alarm in her voice? She led him from the table. He took a step toward the couch, but she carried him backwards with the slightest pressure on his palm towards the inner room, where the bed was. She gave him a little push and he fell backwards like a tree. She knelt on the bedspread next to him. "Let me undo your tie. You look like you've died and gone to heaven. You don't drink much champagne, do you?"

His head shook, no.

"I do. And take it from me, it can get to you if you're not used to it. We have to drink a lot of this stuff in my position. Some nights you come home and you'd lay down your life for a cup of coffee. Here, let me get that." She pulled his tie from his collar with a single fluid tug. "Now we've got a little air, haven't we?"

Her maternal tone melted away the last resistance he could have mustered. Had she given him his pistol and told him to clean his teeth with it, he would have fired away gladly. She slid her arms under his armpits and pulled him higher onto the bed. Then she worked off his shoes. She climbed up, opened his belt and his zipper, and peeled his trousers over his knees.

"Do you prefer the covers?"

He lay perfectly silent, his toes aimed at the ceiling. Oh, Ruth, he thought, why couldn't it have been this way? Teri expertly rolled the bedspread down beneath him, jerked the blanket free of the mattress, and floated it down over him.

"How's that?"

He blinked once at the ceiling and once at her. He was afraid a third blink would make her disappear. "My hand is frozen," he said, pointing with his glance to his naked ring finger, which stirred slightly. "It starts at the hand, where you squeezed it."

She shifted to his side and rubbed his elbow vigorously, working her way towards his wrist. "How far up is it stiff?"

His right shoulder shrugged.

She poked his left.

"Yeow!" He rotated the shoulder carefully. "Wow."

"Uh-huh. I do that to people sometimes." She crawled in behind him and used both her hands. Her right arm reached under his and massaged the front of his left shoulder. Her left thumb and forefinger kneaded the back of his arm. "That's better, isn't it?"

He turned his face to hers. "A little." Their mouths were inches apart.

Her lashes fluttered. He prayed. She kissed him and the stiffness ran out of his arm. His hand touched the skin of her back. He resolved to be patient and gentle. He put his lips to her neck. Her knee shot up between his, hardening his resolve.

He found the zipper on the back of her dress but missed the hook. She stopped to undo it. The free moment frightened him—he set the alarm to distract himself. When she managed to disengage the hook, he was fooling with the clock. She glanced at him, at her beautiful silk stockings, and sat on the edge of the bed to unroll them. He couldn't get the alarm set and phoned the desk for a wake-up call.

While he was on the phone, she spotted the ashtray on the nightstand, opened and closed the drawer, and started for the next room. He asked her to bring him back some champagne. She called in from the next room—the bottle was empty, but she saw a bottle of beer in the refrigerator if he wanted it. He called back—there was an opener in the drawer beneath the window. He heard the drawer open, a quiet click, and a long pause. He climbed out of bed and went to see.

In the next room, his beer sat next to her open purse on the table beneath the window. Its drawer stuck out. The opener was still in it, but the Bible had been removed. Teri was standing in the middle of the carpet in her glasses, bra, and slip, reading intently.

He put the back of his hand to her cheek. She kissed it and kept reading. The Song of Songs. He slipped his hand inside the lace trim of her bra. She kissed his neck, hugged him around the waist, and returned to her book. He lifted her in his arms and carried her reading into the bedroom.

Although Lowenkopf was a great observer of other people's emotions, he did not consider his own feelings about a case of much interest in their own right. Earlier that day, he and Carla had been all over town, conversing with an intimacy that revealed more about their feelings for each other than it did about the murder. Yet his professional detachment was so habitual he could not imagine anyone taking an interest in how he felt about anything to do with his work. It was an attitude that served him well on most cases. But the Hansen murder was proving to be a most unusual case.

When Carla arrived at Shelly's hotel later that night, she was confused, full of doubt. She had received a visit from a New York attorney who had come to award her a role she had earned. Yet, at the apparent culmination of her labors, she hesitated, unable to accept what was hers by right, equally unable to reject it. She had a tendency to self-deception, and was doing her best to fight it. Her acceptance would commit her to an interpretation of what had passed between herself and Shelly, which was growing more uncomfortable daily. She had to admit that he was really a very decent guy, which she had not anticipated. Her previous experiences with men had led her to a different expectation. But her hesitation placed her in several dangers, not the least of which was the risk of feeling very much a fool. This vulnerability made her fingers clumsy in her purse. After what seemed an eternity of fumbling, she slid the key he had given her at Weems's house into the door, where it caught with a sharp click.

The outer room of the suite was empty. Two dirty plates lay on a cart by the window. She picked a stalk of cold broccoli from one of them and chewed it thoughtfully. Two glasses stood on the coffee table, one empty, a ring of flat champagne in the pit of the other. She picked up the glass and swirled the liquid around. A swath of bubbles formed around the edge, where a red semicircle could still be seen. The door to the bedroom was closed. So was the bathroom door—but there was a light underneath it and the sound of running water inside. She turned the knob quietly.

Teri Kern stretched her face in the mirror over the sink, reattaching an eyelash. She wore a lacy green brassiere and a patterned emerald G-string. She glanced up as the door swung open, saw that it was Carla, and returned to her makeup. "I'll be out in just a minute."

Carla sat down on the toilet-seat cover and watched Teri retrace her lips in coral, then kiss a square of toilet paper. Carla stood so she could drop the tissue paper in the bowl, but Teri set it gently on top of the tank. The bedroom door clicked.

"Is Shelly in there?"

Teri suspended her ablutions long enough to listen. "I don't hear him."

Carla dumped the last champagne in the sink.

Teri took down her stockings and gown from the back of the door and dressed herself quickly, stepping into her heels and wobbling past with a smell of cheap taffy to retrieve her purse from the table beneath the window. She stepped gracefully over the champagne bottle and made her way to the door. When she reached it, she touched her finger to her tongue and with a dab of saliva stuck the square of tissue imprinted with her kiss to the peephole. She glanced back over her shoulder—for whose benefit, Carla couldn't guess—and smiled a fond farewell. It lasted long enough to snap her picture.

Carla's eyes turned green in imitation. "Must you sink your teeth in everyone?"

Teri didn't hesitate. "Never use your teeth, dear. That could be your problem." She stepped over an invisible corpse on the threshold and the door clicked discreetly behind her.

Carla watched the bedroom door, hoping something pathetic would crawl out. Nothing did. She considered setting the couch on fire, but decided to be sophisticated about it. She examined the toe of her sandal, flung the champagne goblet at the bedroom door, and stormed out of the suite.

The wake-up call came at eleven. On the fourth ring Lowenkopf sat up and it stopped. He rubbed both eyes with his thumb and forefinger, groping for his glasses on the nightstand. He snapped the waistband of his underpants, opened the door, and cut his foot on the smashed goblet on his way to the bathroom.

He gargled and called Carla for a ride to the airport. And to say a loving good-bye. As he waited for her to pick up the phone, he pushed Teri's image out of his mind. The phone continued to ring. Carla never answered. He found Weems's dinner receipt on the table and slipped it with a note into an envelope he addressed to Oquita.

He shaved, nicking himself on both sides of his chin, and took a cold shower. While he dried, he phoned Carla again, the towel around his waist darkening couch and rug. No answer. He removed a sliver of glass from his heel and picked up the empty bottle on the carpet, turning it upside down into the one remaining goblet on the rolling tray.

What had happened to the other? He dressed, packed his bag, and tried her number again. Five rings. He dialed for a cab and set down the receiver. He picked it up and dialed her again. The phone rang seven times before he hung up and left the hotel room.

He paid his bill in the lobby and found his cab outside. The ride to the airport took four times as long as the ride from the airport had taken Carla in their Mercedes. Nothing he passed looked familiar. He never saw the cabbie's face—

his head rolled from side to side as he drove, keeping the beat of a song that wasn't on the radio.

Once inside the terminal, Lowenkopf set down his bag and tried the phone. A man in a plaid shirt and Levi's kept stepping on the rubber mat that made the automatic door swing open, letting it close nearly all the way, then stamping his foot on the rubber again. Lowenkopf checked his bag and picked up his boarding pass. He remembered his gun just as the metal detector discovered it. Its bell clanged relentlessly. The security men refused to let him pass with a gun no matter what his identification showed. They weren't interested in phoning New York for verification. It was too late to recover his luggage and stow it in his sock. By the time they released him, minus his gun, most of the passengers were already aboard.

He tried one last time to reach Carla, to say at least farewell. No answer. He knew when he landed in New York he'd forget to make the call. It seemed incredible that he'd forget—he felt an anxiety he could not explain, as if his inability to reach her had lent the call an urgency it might not have deserved. He ran from the gate to the postcard rack in the gift shop. He grabbed the top card—Mickey Mouse and Minnie in front of Snow White's Castle at Disneyland —and scribbled a reminder on the back. He dropped it in a slot with his letter to Oquita and convinced a guard closing the boarding gate to allow him on the ramp.

He banged on the plane's aluminum flank and its door opened. He found his ticket and boarding pass in his coat pocket. He took a deep breath as the door was sealed behind him. He had his checkbook and his New York keys. Suddenly he froze. Very slowly he looked down at his side. There, spasmodically clutched in his left hand, was his brown alligator-skin briefcase.

He must have been grinning. The stewardess smiled back, a warm Midwestern welcome.

Everything was about to be different.

Lowenkopf found his seat between a thin man in a pink turtleneck and a window overlooking the wing. As Lowenkopf stood over him, stuffing his coat into the crowded overhead compartment, the man raised a large skull in which two watery eyes floated up, soaking in everything around them—the shuffle of passengers searching for their seats, the long, cool strides of stewardesses up and down the aisle, the fidgety crossing of legs and arms and crooked necks with which any flight begins. Lowenkopf climbed into his seat and pushed his briefcase back behind his feet. Then he reclined his seat cushion and closed his eyes, feeling very much like an experienced flier.

A moment later he felt a tap on his shoulder. The stewardess motioned for him to return his seat to upright position for takeoff. Then she bent her head to the thin man. "The captain would like to see you in the forward cabin. There's something he wants to ask you."

Lowenkopf hoped to sleep through the flight. He pressed his head back and let his eyes close again. The murmur of voices from the passengers around him blended with the rumble of the engines. He was about to drift off when a small shock of light jumped between his eyelids, as the springs in the seat beside him gave way. He opened his eyes. The thin man was back, intently reading a copy of *Aviation* magazine, licking his thumb and forefinger each time he turned a page. Lowenkopf looked out the window. The small flaps along the edge of the wing were tilting up. There was a dry rustle of magazine paper beside him. Lowenkopf closed the shutter on the porthole window and sat back.

The thin man was staring at him. "Would you mind keeping that open? During the takeoff, at least?"

Lowenkopf opened the shutter. "Are you a pilot?"

The thin man was engrossed in his magazine again. "Safety engineer," he said without looking up.

Lowenkopf nodded as if he understood. "Not much to worry about in these big birds, I'll bet."

The man licked his thumb. "I wouldn't say that."

Lowenkopf looked back out the window.

The man rolled up his magazine and held it like a spear between them. "We're sitting in an aluminum cylinder like this," he began, "which has to stay in the air. What do you think keeps it up?"

"The wings?"

The man snickered. "But they don't flap up and down like a bird's wings, do they? They stick out straight. Do you know what would happen to a bird if his wings just stuck out like that?"

Lowenkopf scrutinized the offending wing. "He'd go down?"

"Like a stone." The thin man nodded deeply.

Lowenkopf didn't want to hear any more.

The little flaps on the wing were tilting down now. The plane hadn't moved. Couldn't the pilot decide if he wanted them up or down?"

"So what keeps us in the air?"

The thin man held the rolled magazine with his middle three fingers. His thumb stuck out on one side and his pinkie on the other. "Not much. A little wind rushing past the wings. If the jets don't keep enough air passing the wings fast enough . . ." He opened his hand and the magazine dropped in his lap. He smiled beatifically.

Lowenkopf picked up the magazine and handed it back to him. He closed his eyes for the third time and felt the uneven rattle of the aircraft before it started to speed down the runway. It sounded like the plane would fall apart.

"Here we go," said the thin man brightly.

Lowenkopf refused to open his eyes.

He didn't get much sleep the rest of the flight. Whenever he started to doze he saw a tin can in the air and felt the thin sheet of aluminum between his feet and the clouds. The man beside him commenced snoring about halfway across the continent, a jerky grind full of stops and starts punctuated with sudden swift ejaculations of air. Lowenkopf thought he'd discovered the reason the last flight of the day was called the Red Eye—by the time you landed, that was how you looked.

Before he landed, he learned his mistake. New York at five o'clock in the morning from ten thousand feet resembles a bleak watercolor painting, sky and water and landmass, crowded with buildings, washed a uniform drab gray. But hanging above and before him, a wine-red circle without aureole stared through the grayness, still open after heaven's long night. The thin man snorted so violently in his sleep it awakened him. He leaned over Lowenkopf and peered out the window. "We made it?" He sounded surprised.

Lowenkopf flexed his stiff fingers on the armrests. "Not yet."

To his amazement, the plane bumped down safely. He dragged himself through the drab tile halls to the baggage-claim area and rang Greeley at the precinct house while the circular ramps turned without his bag.

When Greeley said, "Hello?" crisply, Lowenkopf asked without introduction, "Where's the inquest?"

Greeley was evidently drinking coffee—Lowenkopf heard his long, cool sip from the other end of the line. "Shelly? Are you in already? The inquest is not till tomorrow. It's Sunday."

Lowenkopf pushed his coat from his wrist and checked his watch. Five-fifty. "Then what was the rush to bring me home?"

"The captain wants you to see Billy Ringo. He's been asking for you since you left."

The first suitcases pushed through the hanging rubber straps onto the carousel. "I'm not going to see Billy, Homer. I didn't leave a murder investigation in Los Angeles on his account. Billy is a royal pain—he doesn't deserve whatever he wants, and I'm not in a mood to hear it from him."

There was a disapproving silence. "It's not personal, Shelly. Madagascar wants you to see him."

"Tell Madagascar I got held up over Kennedy for sixteen hours. Wait a minute—today's Sunday. He won't be in today."

"He's in now. Do you want to talk to him?"

"No. Don't tell him I called. I'll see you tomorrow."

Lowenkopf hung up and dialed again. "Ruth? This is Shelly. Lowenkopf. That's right, but I'm back. Can I see him today? I know what I told you. Can't you just tell him the truth? No, I'm not criticizing . . . No. Wait a minute, he's my kid too. I know what the judge said. This *is* a weekend. I know what I told you. Look—"

She hung up.

He called back. "Just have him out front in an hour. I'll pick him up. In an hour." He hung up before she got the chance. His bag still wasn't on the carousel. Two skycaps stood at the door, looking out. He asked them for the gift shop. They stared at him blankly for a moment. One pointed.

Lowenkopf followed the finger around a corner and down a flight of wide flat steps. One wall of the gift shop was covered with T-shirts. There was a standing basket of French sourdough breads, and a rack of magazines. Most of the T-shirts said "NEW YORK" or "I'VE TASTED THE APPLE." On the bottom row there was a pile bunched in no discernible order, one on top of the next. "LONDON." "I LOVE MONTREAL." "CALIFORNIA."

The California shirt had a picture of a palm tree on it. Lowenkopf imagined himself standing beneath that palm tree with Carla in his arms. There was another shirt, with a surfer, but no place name. A black teenager at the cash register watched him, sucking a Tootsie Pop. He held up both shirts. "What do you think?"

She shrugged. "For you?"

"For a ten-year-old boy."

She opened a box of chocolates, ate one, and closed the box again. "Why don't you get him a *Playboy* magazine? That's what they all look at in here."

He bought the surfer shirt. Upstairs, his suitcase lay on its side on the carousel, passing unnoticed behind the backs of the skycaps.

Shelly wasn't in Pelham in an hour. Outside the terminal, the world had turned to slush. In front of the East Side Terminal, Lowenkopf saw an unshaven man in a thin coat fold a small pillow over the top of a parking meter and sing to it lovingly, shuffling a little dance on the salty pavement.

It took him an hour and forty minutes on the subway to reach his own place in the Heights, and another twenty to drop off his bag, urinate, and get his car started.

When he reached Pelham, Thom was blowing in his cupped hands and stamping his feet. He was dressed in a football jersey and helmet. The passenger-door button stuck, but Shelly got it open with the key from outside.

"Cold?" He rubbed the tip of Thom's small nose.

The boy shook his head. "It's a little late, though. Not that I mind waiting, but it looks like we might miss the game."

"What game?"

Thom's eyes widened casually. "Didn't she tell you?"

Shelly nodded. "Of course she told me. Only she didn't tell me where and when."

"We're supposed to meet at Mimi's house in Levittown. At eight-thirty." He leaned over to check the car clock. It said eight-ten. "Or else we can just check the fields around there. There can't be more than three or four of them."

Shelly stepped on the clutch and forced the stick into first. "We'll make it."

The trees along the Hutchinson Parkway were bare of leaves. Their roots were buried in unplowed snow that showed a faint black sheen of settled exhaust, and the snow piled on the center divider showed lines of soot. As the road wound around curve after curve, the tires caught on the crack between lanes. "I've got something for you," Shelly said. "It's in the back seat. Open it."

Thom reached around and took a gift box off the rear seat. It had a gold cardboard cover embossed with an apple and a red ribbon. "What's in it?"

"Open it."

Thom undid the ribbon and removed the lid. The T-shirt lay folded with the picture of the surfer on top. The crack caught a tire and the car swerved.

"Like it?"

"It's great." Thom didn't take the shirt out of the box, but he held it up and examined the picture more closely.

"I don't know if you'd wear something like that," Shelly said.

"I wear my other one," Thom assured him.

They were approaching the turn to the Throgs Neck

Bridge. It was crowded. Shelly decided to try the Whitestone. "You've got another surfer shirt?"

Thom nodded. "But don't worry. The one Clem gave me is green."

They rounded the bend and found the traffic to the Whitestone Bridge toll booths backed up half a mile. "You mean your other one is like this? The same design?"

Thom took the shirt out of its box and held it in front of his football jersey. "My other one is green. I like the blue a lot more. And this one's brand new." He smoothed it in his lap. "What happened to your ring?"

Shelly glanced at his bare left hand. "I lost it in Los Angeles. Damn these Sunday drivers! We've got a ball game to catch."

The far-right lanes, where there were exact-change machines, were faster. Shelly didn't have quarters, but the man selling papers by the toll machine did. Shelly gave him two dollars, bought a paper, and asked for change. The man dug both hands in the front of his red sweatshirt, rubbed his mustache, and elaborately doled out seven quarters.

The other side of the bridge was clear. They took the Cross Island to the Long Island Expressway, which was, incredibly, also clear, and turned off at the Meadowbrook Parkway, which they followed to the Wantaugh. It was a drive they had made many times together, and they rode in silence. Thom pushed a cassette with a picture of a football on its case into the machine and sat up on the seat to listen. *"Taxi,"* he said.

Shelly nodded. Bob James was still playing when they found the ramp under the overpass to the Hempstead Turnpike. At the top of the ramp was a traffic light where the turnpike met the ramp. It was red.

Thom looked at the clock again. Eight-twenty-eight. "How much time have we got?"

Shelly consulted his watch. "About two minutes."

"We're almost there."

"We'll make it."

The light was still red. Shelly looked down the road at the traffic on the turnpike, considering whether to risk a right on red. What he saw brought him to the edge of his seat. He looked at the light and prayed.

The hearse crossed the intersection just as the light turned. A long line of cars, headlights on, inched in its wake. Thom sat up next to his father on the edge of the seat. Together they watched the Cadillacs, and BMWs, and Volvos, and Buicks, and Hondas pass in endless succession, hissing as they crossed the wet macadam.

"I know a song about this," Thom said philosophically as a mauve Chevy rolled solemnly by.

"Let's hear it," said his father.

Thom put his hands in his lap and looked up at the sky. "Wait. It goes: *Did you ever think when a hearse goes by that you might be the next to die? They wrap you up in a wooden box and bury you under grammercy rocks.*"

"What are grammercy rocks?"

Thom shrugged. "It's just a song, Dad. *The first few weeks it's all okay, but then you decay and rot away. The worms crawl in, the worms crawl out, they eat your guts and spit them out. Your eyes they turn a bottlegreen, your blood runs out like sour cream. You spread it on a piece of bread and that's what you eat when you are dead.*"

Shelly looked out over the steering wheel. "That's a gruesome little number."

A Mustang rolled by with one headlight out. Behind it, the row of yellow headlights stretched around the bend.

Thom took off his football helmet and rubbed his eye with the palm of his hand. "We're not going to make it, are we?"

A Mercedes crossed. Its windows were dark.

12

There was that dry buzz of courtroom air. The middle rows of spectator seats were all empty—the sunlight on their polished pine hurt Lowenkopf's eyes. From the last row he watched the coroner nod as an old man with waxed white hair harangued the bench from the witness box. In the first row, the deputy medical examiner waited to testify, unhooking his spectacles and cleaning them with a pocket handkerchief. An old woman directly in front of Lowenkopf snorted twice. Lowenkopf slunk lower into the wood, pressing his knees forward into a trapezoid of light that fell on the seat in front of him. He covered his face with a page of newspaper from the floor under the seat.

He could have dozed. Instead, he felt someone sit down hard on the bench beside him. Under the corner of the newspaper page he saw a thin yellow check on a brown pant leg next to his arm. He waited. After a moment of silence, he spoke through the newspaper.

"Hello, Homer."

"Shhh!" Greeley leaned forward in the seat, his forearms resting on the back of the bench in front of them. "Why do you sit so far back? I can't make out half of what they're saying."

"That's my reason exactly." Lowenkopf crossed his arms over the newspaper page, shaping it to his face. "I'm just waiting to be called. You can always hear your name."

"You won't hear yours."

"Sure I will. Unless you're warning me when they call it."

"They're not going to call it."

Lowenkopf sat up. His newspaper fell in his lap. "Why not?"

"The captain doesn't want you to testify. He thinks the jet lag might slow you down."

"That's a crock, Homer. How does the old Turk know from jet lag? It sounds Greeley to me."

Greeley was unperturbed and tried again. "He wants you uptown with Billy Ringo."

"I'll see Billy later. As soon as this is over."

"He said you should go *now.*"

"I'll go when I'm damned ready to go. There are priorities, Homer. You know that. Billy's in the best hotel he's ever seen, in the best section of Riverdale. We're going to have to throw him out of there when the party's over. He'll keep another few hours."

Greeley looked doubtful. He picked up the newspaper on Lowenkopf's lap, folded it on his own, and handed it, neatly quartered, back to his partner. "Did you see this?"

"What?"

Greeley pointed to an item at the bottom of Cindy

Adams' column, on the front of the quartered page. *It looks like Sheik Ibn Amo Znandi won't be moving into the Franciscan Tower after all. The management of the chic co-op announced today their new tenant will be Robert Culpepper, that Hollywood moneyman with a taste for Apple. The top-three-floor living space went for a top price—two million before renovations. Renovations? That's right. Culpepper, in town today, explained, "I just want to get some of the walls out of the way."*

"It's out of my price range, Homer."

"Isn't that the alibi you wanted to check?"

Lowenkopf sat up and reread the item. The head of waxed hair stepped down from the witness box, and the medical examiner was called. Greeley sat forward in his seat and scrutinized the frail bald man with a weaving sideward stoop and enormous hands.

"Where is this Franciscan Tower, Homer?"

"Fifty-ninth between Park and Madison. I want to hear this."

Lowenkopf stood up slowly. He slipped one arm into his coat sleeve and sat down again. "I've got to testify first."

Greeley didn't look up. "Go on. I've got your report with me. I'll read it into the record for you."

"Where the hell did you get that?"

Greeley put a finger to his lips. "The captain gave it to me."

Lowenkopf slipped his other arm into his coat and turned up his collar. "That's what you're down here for, isn't it?"

Greeley was listening too intently to reply.

From Fifty-ninth Street, the Franciscan Tower resembled a black pyramid of glass sloping back at a sixty-degree angle over flat black steps at its entranceway. A tropical lobby was concealed from the street traffic by five rows of kangaroo ivy, suspended just behind the glass from a forty-foot ceiling. Inside the door, rubber trees taller than a man stood to either side as Lowenkopf passed into a jungle of speckled aglaonema and spathiphyllum whose wide leaves hid African carvings of squat figures with wide brows and eyes. Beneath his feet, an Oriental carpet led to a man in a morning suit behind an ebony desk, who directed him along a row of fresh chrysanthemums to the elevators.

At the end of the row, a pretty girl with a green plastic bucket was repotting the last chrysanthemum. He pushed in the elevator button and watched her smooth the soil. She stood, spanked the dirt from her Levi's, and offered him a flower pot she had removed, a yellow mum, not quite as fresh as those he had passed but still far from wilted. He waved it away with his hand but she persisted, slipping it into his buttonhole. The elevator door opened; he stepped in and waited, but it closed on him alone. He pushed the button marked Penthouse.

It opened again to the sound of an electric saw, a buzz of flying chips, and a voice insisting, "Further!" He stepped into a room freshly painted white with a powder-blue carpet and spotless windows, without a stick of furniture. He followed the sounds of activity, the buzz and grind of the saw, through one room and into another where a man in shirt sleeves instructed two bored laborers in the fine points of demolishing a wall, taking the saw from the bigger one and holding it steady while the blade tore out chunks of plasterboard and bit into wood. Overhead, an enormous chandelier trembled, and tiny pools of color danced around the room. A slender man in a black suit stood off to one side with a jacket over his arm. In the far corner, a blonde in a white silk dress reclined in a leather chair beneath the window, stocking feet on an ottoman, gold sandals heaped alongside where she had kicked them off. Her near leg was up, supporting a copy of *Fortune* magazine, which she read while biting her lip. The sunlight tingled delicately on the underside of her thigh.

The unobtrusive man stepped in between Lowenkopf and the girl. "Can I help you?" His boss, in shirt sleeves, swung the saw over his head.

Lowenkopf reached into his jacket for identification, and the other man reached into his. Lowenkopf drew out his badge and held it up, but the man's hand did not reappear.

"Detective Sergeant Lowenkopf," he announced over the saw. "I have to speak to Mr. Culpepper a few minutes about a homicide."

The hand came out of the black suit jacket, palm up. "Step into the next room, sir, if you don't mind." Neither the girl nor the man with the saw glanced their way. The laborers regarded him lacklusterly. Lowenkopf followed into the room through which he had come. With a brief gesture, his guide indicated that he was to wait, and departed. Digging his heel into the blue carpet, Lowenkopf examined his surroundings. Beneath a freshly caulked window he saw an electrical outlet and a cable plug. Covering the outlet that should have been on the opposite wall was a briefcase made of soft caribou leather, stitched over in large yellow thread. It was open. All the papers in it were pressed to one side by a beige plastic box with a collapsible antenna. The briefcase gave off a smell of new leather that seemed to hang in the sunlit dust like an after-shave lotion. Lowenkopf didn't wear after-shave, but if he could have found that scent, he would have started to.

"I'm Culpepper," the man in shirt sleeves declared crisply before he had fully entered the room, offering a manicured, sinewy hand. "I see you stole a flower from the lobby. Good. Sick of those damn things already."

"I didn't—"

The man clapped him on the back. "Of course you didn't. Consider it a gift from me. Robert Culpepper. Angborn tells me you're a flatfoot."

"Angborn, I take it, is—"

"Right. My bodyguard. Didn't say what it was you wanted to discuss."

"I told him a homicide."

"Yes. Mentioned that. But whose?"

"Eliot Hansen's." Keeping his answers short might help him get them out whole.

Culpepper blinked. "Hansen was killed in L.A. You showed Angborn a New York badge. Why are New York's Finest interested in a west coast corpse?"

"I was in Los Angeles when he was murdered, assisting on a movie. At one point I was even the leading suspect."

Culpepper smiled crookedly. "You're Warren's cop, aren't you?"

"I'd like to ask you some questions about a few of Hansen's friends."

"I've heard about you, too. But all right. What do you want to know?"

Lowenkopf flipped out his pad. "Who were you with the night Hansen was murdered?"

"I don't remember."

"Try. It was only four nights ago."

"Why are you asking? Am I a suspect?"

"Maybe."

"Why?"

Lowenkopf bluffed. "You knew Eliot Hansen, didn't you?"

Culpepper wasn't buying. "So did half of Hollywood. Are you grilling Bob Hope?"

"We have reason to believe you can tell us more about the case than Mr. Hope."

"Who's we? What reason?"

"Reports from other parties."

"What parties?"

"Mr. Culpepper, you'd be much more help to our investigation if you just answered the questions. I'll ask them."

"All right. Let's hear them."

Lowenkopf took it from the top. "Who were you with the night of Eliot Hansen's murder?"

"Are you sure it was murder?"

"Yes, we are."

"How?"

"Mr. Culpepper, please. Do you have some reason for deliberately refusing to answer?"

"All right. Just tell me something. How do I know what I tell you will go no further? There are other people involved. To be frank, I'd rather it didn't get out. For my own legal position."

"I'll do my best. If it's got to come out, it will anyway. If not, it won't from me."

"Good enough." Culpepper hesitated. "Did you really tackle Eliot on the set? Insisting he was a stewardess?"

"I really can't discuss the case."

"I don't blame you. I wouldn't either. What's funny is that Eliot probably has been a stewardess at one time or another. If you know anything about his appetites."

"Not much. That's the sort of thing I was hoping you could tell me."

Angborn glided silently into the room. "They've finished what you've assigned them, sir."

"Can you wait a minute, Sarge? I'll be back. If you don't tell them exactly what you want, they give you spaghetti."

Lowenkopf wasn't alone for thirty seconds when the briefcase began to ring. From the other room Culpepper shouted, "Pick that up, will you?"

Lowenkopf lifted the beige box from the briefcase and snapped it open. The voice on the other end was crisp, precise. "Robert."

Lowenkopf wasn't sure how to answer. "No."

"No?" The voice quickened immediately. "Who are you, then? A new *divertissement*? Are you male or female? Or don't you know?"

Lowenkopf put his hand over the mouthpiece and hurried into the next room. "It's a woman. I think."

The two laborers sat against the broken wall enjoying the sight of Culpepper swinging a sledgehammer at the chandelier. As Lowenkopf entered, the hammer missed the crystal and swung within an inch of his nose. Culpepper leaned on the hammer, catching his breath. "Ask her who she is."

"Let me speak to the man of the house," the woman on the other end of the line demanded.

"Excuse me, but who is calling?"

"Mrs. Culpepper."

Lowenkopf glanced at the blonde. "His mother?"

"His wife, you imbecile. Let me at him."

Lowenkopf offered the phone to his host, who waved it away. "I'm out."

"Mrs. Culpepper? Your husband's out."

"Like hell he is. Out where?"

Lowenkopf turned helplessly to Angborn. "Why don't you take it? She wants to know out where."

"Tell her I'm getting my nose blown."

"He's getting his nose blown."

"Like hell he is. You just let him know it's going to cost him thousands a day in knickknacks. If I don't hear from him by Wednesday, he can kiss the Maserati good-bye." She slammed down the phone.

121

When he heard the dial tone, Angborn accepted the phone from Lowenkopf. Culpepper swung his hammer, connecting with the base of the chandelier, scattering bits of crystal in all directions. A maimed chain of glass prismed colors on the ceiling, walls, and floor, as the remaining crystal swayed violently overhead. "How much?"

"She didn't say exactly," Lowenkopf informed him. "Just 'thousands a day,' in round numbers."

Culpepper rested his hammer. "Cheap."

"And she's giving away your Maserati Wednesday."

"She's running out of ideas. Last time, she gave my boat to the Salvation Army. Told them to start a navy. Fifty thousand dollars. Almost a month of my life."

Lowenkopf did some depressing calculations. "If you give me a few answers, Mr. Culpepper, I won't take up any more of your time."

"Go ahead. There's nothing these people can't hear."

The laborers looked intrigued.

"Where were you the night Eliot Hansen was murdered? Four nights ago?"

"I was with a woman. In what they call a compromising position. Several compromising positions, actually. Is that enough? Or do you need her to confirm my movements?"

The laborers savored that.

"Could you tell me who she was?"

"I could. But I won't. Unless I'm convinced I have to."

"Was it Gail Wranawski?"

Culpepper looked up. "She told you herself? So what are we dancing around for? Why the fuck are you asking me?"

"I'm trying to confirm her story."

Culpepper barked appreciatively. "So Gail's the suspect, is she? What did she tell you?"

"That you were together."

"Believe it. She was with me, all right. From start to finish. I don't mind telling you—it takes me some time to get from start to finish. You don't need confirmation of that, do you, Sarge?"

The laborers chuckled appreciatively. Culpepper tossed them a bow. In the corner, the blonde flipped the pages of her *Fortune*. It was impossible to determine if she had been listening. She must have felt their eyes, because she raised her own transparent blues. Her pursed lips opened on tiny pearl teeth. "I want you to read this article on divestitures, Robert. It confirms what I've been warning you about your portfolio."

Culpepper nodded with interest, showing her off. She seemed to understand this and returned to her reading.

Lowenkopf seized his opportunity. "You're sure that Ms. Wranawski never left you that night? You're not close enough to cover for her in a murder investigation, are you?"

Culpepper chose to smile. "Gail's not really my type, as you see. So why do I sleep with her? I'll tell you. She reminds me of the girls I couldn't have in Oceanside High School on Long Island."

The laborers shook their heads in sympathy. Lowenkopf would have pursued it, but a cry of horns from the traffic below suddenly reached the fifty-fifth floor.

Culpepper swung his sledge and smashed the last bit of crystal. "I'll give you a little advice, Sarge. For your investigation. Forget about who loves who. Follow the money. Once, as it passed from hand to hand, the murderer felt its touch. Follow the chain of money. One thing I've learned in this business." With a sudden backward swing, he sank the hammer's head into the wall behind him.

Angborn slipped a jacket over Culpepper's shoulders. The interview was over.

The money chain, as Lowenkopf reconstructed it, ran two links long: Warren Searle spent money as he needed it; Lester Cravit signed the checks. A phone book in the Fifty-eighth Street library listed only one lawyer with that name in the garment district. Less than an hour after he had left Culpepper, Lowenkopf sat across a narrow desk from Lester Cravit, Esquire.

Cravit was dressed for a getaway in red running shorts and a gray sweatshirt on which spidery red letters spelled out "Part of Your Loving." His legs were too long for his desk, and the sole of a blue Nike wavered on its heel pivot inches from Lowenkopf's shoe. In his right fist the attorney clutched a blue pencil stub whose trail of circles and squares Lowenkopf traced across the racing pages that cluttered most of the desktop. Cravit hoisted himself over the desk and stared venomously down at the handicapper's column. "This paper hasn't picked a goddamned winner since DeNonno retired. There's no one you can believe anymore."

Lowenkopf agreed. He had been lucky to catch Cravit in without an appointment. That, at any rate, was what the secretary had crisply informed him, in obvious disapproval. His good fortune was reaffirmed by Cravit a few minutes later, who repeated his secretary's reference to the time of day. Since it was lunchtime, Lowenkopf suspected Cravit would have offered to buy lunch for a client, so the lack of an offer implied a certain shrewdness on the attorney's part. Or a suspicious nature.

"What can I do for you, Mr. Lowenkopf?" Cravit leaned back noisily in his executive chair, which had once been expensive but now showed patches where the fabric was wearing thin. A fine yellow haze shimmered in the sunlight between them, streaming in from two dirty unopened windows.

Lowenkopf leaned forward and put his hand in his jacket. He kept it there long enough to make Cravit nervous, then withdrew it and cleaned his teeth with his pinkie nail. "My friends on the Coast tell me you're a man who finances films," he said. "I'm interested in men who finance films."

Cravit's eyes narrowed considerably. He slid open the top drawer of his desk. "I'm afraid that's something I absolutely cannot discuss." From the drawer he removed a brown paper bag with a dark spot on its underside. From the bag he removed a sandwich in wax paper, almond butter and tofu with sprouts on whole wheat bread. His mouth covered a lot of corner when he bit.

"Of course not," Lowenkopf agreed. "I perfectly understand. These arrangements can be a little unorthodox, after all."

Cravit nodded with a mouthful of sandwich.

"In fact, that is what I was hoping to hear from you," Lowenkopf continued. "I am only interested in men of discretion." He lowered his voice to emphasize his point. "If I had a friend with something to invest, could you arrange one of these unorthodox arrangements for him?"

Cravit offered him a stalk of celery from the paper bag, which Lowenkopf interpreted as a sign of uncertainty. "I guess I know that kind of arrangement as well as anyone in the garment district," he said.

Lowenkopf declined the celery. He leaned closer. "Yes, but—I realize this is delicate, but have you had any actual experience in arranging these things? I mean you yourself. Have you done it before?"

Cravit gnawed the celery. "We don't like to talk about experience."

"And by 'we' you mean . . . ?"

Cravit made little circles in the air with what remained of the stalk. "We businessmen."

Lowenkopf sat back in his chair and counted to ten. Then he leaned forward again, but not so far as before. "I'm afraid I must know. Experience counts a great deal. Of course, it's easy to talk, but I understand these things are tricky to execute discreetly."

Cravit munched slyly. "Not so tricky."

"You speak from experience, then?"

Cravit swallowed. He broke a carrot in half and offered the thick part to Lowenkopf. "I didn't say that."

Lowenkopf stopped the skinny half-carrot just as it approached Cravit's mouth. "Please do. If you've never arranged anything like this before, I'll have to find someone who has."

Cravit tried to shake his carrot free. "I've got all the experience you're looking for."

"Even with money that is . . . unaccounted for?"

"With dirty money, yes!" The carrot, set free, reached his mouth, where it was consumed.

Lowenkopf reached into his jacket again and drew out a worn leather wallet with a badge. "Then perhaps you can help me, Mr. Cravit. I'm most anxious to hear anything you can tell me about those arrangements."

The lawyer looked like he was going to gag. He caught his balance with difficulty and rang for his secretary. "Doris, when am I due in Jersey?"

There was a pause during which she looked from one to the other of them. Finally she said, "Thirty minutes, I think."

Cravit started a nod which ended as a shake of his head. "Sorry about that, Officer. We'll have to continue some other time. Call me next week and we'll set something up. No, not next week—I'm all booked up. The week after. Call Doris and she'll take care of you." He stood.

Lowenkopf kept his seat.

"Of course," Cravit continued, "you're free to take whatever legal action you think you can on the basis of this entrapment. And I'll take whatever action against the city I feel is appropriate."

Lowenkopf refused to rise from his chair. "I don't believe you're expected in Jersey, Mr. Cravit. Please sit down."

Instead of sitting, Cravit moved around to the front of the desk. Then he picked up his desk calendar and shoved it at Lowenkopf. "Look at that." On the top page it read "One o'clock. Jersey." The rest of the page was blank.

Lowenkopf reached up and thumbed through the earlier pages. Each had one or two appointments penciled in. Cravit was a thin man with surprisingly strong hands. He yanked the calendar out of Lowenkopf's grip, leaving only a torn half of a Wednesday morning two weeks earlier.

"I think it's time you went now, Officer. You've violated enough rights for one day."

Lowenkopf rose and stuffed his hands into his coat pockets. "I don't know if you're aware of it, but a man who was working on a film you're financing has been murdered."

"After seeing the way you work," Cravit snarled, "my guess is he's out for coffee somewhere. When he turns up—don't let me know."

Lowenkopf followed Doris out of the office and sat down on the edge of her desk. After a momentary pause, her buzzer rang. Cravit's voice came over the intercom. "He gone?"

"No," she said.

"Then throw him out." The intercom snapped off.

Doris calmly lifted the receiver and dialed 911. She waited, too long. She eyed Lowenkopf as if he were personally responsible for the delay. Then she said, "I'm calling to report an intruder. I've got a full description."

He proffered her his yearbook smile. "How would you like a coffee and Danish?"

She inspected him closely. "About five-eleven. Glasses and curly hair. Wearing—what is that?" she demanded, fingering the material of his overcoat.

"Wool," he said defensively.

"In a gray polyester overcoat. And hurry. He's in the office now." She gave the address concisely and hung up.

Lowenkopf didn't quite close the door behind him. From the hallway he heard her buzzer again. Doris reported, "He's gone."

There was a moment during which all he could hear was the wet crunch of lettuce. "Good," said Cravit at last. "Get me Cecil Rowe on the horn."

"I'll get him later," Doris said. "I'm going out for Danish and coffee first."

Lowenkopf hurried out of her way. The passenger elevator was broken, so he got on the freight. He leaned against soft black padding and listened to himself descend. The cage rang as it hit the first floor. He slid open the gate and followed the side exit out of the building. He walked immediately to the Forty-second Street library and found the bank of phone books. Only then did he open his fist and examine the slip in his palm. He had known what to reach for. Homer wouldn't approve of his method, but Homer was busy at the coroner's inquest. He smoothed out the scrap he had torn from the calendar. He had the top half of a page. It read "Wednesday 24, 10:00 CR and Hansen." Hansen had been in New York for only two days. Lowenkopf had turned to those days as soon as Cravit's calendar was thrust into reach. Had Hansen come to the city on some other business, or just to check out Cravit? He had seen the checks, of course. Had Cravit known what Hansen was after when they met? And why had he arranged for him to meet CR?

At first Lowenkopf had thought it meant "CRavit." But

why would Cravit refer to himself by initials? Why refer to himself at all? The answer was on the calendar on Doris' blotter, with a thick double line through all the Wednesdays and, in a large, childish hand, the name Cecil Rowe. The same name Cravit had asked for immediately after Shelly's exit.

Lowenkopf tore through the pages of the Manhattan book and ran his thumb down the Rowes. Cayman, Cazzie, Cedric. He dropped the tome in its slot and raised Brooklyn. Catherine, Caveman, C.F. Jersey was torn from its binding and Lowenkopf cursed silently. Who would want to steal Jersey? Lowenkopf balanced the Bronx volume across his thigh and held his breath. There were pages missing but the Rowes were intact. In a column after "Carrie" was the name Cecil Rowe, in boldface, followed by "attorney at law." The address was Tremont Avenue. Westchester Square? Lowenkopf's pulse surged ahead and his mind tried to catch up. Physical proximity was no connection—nothing that meant anything. He'd never heard of Rowe before. There was no reason to think, just because he happened to practice out of an office nearby, that Rowe knew anyone Lowenkopf did.

He caught the crosstown shuttle at Forty-second Street just as the doors were closing. At Grand Central he bought a *Post,* changed to the Six train, and settled in against the gray molded plastic for a long, bumpy ride to the Bronx.

This coroner has a nasal voice that whined endlessly. Greeley didn't like what he was hearing. But he was much too good a detective to **jump** to conclusions before the evidence was in. At least that's what he told himself.

The long and the short of it was this: the medical examiner believed Eddie Pepper had been strangled before he hit the ground. The coroner was reluctant to draw the obvious conclusion that the officer's testimony—Shelly's—was entirely inconsistent with this medical fact. If the dead man had been strangled before his fall, the officer had to be lying. The implication was that Shelly had done the strangling.

To protect himself in the event that such a finding could

be resisted, the coroner paraded a string of witnesses, all of whom devoutly placed Shelly alone on the roof with Pepper minutes before the boy was alleged to have been strangled. Most of them had heard the body as it struck the ground and had looked up to see Shelly on the roof, leaning over the edge. A young couple watching a baby had seen him jump like a madman into the circle by the flagpole, climb halfway up a fence, and go bouncing off across the snow. The boy had apparently stolen his car battery. According to the first officers on the scene, Shelly had occupied himself waiting for their arrival in searching for a briefcase.

It all sounded depressingly like Shelly.

Greeley read Lowenkopf's report into the record and decided not to wait around for the verdict. He walked to the car, turned it on, and sat in it for a minute. He turned on a transistor radio Shelly left on the dashboard, usually kept set to the jazz station at the end of the dial, but since Shelly had been in Los Angeles, Greeley had reset the station. Bartok crackled from the speaker. Greeley put the gear in forward and eased out of his spot.

He was interrupted before he reached the Grand Concourse by a call from Madagascar. Shelly still hadn't been to see Billy Ringo. Where the hell was he? Gone to Fifty-ninth Street, Greeley explained, to talk to a producer.

"Another producer? Or the same one? I just got a call from the mayor's office—Lowenkopf's Hollywood buddies are in town. They'll be filming in the streets of our fair city tomorrow. Get down to the Royalton and see if there's anything you can do for them."

Greeley turned on the Deegan.

"And tell Lowenkopf that he gives me a royal pain in my—" The car passed between electrical towers, cutting the message short.

Greeley chose the East Side Drive, but hit traffic on the Willis Avenue Bridge. On the Manhattan side he cut off and followed Second Avenue downtown. He parked the car in a loading zone and propped his Police Department card in the window. There was an old bag of M&M candies on top of the dashboard which lent it a worn, faintly sweet scent. Shelly had left it there, insisting it worked better than the card, a symbol of the secret sisterhood of meter maids. Greeley didn't care for the smell but left it there, in deference to his partner.

Inside the Royalton, the desk clerk sent him to the sixth floor, which Warren Searle had usurped for his cast and crew. A wrangle was already in progress. A cute blonde leaned in an open doorway at the end of the hall, watching a pudgy, wispy-haired man wait out a tirade by the actor Johnny Weems.

Weems's knees poked bonily from the hem of his bathrobe as he paced in and out of the room. Each step kicked open the front of the robe, exposing most of the actor's charm. "Did you hear what I said, Warren?" Weems demanded, slapping a magazine in his hand. "A million dollars. That's what this article says the word 'Naked' is worth in the title of a book. Add that one little word and the book grosses a million dollars more. Doesn't that suggest anything to you?"

"No, Johnny. But I suspect it suggests something to you."

"You bet it does. Just imagine what it could mean at the box office. This damn picture should be called *The Next to Die Naked.*"

Warren answered curtly, "It's not that sort of film, Johnny."

Weems boiled for a minute, then erupted. "This isn't a film—it's a movie! That's the problem with you, Warren—you don't know the difference. You don't know your audience. So you make turkeys like *Pas de Murder* and nobody comes to see them. This is a fuckin' perfect example. You won't add one little word to make a million bucks. And then you cry you haven't got the money when I ask for something I need to work. Have you seen the room they've given me?"

"I haven't had the opportunity," the director said.

"It's just not right, Warren. I've earned someplace to sit and think between scenes. I hate to make a pig of myself, but I've got to have another suite."

There was a green-eyed actress propped on the windowsill, also in a robe, with a hotel towel around her neck. "Take mine! I won't mind. There's no water in the bathroom pipes."

Weems stopped pacing. "Did you try turning the taps beneath the sink?"

"Would you like to give me a hand?"

He threw up his hands. "You see what I mean, Warren. Even this fucking bitch treats me like a plumber. I've got to put my foot down somewhere."

Warren was sitting in a pair of flowered shorts at a portable typewriter on his nightstand. "I've already called the manager about your suite, Johnny," he intoned patiently. "He apologizes for the squeaks in the walls. He apologizes for the traffic in the street. We all have to put up with more than we deserve. Teri can't get water in her bathtub. I suspect she'll switch with you, if you ask her nicely."

Teri didn't hold out for niceness. "Take it! It's no good to me!" She crossed to the bed and reclined dramatically. "If I don't find a place to take a bath soon, I'm going to turn into a raisin."

Greeley stood tactfully in the door frame.

Weems accosted him. "Are you the manager of this place?"

Greeley smiled affably and said, "I'm a policeman."

Searle kept on typing. "My God, we can't be making too much noise already."

"I'm sure you can, but that's not why I'm here. You sent for a detective. My name's Greeley."

They all stared at him.

"I'm Warren Searle," the director said. "I sent for Lowenkopf. You're not Lowenkopf." He rolled a sheet of paper out of his typewriter and gave it to Carla, who carried it reluctantly down the hall.

"He's busy," Greeley said.

"So am I," Searle told him. "Send him along when he's free, will you? He's working on something for me privately. I don't want to bother anybody else about it."

Greeley didn't budge. "New York City police detectives don't take on private cases."

"No, of course they don't." Searle addressed Weems, who was examining his own knees. "Why don't you go to your room and see what the manager can do about those pipes?"

"It's not the pipes. I don't know what it is."

Teri sat forward. "You don't mind if I use your tub for a while, do you, Johnny?"

Weems sneered down at her. "Oh yes I do. Why do you think I'm dressed in this robe? For your fucking benefit? Jee-sus! I was about to jump in a bath myself. What am I supposed to do while you're bathing? I think I'll stuff some cotton in my goddamn ears and go soak."

He would have pushed Greeley out of the doorway, but Greeley took a small step backward. Weems's arm sailed through empty air. He lost his balance and landed on the hallway carpet, rubbing the small of his back.

"Now look what you've done! Warren, when are you going to get rid of this fucking cop? I think something's broken in my back."

Greeley knelt beside him. "Let me see."

"Are you a doctor too? Don't touch me. I'm going to my room, Warren. If those pipes are still singing away tonight, I'm going to crawl in here with you."

He left. Teri watched him go. "Big talker."

Searle cranked another sheet out of his typewriter. "Has Carla come back yet?"

Teri said, "No. But give it to me, I'll take it down the hall. I'm going anyway. Someone along the hallway will take pity on a poor girl desperately in need of bubbles."

"Thank you, Miss Korn." She left with the sheaf of paper. Searle looked up at Greeley. "Guess there's not much for you to do around here, Detective. Unless you want to carry papers too."

"No, thank you, sir. I'll just look around, if you don't mind."

"We're rather busy just now. We'll be shooting outdoors tomorrow."

"I won't be in your way."

Searle looked unconvinced as Carla reentered the room. "Carla," he said, shoving her gently towards Greeley, "why don't you take Detective Greeley to the far end of the hall and show him around? This is really your area, anyway."

"What area?" she demanded.

"You know. Police relations. Introduce him to the crew or show him stills or something."

She glanced at Greeley sourly. "Are you sure you won't need me for anything?"

"Yes," Searle insisted. "I need you for this."

Greeley smiled pleasantly.

"All right." She walked off ahead of him. "Come on."

Greeley chased after her.

Around the corner she stopped and confronted him. "Well—give me a clue, will you? What do you have to see?"

"I don't have to see anything," Greeley said, trying to put a calming note in his voice. "That was Mr. Searle's idea. I'd be just as happy if we sat and talked somewhere."

"Like where?"

"Anywhere. Your room would do."

She smiled unevenly, her suspicions confirmed. "Just what do you want to talk about?"

"About you. The cast and crew. Nothing very intrusive."

"Like what?"

"Well—what did Mr. Searle mean about 'police relations'? Are you the company sleuth?"

"Hardly. It's just that I end up holding hands with all the detectives who come around the set."

"A sort of cop's companion?"

"More like a nursemaid."

"Were you Shelly Lowenkopf's nursemaid?"

The question slowed her down. "Lowenkopf doesn't need a nursemaid. He needs a keeper. He looks so innocent, you know what I mean? I let him out of my sight for a couple of hours one night and that was the end of that."

"The end of what?"

"That girl in the robe got to him."

"Miss Korn?"

"Kern. Are you interested in her too?"

"I'm interested in Lowenkopf."

"Why?"

"I'm supposed to be," Greeley admitted, a little sigh escaping. "He acts like a lone wolf, I know. But he's got a partner, and there's nothing either of us can do about it."

"You're his partner?"

Greeley shrugged. "Or he's mine. Depends on how you look at it."

"Really?"

"Does that make a difference?"

"Uh-huh."

"How?"

"Why don't we go in my room and discuss it?"

"All right. Perhaps you can tell me something about yourself."

"Whatever you want to hear."

"That's very good of you."

"I doubt it." She pulled him along to 609 and felt for the key in her hip pocket. In fishing it out, she dropped it on the carpet.

Greeley retrieved it and opened the door. "Shelly will really appreciate this."

"You'll promise to tell him, won't you?" There was a light in her eyes he took to be the reflection of the fixture overhead.

"On my honor."

She gave him a satisfied smile. He followed her inside.

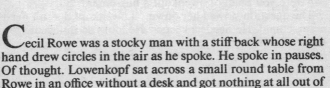

Cecil Rowe was a stocky man with a stiff back whose right hand drew circles in the air as he spoke. He spoke in pauses. Of thought. Lowenkopf sat across a small round table from Rowe in an office without a desk and got nothing at all out of him.

"Did you say, ah . . . Jeffrey Hansen?" Rowe rolled a small cart with a computer on it over to the round table. He punched a few buttons and looked thoughtful.

"Eliot Hansen," Lowenkopf prodded him. "You met him about two weeks ago, in Lester Cravit's office."

"Just a moment." Rowe held up his palm and revealed a watch on the underside of his wrist much too large for his hand. "Did you say Cravitt? With one T or two?"

"One," Lowenkopf said. "Maybe two. I don't know."

Rowe punched two sets of keys and looked deep into the screen. He shook his head in short, rapid shakes. "I don't show a meeting in the last two weeks with either Hansen or Cravitt, one T or two." He invited Lowenkopf to verify the screen's output.

Lowenkopf didn't give a damn about the screen's output. "Could it have been canceled?"

Rowe threw up his hands sympathetically. "I can't get a program that keeps track of that. Once a meeting is deleted, it's gone."

"Mr. Rowe," Lowenkopf pressed, "it was just two weeks ago. Don't you *remember?*"

Rowe's eyes rolled towards the ceiling, then returned to Lowenkopf's face as if descending from orbit. "No, I'm sorry. I don't usually do things like that anymore."

"You don't attend meetings?"

"I'm an attorney. I have to attend meetings. What I don't do anymore is remember them." He typed a string of characters swiftly into the machine. "Your name ends in 'pf,' doesn't it? Now, if anyone wants to know when we met, I have a record to show for it." He angled the screen towards Lowenkopf again. The message read: "2:30 POLICE DETECTIVE LOWENKOPF DISCUSSED ELIOT HANSEN? AND LESTER CRAVIT?TT? NO NEW DATA INPUT."

Lowenkopf had no new data either. He thanked Rowe and left. He bought a slice of thick Sicilian pizza from a storefront with a window on the street. Rowe had had an appointment with Cravit and Hansen—that much the slip of paper in his pocket attested to. If Rowe's computer didn't show it, someone must have deleted the date. Or failed to enter it. In either case, someone hadn't wanted to leave a record of the meeting on the computer disk. That someone had to be Rowe, for his own purposes or the protection of one of the other men in that meeting.

He ordered a medium grape drink and another slice of pizza. Before they came, Cecil Rowe appeared on the sidewalk in front of his office. He moved rapidly to the curb and hailed a cab.

Lowenkopf dumped some change on the counter and grabbed his pizza. A second cab was behind the one that had picked up Cecil Rowe. Lowenkopf banged on the window of the second cab before it had reached the curb. He yanked open the door and hopped in the back.

"Follow that cab!" he ordered as Rowe's taxi moved away from a traffic light.

The cabbie turned to look at him. "Are you kidding?"

Lowenkopf held up his badge. "This is official business. Do what you have to do to stay with him."

The cabbie was less than anxious. "You're paying cash for this, right? I don't take no city vouchers."

"I'm paying cash. Look." Lowenkopf took what cash he had out of his pants pocket. Four dollars."

"That's not going to last very long."

"Maybe he's not going very far. If you don't start moving, we're not going to have a chance to find out. Where is he now, anyway?" Rowe's taxi had left the intersection and was nowhere in sight.

The cabbie looked around. "He turned the corner."

Lowenkopf felt for his gun. The holster was still empty from the airport security check. He slid open the plastic divider that separated him from the driver. "All right," he said. "I'm running you in for loitering."

"Okay, okay," the cabbie said, adding something else beneath his breath. He tipped down the rearview mirror and adjusted the visor on his baseball cap. Then he readjusted the mirror. He rolled down his window, stuck his arm out, and tapped the roof of the cab. He turned back to Lowenkopf. "Do you see him?"

"You told me he rounded the corner."

"Okay, okay. But that doesn't mean he's still there. That was some time ago."

When they reached the corner, Rowe's cab was nowhere in sight. "Where to now?" The street ran underneath the elevated train tracks for miles in both directions. A series of light and dark slashes stretched unbroken as far as they could see. Several blocks behind them, Lowenkopf thought he saw a taxi light.

"There he is," Lowenkopf whispered. "Turn around."

The cabbie yanked his visor down and raised his nose for a sight. "That's not him."

"How can you tell?"

"How can I tell? How can you tell the cops from the robbers? I know the cab you're after. I've driven it hundreds of times. The brakes are low and the transmission clunks. I'd be in it now if I hadn't had to take a piss before we left the garage."

"You mean that car is from your garage?"

"Number seventy-seven. A rolling junkyard. But lucky on tips."

Lowenkopf reached his arm through the opening in the plastic divider and made a grab for the radio.

"Wait a minute," the cabbie squawked, pushing Lowenkopf back through the plastic. "You can't work the radio. Give it here." He took the radio into his own palm and pressed his thumb on the button. "What do you want to say?"

"Just ask him where seventy-seven is going."

The cabbie lowered his head and spoke into the microphone, hailing his dispatcher. "This is sixty-two heading north on Tremont. There's one foxy lady trying to wave down a car going south. Is seventy-seven still around here somewhere?"

The dispatcher, gargling, said, "Nice thought, sixty-two. Seventy-seven's on his way to the zoo. Twenty-three, thirty-one, seventeen, and forty-six are on their way."

The cabbie turned to Lowenkopf. "See? Gotta know how to do these things. Now, you want the zoo."

They entered at the Pelham Parkway gate, a tall bronze set of faded green bars twenty feet high with figures of animals wrought overhead and a small booth at its base to house the guard at the automobile entrance. The taxi dropped Lowenkopf off outside, and he walked in through the parking lot. At the fountain at the far end of the lot he saw a young woman struggling to fit a stroller in the back seat of Rowe's taxi while the cabbie looked on patiently.

Lowenkopf bolted up the wide marble steps and blended with the crowd around the seal pond. Rowe was nowhere in sight. Lowenkopf poked his head into the old bird house, which was closed. He crossed the lawn and entered the monkey house. There was a high shriek, the smell of hay and urine, and the rumbling sound heard over a subway grate. But there was no subway. It was dark, and Lowenkopf was forced to close in on each of the crowds that gathered in front of the glass cages to be sure he had not missed Rowe. The sunlight at the exit on the far side of the exhibit hurt his eyes.

It was a weekday. The pony and elephant rides were slow. Two dusty ponies shuffled around the track with feedbags over their noses, dragging little red wooden carts of children behind them. An elephant stood in the grass under a sycamore tree and munched dead sycamore leaves. Rowe was not in line for the rides. Nor was he anywhere in the stalls of newborn lambs and goats that served as the main attraction of the children's zoo. Lowenkopf followed the long circle of rhinos and hippos with bellies in the mud along the perimeter of the elephant house, and checked out the crowd gathered in front of a mama and baby African elephant pair. He hesitated between the reptile and ape houses. To his right, the cages for the big birds, condors and eagles, were stuck away behind the small mammal house in a less-populated section of the zoo. Around the curve in front of him were the really big attractions: first the bear pits, then the House of Darkness, full of night crawlers, followed by the African Plains, where lion and giraffe roamed open tracts of land, separated from their visitors, and each other, by ditches and low walls. Lowenkopf chose the less-traveled path, and it made all the difference.

He got as far as the antelope cages and crept up to watch them feed. On the far end of the path, beneath a row of big horse-chestnut trees, Rowe was talking softly with another man while a third stood discreetly to one side. Lowenkopf recognized the discreet man. He was called Janice on the street, without a hint of a snicker in anyone's voice. He stood like an infant's toy, doughy rings of decreasing sizes piled on top of each other. His head was a little round ring smaller than his neck, and he wore a wool hat with earflaps to cover his hair. His job was to be mean and he was very good at it. Which was why Keppler never let him wander very far from sight.

Rowe was hovering over a man seated on a bench whose

hands were hidden in the pockets of his black overcoat. Suddenly he drew one out. It rose through the shade in which the bulk of the man was concealed, flashing into the sunlight. Soft, pale, manicured fingers held up something Lowenkopf couldn't quite make out. A peanut. The man pointed it directly at Rowe and tossed it to the pigeons at his feet, who darted like sharks for the shell. He stood in stages, like an invalid, and stamped his left foot to shake his cuff down. The pigeons opened like a sea to let him pass, closing in behind him for the nuts that fell from his hidden hand. He started toward the old rhino house. Rowe kept up with him, a pace or two behind, Janice maintaining a respectful distance. Lowenkopf joined their parade, trying to keep his eye on Rowe and Keppler while avoiding Janice's notice.

He lost them when they made a left and disappeared behind some trees. He ran up to overtake them and saw Rowe and Keppler on the steps to the Alpine Cable Car ride. From the shack at the top of the steps, cables ran fifty feet in the air, bolstered by supports every hundred yards. Along the cables, green, yellow, red, and blue buckets rolled across the park to Asia and Africa. From the dangling buckets, adults could view the entire zoo, while kids enjoyed the terrifying height. It was one place in the park two men could talk briefly in certain privacy. Whatever Keppler had to say to Rowe, he didn't want heard.

Lowenkopf was determined to learn what that was. Janice was nowhere to be seen. Lowenkopf took his place at the back of the line leading to the ride, removed his glasses, and rubbed his eyes. The line advanced rapidly. Keppler and Rowe boarded a yellow bucket. The door was slammed by an attendant and the bucket climbed its cable. Lowenkopf pushed past four kids in front of him and jumped into the bucket after Keppler's, closing the door behind him. The attendant gave him a disapproving scowl and an extra push as the bucket left the ground, swinging unsteadily.

It had been years since Lowenkopf had taken a ride like this, but the fear rushed back immediately. In his concentration on Keppler, he had forgotten his fear of heights. He braced his elbows against both sides of the bucket and strained to make out the murmur from the car in front of his. He thought he heard the word "cough" when his bucket started to rattle more violently than the wind could account for. The mechanism that held his bucket to the cable was passing over one of the towers guiding the cables through the air. He looked down, a mistake he recognized at once, but too late. Beneath him were giraffes and what looked like pigs in open areas. Far beneath him. From deep in his windpipe he felt something rise. Not until it forced its way through his teeth did he recognize it as a laugh. Soon he was giggling uncontrollably. The two men in the bucket in front seemed to be turning his way. The only way he could stop the noise was by balancing in the center of his seat, slumping low, and covering his eyes. His bucket passed over the second support tower with a sharp lurch, swaying a bit wider in the wind. Overhead the gears rattled and missed. He knew he would fall. He *knew*.

When his bucket arrived at the Asian station it seemed to be empty. The attendant opened the door to let a little girl in and found Lowenkopf kneeling on the floor of the car. He held up the bows of his shoelaces in explanation. The little girl stepped over him, crawled up on the seat, and stuck her head over the side, looking down. Lowenkopf closed his eyes and exited, accepting a helping hand. When he opened them, the hand had turned to a vise and his arms were pinned behind him by Janice.

"Put me down. I'm a police officer." The massive arms around him tightened. Janice's mouth opened. Lowenkopf thought he was going to speak, but when no sound emerged, he feared he was about to be bitten. Janice yawned. His teeth were perfect—white, clean, enormous.

Lowenkopf stopped struggling. "Where are we going?"

The big man struggled to remember the words. "Feeding lions," he said, bearing Lowenkopf over the crowd.

When they reached the African Plains, Rowe was gone. His client stood gazing into the lion pit. A great yellow cat lazed in the pale winter sunlight, his back to the subdued visitors. Keppler studied the lion. Now and then a hand emerged from his overcoat pocket, flung a peanut at the big cat's flank, and disappeared into the pocket again. The lion lifted his head, looked around. Its gaze settled on the man in black. Keppler returned the stare. The lion broke first, lowering its massive head on its paws. As soon as it did, Keppler threw another peanut at its rear.

"Sergeant Lowenkopf." It was a fact, not a term of address. Keppler's voice was deep and hushed. "As a taxpayer I am distressed to see how you spend your working hours. Have you uncovered the lion's plot to devour the lamb? Or are you here merely to harass me?"

Lowenkopf hung sideways in the air over Janice's head. "Tell him to put me down."

Keppler made no signal that Lowenkopf could see, but the big man obeyed immediately. Keppler's face was large and wrinkled as a lion's, and only half as encouraging. "But you do not put me down. These are my last hours of freedom, you believe. Why do you follow me around the park?"

They were alone except for a group of schoolchildren making their way from the giraffe exhibit a hundred yards away, where their teacher still conferred with an aproned zoo-keeper. The ground felt secure beneath Lowenkopf's feet. He assumed his toughest stance. "I haven't got time to be following you, Keppler. I've got new fish to fry."

Keppler's lips drew back from his teeth. "Since your trip to Los Angeles you haven't had time for any of your old friends. But you see, we are all still here, waiting for you."

"What do you know about my trip? For that matter, what do you know about the murder of Eliot Hansen?"

"Eliot Hansen?" Keppler raised his head. "You will have me implicated in the death of Abe Lincoln soon. You would like a connection there, wouldn't you? But I have been in New York all this time. I am not permitted to travel just now, a result of that other unfortunate business between us. It is a great inconvenience to me, Lowenkopf. Why don't you give it up? Why don't you listen to your partner, Homer Greeley, and put your energy into police work that will do something for you? My little case will do nothing for you. I will be absolved, and everyone embarrassed by it will then blame you. This warning I give you as a favor. Why don't you take a little vacation? You can go away with one of your new Hollywood friends. When the grand jury learns you have nothing on me, you will return, well rested and clear of responsibility. You can be a free man."

Lowenkopf smiled grimly. A warm thrill ran through him,

as if the sun had suddenly broken through the gray. "Let me tell you something, Keppler. You're not going to dance out of this indictment. The principal witness against you this time is no two-dollar crook you can scare or buy off. This time, I'm the principal witness against you, and I'm a professional testifier. I was under the table when you made the deal, do you understand? I heard every dirty word. I've got it all on tape. I saw your face when you came in and the back of your head when you left. I saw you scratch your ankle with your pinkie nail. I could have unraveled your checkered socks. You wouldn't get off if I were the only witness against you. And I'm not the only witness."

Keppler laughed, a sound like metal drawers scraping. "Have you seen Billy Ringo lately, Lowenkopf? You should talk to him." He took a peanut from his pocket and held it up.

At the signal, Janice gurgled and lifted Lowenkopf, struggling to free his arms, eight feet off the ground. A brittle wind passed through him, tousling the heads below, as the sun frosted over and the air thinned. A tremor beginning in Janice's arm coursed violently through Lowenkopf. "Now you're courting a charge of police assault," he warned horizontally.

Keppler waved his hand at the crowd of possible witnesses. All were under ten years old. "I'd rather face their testimony than yours, Sergeant Lowenkopf. Janice, put him down somewhere." He tossed his peanut in a careful arc at the lion and the big man tossed Lowenkopf after it.

Lowenkopf landed in the dust on the lion's side of the pit just as the cat was struck by the shell. A shriek froze in his gut. Keppler wagged a long finger at Janice. He shook his head and addressed a small boy. "Now, I didn't tell him to put him *there*, did I?"

Intrigued, the boy nodded in agreement. The children clustered to see the man in the lion pit. Something in his paralysis inspired curiosity. Sensing their excitement, the lion rose languidly and decided to investigate. Keppler waved a genial farewell as the scrappy old lion paddled over, grumbling. He rolled his head, wrinkled his nose, then sank his teeth into the seam of Lowenkopf's trousers and tugged.

Lowenkopf was terrified. He hollered for a zoo-keeper, but only a peep escaped. The lion growled at the noise. There was a scream welling in his throat—Lowenkopf caught it with his teeth, which rattled to contain it. The lion scowled at him. He stretched his hand behind the lion's back and gestured desperately to the children, his fingers furiously imitating legs running for a keeper. No one seemed to want to miss the drama in the pit. The lion bent his head at Lowenkopf's cuff and began licking his sock.

Behind the old lion, across an open field, a lioness sunning on a rock yawned hungrily and sat up. When she spotted her mate, her eyes narrowed. She stood. An adolescent cub imitated her, ignoring his father's play and gauging Lowenkopf with the same calculating stare.

Lowenkopf saw them advance. Suddenly a piercing pain caught him in the back of the thigh. As he went down he heard a soft whiz pass his ear and felt the body of the beast in the dust behind him.

15

He opened his eyes on a hard green bench on the safe side of the wall of the lion pit. A man in a dirty white apron knelt in front of him, and an indeterminate crowd wobbled noisily somewhere beyond him.

"Sorry about that first dart," the aproned keeper apologized. "Haven't had to use that gun in a while. You'll be fine now. It hardly grazed your knee. Look."

Lowenkopf tried to sit up but his knee swam out of focus. He laid his head down softly, but not softly enough. A swarm of bees changed position between his ears. His tongue was thick when he spoke. "Lion?"

"Oh, don't you worry about him," the keeper assured him, chuckling. "We've got him in the veterinary hospital with every sort of luxury you can imagine. He'll enjoy the life of Riley for the next few days, believe me."

Lowenkopf had hoped the lion was dead. "You got him with a tranquilizer?"

"Right in the flank, on the second shot. Sorry about that first one. Your eye gets a little rusty. Let me help you up."

"I can manage," Lowenkopf insisted, but he couldn't. The keeper lifted him to a sitting position. "Thanks."

"Nothing to it. I carry animals all day long."

"For saving my life, I mean."

"Oh, that. Well, you know—wouldn't do to let them get used to that kind of meat. Makes it harder on us who have to feed them, if you see what I mean. Got to look out for each other around here."

When it became apparent that Lowenkopf would recover, the onlookers lost interest and dispersed. The zoo-keeper helped him to his feet and into an electric car with a red-striped awning, drove him to the south gate of the zoo, and deposited him in a cab on Southern Boulevard, easing him into the back.

"I'd go home and sleep for a while, if I were you. That tranquilizer isn't finished with you yet."

Lowenkopf thanked him again and promised he would do as the keeper suggested. As soon as the stripes of the awning rolled between the zoo gates, he gave the cabbie an address in Riverdale.

Billy Ringo had never had it so good. His bed was soft and the view from the living-room windows spectacular, a panorama of ships moving graciously up the Hudson. The days were long and the two plainclothes detectives who shared his suite had no memories at all for gin rummy. He had all the beer and pizza he could consume, and the television set in his bedroom carried blue movies on cable at night. The luxury he had failed to find as a runner on the street for Keppler had come to Billy at last as a guest of the district attorney.

It hardly seemed to matter that he no longer had any intention of testifying. He had thought about it carefully when he heard the news about Eddie—weighing present luxuries against future costs, and his chances for survival against both. He had expected to lose everything when he first told the cops about his change of heart. But nothing happened. The plainclothes detectives must have passed the word to the district attorney, or at least to the precinct house, but nothing in his situation seemed affected by his recantation. The pizza and beer arrived every lunchtime, the movies flickered on every night. He knew they were all waiting for Lowenkopf. The cop who had arranged the deal had to be the one to square it. At first Billy had been anxious to get on with it and had called for Lowenkopf whenever they reported to the precinct house. But the days passed comfortably, the ships continued to glide up the Hudson, and Billy Ringo decided to give Lowenkopf all the time in the world.

So it was with a touch of dismay that he heard Shelly's "Coming up" over the intercom speaker. And it was with more than a touch of fear that he apprehended Lowenkopf's weary face in the suite's inner room. The cop's skin was ashen, his cheeks were bruised, and the eyes behind his crooked glasses were pasty yellow half-moons. His pupils were tiny specks in his irises, from which all color had been washed away.

The little runner fluffed up the pillows on the bed and eased Lowenkopf onto it. "What the hell did they do to you? You look like a pile of birdshit."

Lowenkopf sank into the pillows without a protest. "Keppler fed me to the lions."

Billy whistled. "Like one of those emperors. Got to hand it to the man. He's got class. Didn't mention what he's got in mind for me, did he?"

A detective guarding Ringo came into the bedroom with a cold slice of pepperoni pizza on a paper plate, which he bit into, munching pizza and plate together. "S'bout time you got here. Billy's been having a helluva time with just us two." A second detective poked his head into the room, followed by a long, rubbery frame.

Lowenkopf eyed the pizza covetously. The slice he had grabbed in Westchester Square had only sharpened his appetite. "I got here as soon as I could."

This seemed to amuse the detectives. "I told you he'd say that." The paunchy one elbowed his partner, who plopped on the foot of the bed and switched on the TV. A toothpaste ad came on, which they both watched closely. When it was over, the round one opened his mouth to say something but savored a pepperoni first.

"I'd like to talk to him alone," Lowenkopf murmured.

With his mouth full, the detective replied. "You do that. We'll be in here if you need us. Just holler and we'll come runnin'." He crammed in the last of the pizza crust and twisted the knob on the television set. Lowenkopf heard a buzzer, giggles, and the cued applause of a game show as he led Billy into the next room.

Ringo dove for the softest seat and stretched out on the sofa. His features were as Lowenkopf remembered, too large for the size of his head, as if a man's face had been plastered onto a boy. There was a new flush to his cheeks and his chin seemed rounder—two cushy weeks had erased the pallor of an adolescence in the gutter. But his eyes were still disturbingly alert, pale gray and flat as an iron.

"Now you're gonna talk to *me*, Lowenkopf? What are you gonna say? That the world would be a better place without Mr. K. in it?"

"Well, wouldn't it?"

"Maybe. But it's none of Billy Ringo's business to make it that way. They tell me you offed Eddie Pepper."

"Who told you that?"

"Word on the street, man. They say you shoved him off a roof."

Lowenkopf sat gingerly on the edge of his chair. "In the first place"—he held up his thumb—"I didn't shove anyone off a roof. And in the second"—his index finger—"that kid wasn't Eddie Pepper."

Billy studied the heel of his shoes as he cleaned it on the sofa's arm. "What kid? If you didn't shove nobody."

Lowenkopf knew that averted look from the first time he saw Billy—eleven years old, hiding in a trashcan. He had opened the lid and found the boy pretending he just wasn't there. "I didn't. Especially not Eddie. The kid they say I shoved was wearing a bracelet with the name Waldo on it."

Ringo couldn't conceal his grin. "What's the matter, Lowenkopf, you never heard of the Great Waldo Pepper?"

"What are you talking about?"

"Eddie wore a bracelet just like that. Jingled all the times we played craps."

Lowenkopf leaned forward over the coffee table. "I don't care what he was wearing. I know Eddie Pepper. And that wasn't him on the roof."

Ringo held up both hands in surrender. "Hey, I'm with you. You say that wasn't Eddie you shoved, *I* believe it. Sure. But that's who they found on the pavement." He studied the ceiling. When he looked down he wore a jagged smile but the hollowness returned to his cheeks. "And they're gonna find me there too."

Lowenkopf felt Billy's desperation shiver through him. Softly he said, "We had a deal."

Billy responded with restrained fury. "You bet your ass we did. I was gonna talk and you were gonna keep me safe and happy. You blew that when you let Eddie down."

Lowenkopf nodded. It made him feel dizzy. "Eddie wasn't part of our deal, Billy. He changed his mind about testifying. If he hadn't changed his mind, he'd be here with you. You don't want to do the same thing, do you?"

Ringo shook his head vigorously. His straight black hair swung a wider arc than his ears. But they both knew it didn't mean what Lowenkopf hoped. "You got to figure, Lowenkopf—I'm not gonna be testifying forever. If no one was there to help Eddie, who's gonna be there for *me?* Much fun as I'm having here, I've got to think of my future. You should be able to get behind that—you a father and all."

"What makes you think I'm a father?"

"He knows a lot, Mr. K., don't he? That's why I gotta protect myself. I know you didn't drop Eddie. We both know who did. And I can tell you why he did it. To tell me something, man, to make sure I was listening. Well, I listened and I heard. Either way, I'm in the shithole, but I figure my odds are better without you. So, thanks for a slick week but I got to fly."

He looked suddenly uncomfortable in all those cushions. Billy leaned forward to get up, but Lowenkopf grabbed his elbow. "You might as well testify, Billy. Keppler will kill you anyway, for even considering it."

Billy yanked himself free and headed for the kitchen. "Thanks for the advice, Lowenkopf. Just wish I could share it with Eddie. That wasn't real smart of you, letting Mr. K. set you up so you delivered the shove. But that's Mr. K. all over. Nice touch."

Lowenkopf found Billy at the refrigerator, tearing a slice of pizza from a pie in a gray cardboard box. Ringo looked up expectantly, but Lowenkopf couldn't think of an answer. He waved at the pizza. "You mind if I have one of those?"

Billy shrugged. "It's your pie, man."

Gobbling cold pizza, Lowenkopf followed Ringo back into the living room. He was starved and his head rang from the tranquilizer, but he wasn't going to get another chance at Billy Ringo. Time to get tough. "I don't want to have to put the screws to you, Billy. But I will if I have to. I can make you sweat."

Billy didn't glance back. "Turn your screws, man. Screw away. The more I sweat for you, the better my credit with Keppler. What can you do to me in the end? Two years? I'll take that lying down and come out roses."

A thought rumbled through the fog in Lowenkopf's head. He shook his head and smiled. "No, Billy. Not two years. No time at all. I'll let you off like that." He snapped his fingers. "Free and clear."

"You can't do that!" Ringo shrieked in indignation. "I'm a *criminal*. You've got to treat me like one. Those guys in the next room—they won't let you get away with it."

Right on cue, the phone rang. They waited. One of the two detectives in the next room hollered through the crack in the door, "For you, Lowenkopf."

It had to be Madagascar. Billy pointed to the kitchen. There was another extension on the wall by the refrigerator, which Billy opened and took out a beer. Lowenkopf picked up the receiver.

Over the line, the captain's voice sounded tinnier than usual. "Glad to learn you finally took the time to see your witness, Lowenkopf. Making any progress with him?"

Lowenkopf watched Billy twist the cap off the beer bottle, and felt the dryness in his own throat. "Some."

"Is he going to testify?"

"He hasn't really decided yet," Lowenkopf said softly.

"Oh yes I have," Ringo insisted. "Not in this life."

"What was that?" Madagascar had ears like a donkey.

Lowenkopf twisted away from Ringo. "Can I get back to you, Captain? We're right in the middle of discussing Billy's testimony. I'd rather keep him at it while we're going strong. You know how these things are. I'll fill you in as soon as we're done here."

"We're done now, Lowenkopf." Ringo upended his beer.

There was a long pause from Madagascar's end of the line. "All right, Lowenkopf," he said finally, his voice laden with unexpressed doubt. "Don't be too long about it. I want you back at the Royalton as soon as you can get there. There's been some trouble."

"What kind of trouble?"

Lowenkopf's question came too quickly. He heard that himself. So he understood Madagascar's hesitation, and the answer when it came. "On second thought, Lowenkopf, stay with it there, with Ringo. Homer's at the Royalton already. He can handle it as well as you can."

Slowing his breathing, Lowenkopf asked again, "What kind of trouble is it, Captain?"

"Homicide." Madagascar sounded irked. "One of the girls was found floating upside down in a bathtub."

Lowenkopf clung to the phone as if it were a life preserver. "Which one of the girls was it, sir?"

Madagascar said, "I don't have her name in front of me."

"Could you get it, please?"

When he returned to the phone after the longest minute in Lowenkopf's life, the captain's tone was brusque. "Here it is," he announced as if he had dredged the name from the Pit. "Theresa Korn. A.k.a. Teri Kern, on-screen. It ought to have been the other way around, oughtn't it?"

No, it oughtn't, Lowenkopf thought, it oughtn't be any way. He was caught up in a snare of memories which flung him back to their dinner together. She kept dropping the cauliflower in the cheese. Or had he? He couldn't remember, and it disturbed him deeply. There was another feeling, too, one he didn't care to examine, a mix of guilt and, well, ready acceptance. The ease with which it came horrified him. He concentrated on Teri, the last he had seen of her—falling asleep on his shoulder, her cheek pressing his collarbone, the sweet smell of hair and sweat as she kissed him, for the last time, on the throat.

Lowenkopf lowered the phone. Madagascar was asking him something about Warren Searle. He set the receiver on its cradle with a soft click that released something inside him. He looked at Ringo's scarred purplish lips.

Billy raised his beer bottle. "Want one?"

Lowenkopf shook his head.

Ringo drained his own and set the empty bottle on the counter. He returned to the sofa and swung his feet up on the coffee table. "There's no point dragging it out forever, blood . . ."

Lowenkopf didn't hear him. He didn't see or hear the apartment door until it slammed shut behind him. The noise was as loud as his own pulse in his ears, and that was very loud. In his mind's eye, Teri lingered in the doorway, regarding him with an expression he could not decipher. A pair of luminous green eyes blinked at him, receding into darkness as a shadow fell on her nose, her lips, her delicate chin. He felt the imprint of her kisses on his mouth, a sweet taste slowly bittering. *There was nothing I could do*, he swore silently, but knew it for a lie. Her form slipped into shadow and the door closed. He became aware of something hidden behind him, a secret, obscene, creeping around from behind. His heart, grieving for Teri, brushed a sharp twig of joy. He could not say when she had become so dear, but a thrill of gratitude stole over him each time he realized Carla was alive.

The blond mass of Carla's hair rose over Greeley's chest like the sun over a field of wheat. His stomach was firm and bare except where a row of blond hairs ran straight from his solar plexus to his navel. His nipples were still brown and wrinkled, set far apart, each pointing in opposite directions away from his heart. He watched her through barely opened lids as she pressed her cheek over the left nipple and counted four, five, six deep breaths. She blew softly on the tiny hairs which stood against her lip and rubbed his chest with her jaw to feel the tickle of recovering hairs. His fingers slipped loose from the brass bars of the headboard and his arm slumped over her shoulder. He heard his watch as it passed her ear and landed roughly beside hers.

She kissed his solar plexus, which caused him to draw deeper breaths. She began to nibble her way down his belly but was stopped short an inch above his navel by the length of her arm, which had reached its full extension from the wrist handcuffed to the headboard.

She raised her head. "Homer, you've gotta let me out of these things."

He put his hand to his chest for the key, but his shirt pocket was gone with his shirt. His head swept the room like a searchlight. He chewed his lip thoughtfully for a minute. "The key was in my shirt. Or my vest. One of those."

Those were further apart than usual. His vest dangled over the edge of the bathroom door, while his shirt was bunched in a corner.

Carla tried to prop her head but the chain was too short. "Why don't you get it?"

He swung his legs over the side and set one foot down on a block of chill marble. The room was decorated in an old idea of luxury—velvet draperies over fluted columns, inset into the walls, two doors, one to the next room and one to the hall, padded in red leatherette with buttons, and a solid rectangle of what looked like black marble on which rested the bed. His pants hung, one leg inside out, across the radiator, an accordion of brass tubing that hissed and spat, warming the change in his pockets. But the marble remained imperturbably cool.

Rather than placing his second foot down, he retracted the first. "I've got a better idea." He slipped below the blankets and nibbled the side of her knee. He felt her hand close on his ankle and admired her grip. Her right wrist was still cuffed to the headboard, but she wouldn't need it now. Suddenly he felt her teeth on his ass. He bit back softly underneath her thigh but heard a terrible shriek in response. "I didn't mean to hurt you. . . ." he started to say, when he realized that Carla's mouth was occupied. And he heard a scream.

He was out of the bed in a flash. Carla emerged from the blankets to find him jumping at the chandelier where his shorts hung tauntingly out of reach. There was another scream, which did not end. The first surprised shriek had matured into sustained wails of horror.

He tilted his head as a shepherd dog would, listening. "It's coming from next door," he decided.

Carla glared at the door resentfully. "So what?"

The screamer struck a strong, clear note and held it. Greeley gave up on his shorts and leapt too quickly into his heated trousers. "I'm a police officer. I can't just let a woman scream." He scanned the room for his gun—the empty holster was wrapped around the lampshade on the night table—didn't find it, and set his shoulder to the connecting door. He bounced off the red leatherette, spotted his shoe in a potted plant, and banged with its heel on the knob. "Open up! Police!"

"Homer! At least open the handcuffs!" Carla protested as the door gave way and he fell through. The room trembled for a moment of tinkling crystal and prismed light. "Homer to the rescue," she mumbled, "without his gun, his bracelets, or his sidekick."

In the next room, Greeley found Gail Wranawski in a red satin camisole, clinging to the bathroom doorknob, her narrow limbs trembling, and not with cold. She pointed a crooked finger. "In there."

Greeley cracked the door. The taps on the porcelain sink gleamed dull yellow. The white tile floor was chilly, colder than the marble had been. A trickle of water ran across the floor and touched his instep. It was lukewarm, a spill that lapped over the side of a claw-footed bathtub. He peered over the edge. In the tub, a naked woman was practicing her crawl, face averted for the gulp of air. But instead of turning down, the head rolled upward, and Greeley found himself admiring the brilliant green stare of Teri Kern, somewhat diminished in death.

The head rolled down and stayed there. At his elbow, Gail loosed a cadenza of *eee's,* her eyes fixed on the tub. Greeley deftly removed the living woman from the room by her elbows, standing between her and the corpse. It made no difference—she seemed to see right through his body to the other in the tub.

He pushed her towards the connecting door to Carla's room. "Call the police, ma'am. Nine-eleven. On the double."

The command seemed to calm her a little. For the first time, she looked at him and whispered hoarsely, "What should I tell them?"

"Tell them there's a body in your bathtub and it isn't yours." He shoved her gently through the doorway.

In a moment, she reappeared. "Shouldn't I try to reach Lowenkopf?"

Greeley shook his head. "Not our jurisdiction. This is Midtown."

He shut the door behind her and returned to the bathroom. The corpse was still face down. There was a towel on a hook behind the door—the same one she had been wearing in Searle's room when he first saw her. He approached the tub attentively. There was a small puddle of bathwater at the left-front claw; a pair of black Chinese slippers sat at the puddle's edge, soaking up water. Her robe was folded on the closed toilet seat. With the tip of his fingernail he lifted the lid and found the bowl clear. He peered into the drain. A full set of towels, less one washcloth, which he found daubed with a bit of mascara above the sink, still hung on the racks beside the wall mirror. He couldn't tell through the bathwater whether the lipstick on the glass and mascara on the washcloth matched the makeup on the corpse.

There was a book on the bottom of the tub, a paperback. He could make out the title: *In Front of the Camera: How to Make It and Survive in Movies and Television.* There was a set of contact prints of a pretty girl on the cover. She looked up at Greeley from twenty different poses through the bathwater. Something floated between the model's forty eyes and his own. A trail of black specks. And some brown ones. He leaned over the tub to investigate and found a cigarette on the bottom, an inch and a half long once but now almost entirely unrolled, with a filter holding what paper remained intact. A pair of reading glasses rested on the plug. The tub stood two inches from the wall, but Greeley could not see into the space between the tub's far corner and the wall. He crawled beneath the tub, careful to avoid the puddle, and found—nothing.

He stood up and thought a moment, returned to his hands and knees, and examined the tiles conscientiously one more time. He found nothing more.

"Ma'am . . . ?"

No answer.

Striding to the connecting door, he pushed it open. Subliminally, he took in the scene—Carla reclining in bed, Gail searching the floor beneath the radiator, dresser, and bed—but his mind was in the bathroom next door. "Ma'am, could you come here for a moment?"

Carla groaned. "For Chrissake, Homer. Take your time." He didn't seem to hear her sarcasm, or to notice her at all. She fell back on the bed, exasperated.

Gail looked up from the floor midway between the bed and the big blond detective. Carla's predicament had punctured her hysteria: she was still trembling but breathing regularly, and her eyebrow arched with amusement. She flicked Carla's bra off the corner of the dresser and sauntered across the room. "You must excuse us, Carla dear. Your friend and I have a little police business to discuss. We'll be back as soon as we've finished, won't we?" She smiled and Greeley could see all her teeth. She tapped his shoulder as she passed back into her room, pulling him in after her. "There's something to you undercover boys after all, isn't there?"

Greeley suddenly remembered his shirt, but not where he had left it. Evidently the shock had worn off, but Gail made no effort to cover herself. She removed a cigarette from a purse on her night table, lit it, and sat on her camisole on the bottom of her bed, swinging one leg over the other. "Can I get you a drink?" She shivered and motioned toward an ice bucket on the dresser.

In twelve years on the force, Greeley had seen a lot of reactions, but hers unnerved him. Her composure deprived him of his favorite tone, firm and reassuring. He stood awkwardly before her, his hands folded behind his back. "No. Did you call the police?"

She nodded dutifully. A tremor of fear might have narrowed her mouth, but he wasn't sure.

"Did you mention anything to . . . ?" He jerked his head towards Carla's door.

Gail shook her head, averting her eyes.

He stared at the door quizzically. "I have a few questions."

She cleared her throat, uncrossed her legs. "Go ahead then."

Greeley reconnoitered—a room more cluttered but styled like Carla's, its furnishings fixed irrevocably in place and time. Two items marked the management's grudging acknowledgment of the calendar: a plastic television on a rolling stand and a digital clock, halfway between 5:06 and 5:07, on the night table next to her purse. "Did Miss Kern ask you if she could bathe in your tub?"

Gail didn't hesitate. "No."

"What do you suppose she was doing in it, then?"

"I suppose she was bathing. Other than that, I haven't the slightest idea. I've been out for the last three hours. A dozen storekeepers will confirm my progress up and down Madison Avenue. When I left, Teri was as healthy as a horse. When I returned, I put down my packages and took off my clothes, planning to slip into a bath myself for an hour. I went to turn on the water and found that." She shuddered theatrically, shaking the ash from her cigarette.

"Then you were back not more than five or ten minutes when you found Miss Kern?"

"Not more than five."

"And what did you do then?"

"I screamed. Didn't you hear me?"

"Yes. You didn't use the toilet, did you? Since your return?"

"Is that really pertinent?"

"Yes."

155

"Of course I didn't. Do you think I'd just sit on the can with a dead body banging around in the bathtub next to me?"

"I wouldn't have thought so, ma'am."

"She was *dead*, wasn't she? I mean, there's nothing I could have done?"

"Quite dead. What I'd like you to do now is this: look around, and without touching anything, can you tell me if anything is missing?"

"You think I've been robbed?"

"I'd rather you told me."

Gail glanced around the room. There were a few bottles of perfume on the dresser, her purse on the night table and dress on the bed, shoes below the dress, boxes piled near the door. She squatted and lifted the bedspread's brocaded skirt, uncovering a leather suitcase and examining the lock and handle. "Without touching, you said?"

"That's right."

She stood and faced him. "There's nothing I can tell is missing without touching anything. There wasn't a lot in here to steal. I had my traveler's checks and credit cards in my purse with me. All I left here was some jewelry in the suitcase under the bed, but I can't check that without opening it, can I?"

"Once they dust for fingerprints, you can open it."

"Now you've got me wondering."

Greeley shook his head. "A thief would probably have found the case, but I doubt he'd have been considerate enough to close it and push it back under the bed once he'd gone through it."

Gail surveyed her room. "It doesn't look like anyone's been here, does it?"

"No, it doesn't."

"I'll bet no one has. Poor Teri must have slipped on the soap."

Greeley sat in the desk chair and stretched his arms. "I wouldn't go that far."

Gail shivered and reached for her dress. "You think someone has been in here?"

Greeley opened the door to the hallway and examined the outside lock. At the end of the hallway an elevator opened and five suited men emerged. Gail moved behind Greeley's shoulder. "We'll see what they say." He pointed. "It's their case."

Gail slipped the dress over her head and worked it down to her knees. In the dark blue silk she looked elegant and confident. "But what do you think?" she demanded.

Greeley moved away from the door. He stopped in front of the mirror over the bureau and parted his hair with his fingers. He ran his thumb down the middle of his abdomen, smoothing the fine hairs. As the footprints on the carpet approached the door, he said, "As far as I can tell, there's very little doubt. She was murdered."

The men from Midtown weren't so sure. Detective Sergeants Stearns and Baedecker questioned Gail, each of them noting in his own pad the names of the stores she had visited, approximate times, the route, and purchases she had made at each stop. They verified the sales receipts in the packages on the floor against the account she had supplied, passing each receipt from one of them to the other, where it was checked off in separate notebooks. Stearns was short with a single eyebrow that did service over both eyes, Baedecker tall with a flat nose. They released Greeley at a signal from Pound, a lieutenant from Homicide, who followed the medical examiner and a lab man into the bathroom, directly overseeing the dusting and examination of the body. Greeley went with them.

The lab man found two sets of fingerprints. The prints on the tub matched the victim's, and the prints on the glass matched Gail's. The medical examiner discovered a bruise at the base of the scalp above the hairline. While Pound inspected the wound, Greeley retreated to Carla's room to dress. The handcuff key was in his pants pocket. Carla had only the iciest stare for him while he unlocked her wrist, but he was still too caught up in his thoughts to notice.

While he was reknotting his tie and parting his hair for the fourth time, a sharp rap shook the connecting door. Carla sat up, rubbing her right wrist. Greeley opened the door crisply, at once inviting Lieutenant Pound to sit. The lieutenant regarded the desk chair as if it were a trap. In volume he was the largest of the five men; the legs of the chair shrank to matchsticks beside his own massive trunks. He declined the seat suspiciously and shifted from one huge shoe to the other as he paced a little dance in place.

"I understand you were both in here at the time of the incident," he began, addressing the floor. The steps of his little dance were apparently trickier than they looked.

Greeley spoke for both of them. "That's correct."

"Where did you hear that?" Carla was speaking for herself.

"We . . . can't reveal our sources, miss. Not until the trial."

She didn't care about the trial. "Did someone tell you we were in here together?"

"Yes, miss, someone did."

She swung on Greeley. "You see? No one minds their own business around here."

"Right," said Greeley, ignoring her. "Anything else?"

The big man thought a minute. "Did you hear anything, sir?"

Greeley knew Pound outranked him, and the term of respect rankled. He showed his own badge and identification. "I'm on duty here, Lieutenant, helping out the production. I was conferring with Miss Hollie about her needs. Twenty minutes ago we heard a shriek, followed by two sustained screams. I banged on the door with my shoe and Miss Wranawski let me in. When I saw the victim's body in the tub, I instructed Miss Wranawski to phone your precinct immediately."

The lieutenant studied the badge. "You're with the two-five?"

"In the Bronx."

"Long way from home, ain't ya?"

"The victim is even further."

Pound's brow furrowed and his lips pursed. "You might say that. Only we're not sure there is a victim. In Midtown, we don't call them 'victims' unless we think someone else is responsible for the death."

Greeley hesitated but couldn't resist. "And you still haven't decided that someone else was responsible for Miss Kern's death?"

"No, we still haven't." Pound risked a perch on the edge

of the chair. "We may be slow down here, but there isn't much to suggest foul play. Unless *you've* noticed something?"

It was more of a threat than a question, but Greeley saw his opening. He undid the button of his suit jacket. "Want to go over our story again?"

Pound glared and leafed through his notebook. "You heard three screams twenty minutes ago?"

"That is what I said."

"And nothing at all before that?"

"No," Greeley agreed. "But that doesn't mean there was nothing to be heard."

The lieutenant gritted his teeth. "What the hell are you driving at?"

"There might have been a sound we didn't hear."

Pound opened his mouth like a sheepdog sneering. "That how you think in the Bronx? Sounds like crap to me. If someone surprised Miss Kern in her bath, she'd have let out a holler you could've heard in your sleep."

"If she had time to scream," Carla interjected, drawing the attention of both men. She was propped on two pillows against the headboard, buttoning the cuffs of her blouse. "Maybe she didn't."

"That seems unlikely from the layout of the bathroom, miss. He'd have to walk straight at her across a tile floor for at least a few seconds. Even if she'd been reading, she would've had to hear him coming. And she couldn't've been asleep. We found a cigarette in the tub that had just been lit."

"She might have known him," Carla persisted.

"It wouldn't have made a difference. Take a look at Sergeant Greeley over there. Now, imagine him trying to get you by the throat. You see? You always have time to holler, no matter how fast his hands are. The only way for him would be to stuff a pillow over your face, but none of them in the next room have been bothered. And you were using yours, I understand."

Carla blushed.

"If she'd been choked, she would've had time to scream. And you would've heard it. Unless of course you had a reason not to hear."

Greeley couldn't ignore the implication. "Miss Hollie and I met two hours ago. We've been together ever since. If one of us killed Miss Kern, the other would know it."

Pound looked at Carla on the unmade bed. "Two hours?"

She nodded without meeting his eyes.

"You can verify that with anyone in the company," Greeley insisted. "We can't be working together, and neither of us would cover for the other. So your list is two suspects shorter. Now—were there people in the next room, Lieutenant?"

Pound paused. "On the other side of Miss Wranawski's, yes."

"And they didn't hear anything either?"

"It was just Mr. Weems, the actor, who says he was in bed with the Magic Fingers on."

"The machine in the bed? Then it's possible he couldn't hear her scream."

"But the two of you had to, didn't you?"

Greeley hesitated a moment. His carriage was erect, his voice controlled. "Lieutenant, it is possible that we didn't hear her scream."

"I don't see how."

"We were rather noisy ourselves."

"How noisy?"

"This is too goddamn embarrassing," Carla groaned, covering her face with a pillow.

"We might even have screamed a few times. Miss Hollie certainly did. Miss Kern's screams might have been muffled by our own."

Pound mulled that over. "So?"

"It explains why no one else answered Miss Wranawski. Weems must have heard us earlier. He simply mistook Gail's scream—as he did Teri's—for one of ours."

From under the pillow Carla moaned, "Oh, God."

Pound chewed his lower lip. "That still doesn't mean Miss Kern was murdered. Even if she could've screamed."

Greeley sat down on the corner of the bed in front of Pound. "What other explanation have you got? That she slipped getting into the tub, hit her head on the side, and slid under the water?"

"We thought of that."

"Let's consider that. You said she was smoking. People don't light up *before* they step into the tub. Especially if they've brought only one cigarette with them. They relax, settle back, and prepare to enjoy it first."

"I wouldn't know about that. I don't smoke."

"I smoke a pipe. But here's the question: what did Miss Kern light her cigarette with?"

"We didn't find a match near the tub. But there were two burnt matches in the ashtray by her bed."

"I saw Miss Wranawski light one while we waited for you to get here. I'll bet she lit the other before she went shopping. Ask her."

Pound clamped his jaw. "So we can't find a match. So what? If there was someone with Miss Kern, why would he have taken her burnt match?"

"He didn't. He took her lighter."

Carla peered over her pillow. "Don't be so smug, Homer. He might have lit it for her. If she knew him."

Greeley shook his head violently.

His certainty irritated her. "Why not?"

"She would have had to enter the tub with a cigarette but no light."

"She might have forgotten a light."

"She might have. But she would have remembered when she set the cigarette down by her book and slippers, don't you think?"

"And what does that prove?" There was a growing note of hostility in her voice.

He missed it. "It proves she must have been murdered."

"Wait a minute," Carla insisted. "You haven't explained anything. She didn't have an ashtray with her either."

"She used the floor," Greeley said.

"But how do you know she didn't use the toilet? And flush the match before?"

"Because the seat was closed," he told her. "With her robe folded on top of it. The lid must have been down before she had her robe off. That means before she got into the tub. Since we found the cigarette in the tub, she must have been smoking it after she dropped her robe on the closed toilet lid."

"That doesn't prove anything," she said peevishly.

"The fingerprints on the plunger will."

Carla turned to the lieutenant for help but Pound had run out of objections. His red eyes hung on Greeley, searching for a vulnerable spot. "We'll see how the case goes," he said finally.

"This case should be gingersnaps from here," Greeley gloated. "As we say in the Bronx."

Pound raised himself on his two large hands. "I said we'll see. You'll both be available for further questioning, won't you?"

Greeley nodded. Carla said, "Yeah."

"And I can reach both of you at this address?"

"I'll be here," Carla sputtered, anger and frustration having jelled into dislike. *"He* won't. You can bet your gingersnaps on that." She threw the pillow at Greeley and marched off to the bathroom.

The lieutenant's paw fell on Greeley's shoulder with the warmth of a billy club. "If you don't mind a word of advice in exchange for your own," he said with relish, "I'll offer you this: some of them may ask for 'em, but I've never found a woman who really appreciates handcuffs."

17

If Homer Greeley's detective work was an art of details and their logical relations, Shelly Lowenkopf was as usual mired in the messy business of human motives and relationships. He had trouble abstracting the corpse from the spirit it released. The long, bumpy cab ride from Riverdale to the East Side of Manhattan gave Lowenkopf's head a chance to clear. His rush of guilty relief evaporated rapidly, and he found himself thinking professionally. It was not Homer's discipline of thought. The permutations of minutiae did little for Lowenkopf; he preferred emotion recollected in pugnacity, a formula ensuring that each reaction was followed by an action of equivalent intensity. Teri Kern was more than the sum of her remarkable parts. He remembered her eyes over the simmering fondue pot; saw her standing naked in the middle of his suite, in her glasses, reading a book. He knew the questions to ask, the prescribed police procedures, but there was also a truculent sadness welling in some part of him that always responded unprofessionally at this moment in a case.

He did what he always did in that moment. He stared out the window and let the sadness harden into anger. They were just about to cross the Henry Hudson Bridge, a high, brief span over the Harlem River into Manhattan. To his right, the much larger Hudson separated New York from New Jersey. A relentless tide of gray-blue water flowed without end beneath the George Washington Bridge. They passed a long curve of thick brown trunks, clambering down from the peak of Fort Tryon Park, where the Cloisters Museum, an old stone castle, stood guard. The museum was a gift of John D. Rockefeller to the City of New York, as the Palisades Park on the far side of the Hudson was a gift to New Jersey—for the sake of Internal Revenue, public relations, and his fellowman. Lowenkopf recognized the cynicism of his attitude as the catalyst necessary to work the change, and considered the social distance between Rockefeller's estate and the ghetto they would soon be approaching as the taxicab rattled on south.

When Lowenkopf reached the Royalton, the lobby was crowded. The unit publicist, a tall, wiry, mustached man named Scofflaw, was desperately entertaining a few reporters, kept from the elevator by a police barricade. A woman in front demanded, "Will the picture continue?"

"Boys," Scofflaw answered her, "you know Hollywood. The show must go on."

They didn't know Hollywood, but since it was a Broadway line, everyone wrote it down.

Carla was at the barricade, allowing guests with room keys towards the elevators. Lowenkopf joined the line and showed his badge. When she read the name she glanced up.

"What happened?"

She ignored the concern in his voice. "Ask your partner. You're supposed to be the experts."

He caught the unmistakable chill in her tone. "Is Homer here?"

"Not anymore. Rode off into the sunset. With a hearty 'Heigh-ho, Silver.'"

The elevator door opened. A tall blonde exited, dragging a fur coat. The elevator operator stepped out of the car, surveyed the lobby, and addressed Lowenkopf. "Sir?"

Lowenkopf turned to Carla, who avoided his eyes. "I'll see you," he said, trying to sound casual. She didn't answer and he entered the waiting car. On the sixth floor Lowenkopf found Stearns and Baedecker on their knees minutely examining the carpet from 604 to the elevator.

"I think I've got something," said Stearns, puckering his pudgy lips. He held up a tiny fragment of black smudge for his partner's inspection.

Baedecker accepted the smudge and held it at arm's length. The gash that served as his mouth creased, showing small gray teeth. "I think you've got something here, all right," he confirmed, opening a plastic Baggie with a practiced snap of his wrist and dropping the smudge delicately inside.

"Why don't you look at your shoes?" Lowenkopf suggested as he passed the two detectives. Baedecker was right behind Stearns. On his partner's left heel was a familiar black smudge with an even more familiar scent.

Lowenkopf found Lieutenant Pound at the medicine cabinet in Gail Wranawski's bathroom, inspecting the razor-blade disposal. "Does that look like carbon to you?" The lieutenant indicated a small line on the lip of the slot.

Lowenkopf rubbed it with his thumb. "It's a scratch."

A fleshy man with red cheeks and a camera bumped the door. "Just once more, Lieutenant. To be sure." As the strobe flashed and the automatic advance whined, Lowenkopf looked into the tub. Teri's face stared back from a three-foot depth of water with a sad, soft expression on her open mouth. Her hair moved about her face as if it were still alive, though her eyes were dull as stones.

Pound considered the corpse's generous breasts. "Did you know her?"

Lowenkopf nodded.

"Too bad," Pound said enviously.

In the next room, two men waited with a plastic body bag. When the photographer was satisfied, they entered. Pound sat heavily on the side of the tub and scanned the floor, streaked with black heel marks and dirty water. "You don't see anything burnt-like, do you?"

Lowenkopf glanced around. "Like what?"

"Like a match."

Lowenkopf hated to disappoint him. "Is that what those bloodhounds in the hall are sniffing around for?"

Pound wagged his head. "They won't find anything there. The rug was just vacuumed. We passed the maid at the elevator on our way up."

"What did she tell you?"

"That there was an extra towel in this john and one missing from Teri Kern's."

Both men sprang to their feet at a crash in the hall, followed by a wail. As it waned, Lowenkopf recognized Johnny Weems's nasal tone. "Warren! Get these fucking creepers out from under my feet. It's impossible to work here."

Searle was walking from his room at the end of the hall towards Weems, who sat on the carpet twittering. His hair was slicked back and its deep red color made him resemble a cardinal. In his singleminded zeal Stearns had backed into Weems, catching the star behind his knees, which had given way, dropping him on the hard black heels of Stearns's shoes. The crash had come from something in the brown paper package wrapped with string cradled in Weems's lap.

Searle could not entirely repress his smile, but he recovered quickly, drawing his thin lips over his teeth before speaking. "They'll be out by this evening, Johnny. They've got their job to do, just as you have."

Pound's head and shoulders filled the doorway to 604. "They're nearly done with it now," he said, glaring at Stearns and Baedecker. The two detectives crawled off in opposite directions along the juncture between carpet and wall.

Lowenkopf lifted the package from Weems's lap and helped him to his feet. The package was heavier than it looked, addressed to Weems himself at a Malibu residence. Lowenkopf shook the package by his ear and heard a muffled metal rattle. Silverware and towels.

Weems snatched it away. "Look who's back, Warren.

Inspector Clouseau of the Brooklyn Navy Yard. New York's Finest have sent in the big guns."

Searle blinked briefly. "Hello, Sergeant. I'd be grateful if you would see to it that Teri gets every consideration from the coroner."

The two men emerged from 604 with the body bag on a stretcher. "We try to take care of them all," Pound muttered.

As the director began moving down the hall, Lowenkopf called after him, "If you don't mind, Mr. Searle, I'd like to ask a few more questions of your cast."

Searle rubbed his face with both hands and massaged his temples. "I can't afford to have Gail distracted now. We need a new Teri and fast. You don't know anybody in town, do you?"

Lowenkopf hesitated—who could he make a star? He thought of Ruth and Isabelle and shook his head. "Just a few more questions."

Searle shrugged and turned away. "Go ahead. Whatever will help."

Lowenkopf caught Weems at the elevator as the door opened in front of him. Two men and a woman were in it. "I'm on my way, Lowenkopf. Can't talk now."

"It'll just take a minute."

"Like hell it will. I've talked to you before. It's like coaching Elmer Fudd in diction."

Lowenkopf persisted. "A woman was killed in the room next to yours. Unless we find out why, there's no way we can promise that you won't be the next to die naked in your bathtub. That ought to concern you. Unless, of course, you know something I don't."

Weems stuck his foot in the elevator door. The rubber safety bar on the closing door bumped his instep and retreated. "I know a lot you don't know, Lowenkopf. But nothing to do with murder. I went out for lunch at Sardi's, came back, hit the sack, and dropped some quarters in the Magic Fingers. I didn't hear anything or see anyone. Why don't you ask your friend Greeley what he heard? If he could hear anything over his panting." It was a performance he must have rehearsed to the last breathless pause, delivered tight-jawed, through the nose.

Lowenkopf was getting used to Weems's performances. "Greeley was *here* when it happened?"

"Christ, didn't you even know that? Sure he was here. With Carla." The trio in the elevator followed the conversation with growing interest. "Didn't he tell you that? I thought you partner cops shared everything."

Lowenkopf said defensively, "We do."

Weems jeered. "More than you think." The elevator door closed between them.

Lowenkopf stared at the metal door. There was a hum and a sudden stop. The second elevator car opened. Lowenkopf and a woman in a maid's blue uniform regarded each other silently before the door closed between them as well.

Lowenkopf started. He found the stairway and dashed down three flights. The stairwell door on the sixth floor had not slammed before the third-floor door was open. Lowenkopf rushed back to the elevators and punched the button. He waited a moment, painfully. The elevator opened and the maid jumped, startled to see him in the entranceway.

She had a cart on which something was covered with a white linen cloth. She wheeled past him and knocked at the first door. She was a young woman with a round face and straight dirty-blond hair. Her stillness made her seem to disappear against the gold-flowered wallpaper. She knocked again, softly. Lowenkopf knew that noticing her was only half the battle, and took care not to patronize her. In a brisk, professional manner, he said, "Got a minute?"

"I'm kinda busy now," she said, eyes averted. No one answered the door.

"I know you are. Your job is demanding. But I won't take much of your time."

He said it with so much conviction, she couldn't help peeking. He felt invincible as Greeley. He was ready for her, meeting her glance and holding it patiently—allowing her to decide. She looked down the hall. "What do ya want to know?"

"You're with the housecleaning service?"

"Uh huh." There was a towel perfectly folded over her left arm, which she smoothed while he spoke to her.

"I'm a police detective investigating the death of a guest on the sixth floor. Have you heard about that?"

"Oh yes, sir. All of us maids've been talking about it."

"What have you been saying?"

"Nothing. I mean nothing that would interest you policemen. Just how terrible it was and all. They were new arrivals here. None of us really met the lady yet."

"But you've seen her?"

"One of the girls named Alice says she seen them come in. They're movie people. We get a lot of movie people in this place, what with the discount for union cards and all. And she wasn't really a star or anybody, was she?"

"How do you work the floors? Top down?"

"Yes, sir. Also from the bottom up. Two girls usually meet in the middle, around five."

"Do you know the name of the girl who vacuumed the sixth floor today?"

"That's me today. That's my luck. It really gives me the willies knowing someone died in a room today while I was outside doing the carpet. It makes you wonder."

"Did you see anybody go into 604?"

"No one at all, sir. And no one coming out either. There was hardly anyone in the hall the whole time I was working. Just the man knocking on 605 and getting no answer."

"Who was that?"

"The man in 601. The director, Alice says."

"You came by the elevator?"

"Not the front ones. I had my vacuum with me, so I had to take the back elevator. Down at the other end of the corridor."

"So you couldn't see into this part of the hallway until you turned the corner. What time did you reach the sixth floor?"

"I don't know exactly. Lunchtime. If you asked the delivery boy, I bet he'd know."

"What delivery boy?"

"The flower boy. He was getting on the elevator when I got off. He had on one of those T-shirts—you know, with the name of a flower store on it."

"Can you remember the name of the store?"

She thought a minute. "His shirt didn't have a name exactly. It said, 'Nothing says it like flowers.' He had hair the color of straw and yellow teeth."

"How did you see his teeth?"

She blushed. "He gave me a real big grin."

"Is that all?"

"I think he winked at me too."

"You're not sure?"

She hesitated. "I saw his eye close. But afterwards it didn't really open wide again. It just hung there, kinda droopy."

The door to 302 suddenly opened and a man in silk pajamas jumped to find them waiting. "There you are, Mr. Pinski," the maid said cheerfully, catching the man by his striped sleeve. "Did you have a good nap?"

Mr. Pinski's bulging gray eyes rolled a little. "Who are you?" he asked Lowenkopf.

Lowenkopf held up his badge, and the man slammed the door in their faces. The maid frowned and knocked again, but Pinski wouldn't open. "You've frightened him," she reprimanded. "Now what am I going to do with these?" She lifted the linen cloth on her tray to reveal a pith helmet, a gorilla suit, and an uninflated inflatable doll.

Lowenkopf pushed the tray against the wall beside the door. "Leave it here." She seemed reluctant to do so; Lowenkopf tipped her, wrote down her name, and thanked her more than once. There was a touch of abandon in his manner, a grim satisfaction, like a father at the wedding of his eight-months-pregnant daughter.

"Are you all right, sir?"

"Yes," he said, suddenly focusing, but not on her. She peered at him doubtfully. He gave her a brief nod, forced an uneven smile, then clumped off awkwardly down the corridor. When he looked up, the twin doors of the back elevator confronted him. He stared at the line between them as if reading a face he saw there.

And, in a way, he did. The maid's description of the delivery boy fit no one he knew by name. Just a face he had glimpsed on a rooftop, grinning at him from the neck of a red flannel shirt.

The elevator never came. Lowenkopf walked back to the sixth floor, one heavy step at a time. On the sixth-floor landing he found Gail Wranawski at the cigarette machine. With a sudden violent jerk she snapped back the knob and a red pack of cigarettes fell out. When she saw Lowenkopf, she said, "How's the case?"

"Solved," he said, walking past her.

"Really?" She was dressed in a dark blue serge suit, ruffled shirt, and string tie, which swung as she turned to face him. "So tell me—whodunit?"

"A kid I'm supposed to have pushed off a roof a few days ago."

"That must've made him mad, I bet." When he didn't laugh, she said, "You look like you need a drink. I know I do."

He didn't know if he did or not, but when she marched to her room, he followed her. For a few final questions, he told himself.

The room had changed considerably since he'd last passed through it. Drawers teetered from the bureau, their contents emptied on the carpet—folded skirts and sweaters and a heap of underclothes, which Gail stepped over neatly on her way to the bottle in the desk. She poured two stiff bourbons, stepped back over the clothing, and handed one to Lowenkopf.

He accepted it. "Replace Teri yet?"

"Yep. Took all of fifteen minutes."

He held his drink inert while she gulped. She set her empty glass on the bureau and noticed his. "What's the trouble? You're not on duty now—this is Midtown's case."

He set his full glass next to her empty one. "There are still some things I'd like to know for myself."

"Just like your partner," she said. "You should've seen him whiz in here when I called."

"From where?"

"He was next door," she said, reluctant to continue. "With Carla."

"When you found the body? Or before?"

She trembled at the memory. "Both, I think."

"Why do you suppose he didn't hear her scream when a strange boy entered her bathroom?"

The question seemed to divert her. "Maybe he wasn't a strange boy. Maybe she knew him."

Lowenkopf shook his head. "He was strange, all right. Believe me. So why didn't she scream?"

Her gray eyes darkened again. "Maybe she did and no one heard her."

"But Weems was on the other side of this wall. And you just said Homer and Carla were through that door."

"Maybe they couldn't hear her."

"They heard you. She would have been more desperate."

She shook her head resentfully. "When Johnny's asleep, a siren at his ear wouldn't wake him."

"But Homer and Carla weren't sleeping, were they?"

She avoided the question by fitting a cigarette to her lips and waiting. Lowenkopf thought fleetingly of Teri's pearl lighter with the gold works while he dug into his jacket for a match. He didn't have one. She gave him the book that had come with the cigarettes, and he offered her a light.

When she exhaled, he persisted. "But they didn't hear anything, did they?"

She shrugged, crushed out her cigarette in an ashtray, refilled her glass, drained it, refilled it again. She didn't look up when she mumbled, "They were making a bit of noise themselves when I came in."

"What kind of noise?"

She picked up the bottle again, but before pouring, offered it to him. His glass was still untouched on the bureau. He lifted it to demonstrate and set it down again.

"Look," Gail said bravely, "you're a sweet guy, Lowenkopf. Do yourself a favor. Don't ask. Leave this case to Midtown and go home."

"What kind of noise?"

She lifted her glass to empty it, sipped it instead, and placed it gently next to his. He watched her intently, bracing himself. Her troubled eyes met his squarely. "Moans. Sighs. That kind of noise. In their case it sounded less emotional than theatrical, if you get the difference."

He didn't. Or wouldn't. He felt the top of the dresser against the base of his spine. "It doesn't sound like Carla to me."

"How well do you think you know her?"

"It doesn't sound like Homer," he persisted, weakening.

She decided to do it cleanly. "When I screamed," she said, "he beat on the door until I opened it. His shorts were hanging from the chandelier with little blue engines on

171

them, but he still called me 'ma'am.' Carla was just warming up again. But he was so damned eager to investigate, he left her handcuffed to the bed. That sounds like your buddy, doesn't it?"

Inescapably. Lowenkopf's body sagged. Gail helped him to a chair. "Let me get you some cold water from the faucet in the bathroom. Just sit here a minute."

Lowenkopf felt no inclination to move again. She reappeared with the plastic bathroom cup. "Drink." She stood over him and tilted the cup at his lips until a few drops wet his tongue. He took the cup in his own hands. She watched him closely until he forced a crooked grimace. She smiled to encourage him. "Really got you that time, didn't she? If you don't mind my asking—how old are you?"

"Forty-two," he said hoarsely.

"You ought to know better."

Lowenkopf tried to nod, but his head wobbled between his shoulders. "I didn't know I felt this way. And I don't know what to do about it."

She patted the back of his hand and removed the empty cup, then retrieved his bourbon from the bureau top and wrapped his fingers around it. "There's only one thing ever to do at a time like this." She tapped the bottom of his glass.

He drained it.

She refilled it, still in his hand.

"The Next to Die," he said bravely.

"That's my boy."

An hour later, Lowenkopf found himself in a telephone stall on the corner of Fifty-ninth and Lexington. The telephone was off its hook. On the shelf at his elbow were his handkerchief and a few coins—a token, two nickels, a quarter. The wind was blowing, and now and then a gust hit the panes forcefully. There was no light overhead or telephone directory in the binder, but that didn't matter. He knew the number by heart.

He heard a dial tone. Fitted the coins into the slot with care. Pushed the buttons. Beep-beep-beep-beep. Silence. A click. Then the nonchalant hiss-buzz of a ringing line. Two rings were a very long time. A third ring. No hope. The receiver dropped from his neck.

"Hello?"

He recovered the receiver, stared at the mouthpiece, set the speaker to his ear.

"Hello-oh." Ruth's voice had taken on that sharpness already, after one unanswered "hello." He knew that tone—it was not the one he had called for.

"If there's someone out there, you'd better speak up or forever hold your piece."

He decided the woman he wanted to speak with wasn't home anymore. The receiver slid to its hook and he leaned against the glass. The side of a newspaper stand was covered in posters, their edges flying loose, advertising massage parlors whose names promised comfort. Taj Mahal. Shangri La. Each poster showed a scantily dressed woman inviting attention. His forehead was pressed to the window and the rim of his glasses rubbed the pane. He smelled the bourbon on his breath, a sweet, unpleasant taste.

A woman stopped at the newsstand to buy a paper, holding her skirt closed against her thigh. The wind reached for her hair as she sank into the subway entrance on the far side of the corner. Lowenkopf thought of Homer. He dropped the quarter into the change slot and punched Greeley's buttons. There was another endless wait. On the sixth ring, he pushed open the door and left the receiver dangling on its silver cord.

The wind was bitter. Good. The newspaper vendor eyed him expectantly. Lowenkopf lifted his arms and let the air rush under his coat. Then, with a purposeful grip, he took hold of the handrail and descended into the subway, one step after another.

18

Greeley emerged from the subway on Sixth Avenue just below Eighth Street and waited in the protection of a bank for the Don't Walk light to change. He had gone uptown to type up his report, waited a few minutes for Shelly, and then signed out. In the precinct, Shelly's problems were his as well. Now he was on his own time. A brisk wind kept people off the street and agitated the litter at the curb. He kicked a crushed plastic cup from its berth against his shoe. It was caught at once by the wind and carried smoothly into the gutter. He watched it avoid the tires of a cab and a laundry truck; a bus certain to crush it stopped suddenly short, and Greeley realized that his light had changed.

He stopped at the fruit stand on Greenwich to buy a bottle of orange juice, squeezed for him from the oranges in a bin beside the squeezer. He tucked the bottle under his arm and lowered his head, checking his image in the window of a pastry shop for the proper mix of casual but deliberate intent. There was a woman waiting in front of the Peacock Café, holding a package with both hands while she stamped the pavement softly with a red boot. She saw him watching her, or the cold touched her, and she retreated into the café. It was almost six o'clock. He turned up his jacket collar in the window of a men's store, and considered whether to walk the half-flight up to a coffee shop across the street or the half-flight down to a restaurant on the next block. Feeling chilled, he decided to put off the decision until he had reached his apartment and changed his socks.

He bought a paper and scanned the headlines for an item on the case, holding the corners taut against the wind. Nothing yet. Too close to deadline. He knew what the afternoon papers would do with a victim who looked like Teri Kern. Too bad she wouldn't be around to enjoy all the publicity.

Only nine of the ten seats in Chez Brigitte were occupied and he thought he might finally get a chance to taste their food, when he saw Mr. Olio, the superintendent of his building, standing at the corner, waving him home. Mr. Olio was a cautious man. He wore buttoned pants, instead of zippers, in case of lightning, and protected his allotment of Christmas gifts with a dedicated courtesy. Greeley had paid him three hundred dollars for the right to rent his apartment, and that largess, though expected and necessary, was still appreciated.

"Your friend was here," Olio lamented, his breath visible

in the air. "With the eyeglasses and red nose. Ringing the buzzer like this and this. When you didn't answer, he banged the glass with his fist."

Greeley said he was sorry he had not been home to receive his friend, then apologized for Shelly's enthusiasm.

"Mrs. Solomon didn't know whether to let him in. I opened the door but then he wouldn't come inside. You see this on the glass? That's from him." Olio pointed to an invisible smudge on the doorpane. He removed a handkerchief from his pants pocket and rubbed the spot furiously.

"Did he say where he was going?"

"He said he could eat alone—he could make it alone if he had to. He didn't look like a man who should be eating alone. He had whiskey on his breath. I said he could wait in the lobby, but he wouldn't come in."

Greeley nodded to show he appreciated Shelly's ingratitude. He wondered where Lowenkopf would go. The veal at the Casa di Pre was good, but it wasn't a place to sit after eating, and it sounded as if Shelly felt like sitting. Olio was still waiting for a reply. "Thank you," said Greeley. "I'm sorry if he disturbed the building."

The superintendent nodded. That was enough, until Christmas. Greeley followed him into the building and pressed the button for the elevator. He'd change his socks first. He'd find Shelly, have some wine with him, discuss whatever was causing him to make an ass of himself. Then he'd stop by Brigitte's for supper. He was in no hurry. There was only one place Shelly could be.

If there was anything Lowenkopf hated with a blind impulse to get up swinging, it was a kid who thought he was better than the people around him. Kids like that inevitably included Lowenkopf in the class of people beneath them. All over the city he saw them, kids whose general good luck in health, looks, money, and sex led them to believe that the function of other people was to provide comic relief to their own charmed lives.

Four of those kids sat at the next table, laughing at some private joke that lifted them above the struggle in which his own life was submerged. A blond boy in a thick turtleneck sweater smiled, his soft lips revealing expensive teeth. Lowenkopf stared at the plate of rice in front of him. *He probably thinks I envy him,* he thought, knowing the kid was right and resenting him for it. Where was that waiter? Alcohol usually made him sullen, but this time he felt he had good cause. He lifted his empty sangria pitcher and waved it in the general direction of the kitchen, while the laughter of the four snotty kids spilled all around him.

The restaurant's Spanish food drew Lowenkopf from the busier central Greenwich Village area to the darker, occasionally cobbled streets further west, where trucks sit behind warehouse doors all night and parking is less of a life-and-death struggle. A repair shop nearby kept the side streets unusually dense in Rolls-Royces, and the sidewalks, closer to the river, seemed colder than a few blocks east. A long oak bar filled more than half of the front room; dark paintings hung over booths and tables close together in the back. *Too close,* Lowenkopf thought as he lifted the iron top of his pot of *paella marinara* and spooned out two shrimp and a clam from the steaming saffron rice. *Is that what I'm keeping the streets of this city safe for?*

The turtlenecked boy leaned forward and squeezed the thigh of a girl in a tailored white shirt, open two buttons at the throat. The second boy was slender and dark; the crisp collar of a lime shirt peeped out from his cashmere sweater. He asked the waiter something in Spanish. His date cradled her wineglass in both hands and sipped at it methodically, now and then sweeping her long brown hair over her chair. The blond boy whispered something to the girl beside him, who turned towards Lowenkopf, whispered something to the other girl, and all four laughed.

Maybe a junkie'll mug them before they get back to Fifth Avenue, Lowenkopf speculated uncharitably. *Maybe their car is gone.* The girl with brown hair stood dramatically. Her hair fell to the back of her thighs. Who were these people? How did they get so lucky? She smiled at the blond boy, who dimpled. Like Weems—a prick who had everything Lowenkopf ever wanted. At least the sonofabitch was short. But Homer wasn't short. He wasn't rich either, but he usually got what he wanted. *Even the man with the fur collar in the deli got what he wanted,* Lowenkopf thought suddenly. So why should he risk his neck for them? Let them get their wallets lifted, their batteries stolen, their heads busted. Let them get murdered in their baths. The image of Teri swam up out of his drink, evoking a sudden warmth he associated with Thom. He could make the city safe for Thom. And Carla. But she didn't care if he made it safe for her. So why should he care?

The waiter replaced his empty pitcher with a filled one, glimmering purply in the weak light.

To hell with Homer, too, in his houndstooth suits. Lowenkopf examined the woolen sleeve of his coat. If that's not good enough, who needs her? It would have been good enough for Teri. That warm feeling pressed at his rib cage. He should've made the city safe for Teri, instead of chippies like Carla.

He winced at the sound of that. Once again he was amazed to discover how strongly he felt about her. His last night in California played cinematically before his eyes. She had done this delibertately to hurt him. She had spotted Homer as his partner and knew how to make her feelings known about the night he spent with Teri. *How the hell did she find out? They always find out,* he thought, *always. Like pigeons, coming home to Homer.*

Lowenkopf couldn't find it in him to blame his partner. Homer couldn't help being golden-haired and well-dressed. He couldn't help it if he smiled a lot, if women went for that easy Howdydoo-ma'am line. Lowenkopf felt his own share of the blame for not telling Homer how he felt about Carla. Not that he knew it himself. But a flash of anger welled up inside him anyway, and Lowenkopf wished Homer hadn't found her, wished Homer had called him from the hotel and said, By the way, there's a blonde named Carla here who wants to jump in the sack—you haven't got a thing for her, have you? But what could he have answered? He wished Gail had been around to gobble Greeley up before Carla got to him, or even Teri—it would've saved her life. Now Teri was dead and Carla was gone and Homer was probably walking around like everything was fine with a big shit-eating grin on his face.

How did the pitcher get filled again? Lowenkopf found his plate empty and couldn't remember if there was any more in the pot. He grasped the lid. Still hot. The warm smell of saffroned shrimp, and the last clam still in its shell, made the next few minutes happy for him. Two peas and some rice missed the plate. He looked up. The blond and his girlfriend were watching him. The boy's thick features seemed to have been pressed into his face by a thumb. The girl had cool green eyes.

Lowenkopf turned his back. What the hell were they staring at? Weren't there enough waiters with funny accents and grotesquely swathed shopping-bag ladies without turning to him for entertainment? Enough miserable unfortunates without adding him to their host of clowns? He'd be damned if he'd amuse them. He dunked a napkin in his wineglass and tried to clean his shirt where some rice had fallen, when he felt a hand on his shoulder. A clean hand, with trimmed nails. If it was attached to that blond kid, he'd flatten him.

It was Homer, unbuttoning his dark leather coat, his hand slipping from Lowenkopf's shoulder to an empty chair at the next table. "Is this taken?" Homer asked the girl sipping wine, who smiled at him, a mouth full of pearls. Greeley pulled the chair to Lowenkopf's table and signaled to the waiter for a second wineglass. It arrived at once. Greeley extended a friendly smile to his partner. The leather of his jacket looked like butter. "Howya doing?"

Lowenkopf stared at him dully. "How do you think I'm doing? Four days ago, a kid I was chasing for stealing my battery jumped off a roof. Three nights ago, a man I nabbed for stealing my briefcase lands facedown in a fire. Today a woman who gave me a night I'll never forget sank in her bathtub forever. And I don't know the first fuckin' thing about any of it. A little while ago, Billy Ringo accused me of throwing Eddie Pepper off that roof. But that wasn't Eddie Pepper I saw jump off—it was a kid in a red flannel shirt. So how come they found Eddie Pepper on the ground? And how do I call in an APB on a kid I saw fall to his death four days ago? I don't understand any of it, and I feel rotten about it. How do you feel?"

"Thirsty," Greeley said, filling his glass. "But I've got some news that should cheer you up. LAPD's got your man McDonald. They caught him with someone named Charles Fierce on a sailboat at Catalina, as you suggested. The D.A. out there feels he's got enough to go to court, so that case at least is closed."

"The hell it is."

Greeley's face registered gentle disapproval. "It is for the LAPD, so it should be for you. Hansen's their problem and McDonald's their man. What more is there?"

"What happens to Searle and his movie?"

"Insurance takes the loss. What do you care?"

"And what about Weems? I saw him, don't forget, in the parking lot after Hansen was hit with the firewood."

"Nobody's interested."

"Not even you?"

Greeley hesitated. "Are you sure it was him? They tell me everyone in Hollywood looks like him."

"Who told you that?" Lowenkopf demanded, remembering his resentment. "They look like *you*. It's all the girls can do to wait till you show up and climb aboard."

Homer was the soul of patience. "Why don't you go home and get some sleep? You've got a big day in court tomorrow. You're our heavy hitter, Shelly, the only one we've got now. Madagascar won't be happy if Keppler gets off because our star witness has fallen asleep on the stand."

Lowenkopf recognized Greeley's attempt at kindness. But he wasn't in the mood for it. "Don't give me that star crap, lover-boy," he said, raising his glass bitterly to his lips.

It dawned on Greeley just how drunk Shelly must be. He stood up and pulled out Lowenkopf's chair. "Let me help you out of there."

Lowenkopf grabbed the table's edge. "I don't need that kind of help."

Just then a paper straw sleeve sailed over from the next table, looping through the air. That was it. Lowenkopf was on his feet in a flash. He spun the dark-haired boy around and seized a fistful of cashmere. The boy clung to his chair with both hands and left his face and stomach open to the punch Lowenkopf would have thrown had not Greeley caught his big right hand in the windup and held it. The chair went down and the boy with it, in a little flurry of cashmere.

"Excuse us—" Greeley began, but never finished his apology. Lowenkopf shook his right fist free and used it to stop up any nicety Greeley might have uttered. His swing went wild, and the back of his knuckles caught the front of Greeley's teeth. Lowenkopf swung again, but Greeley was a pitcher-and-a-half behind him. He ducked Lowenkopf's flailing fist easily and swung up, connecting with his partner's jaw from below. There was an instant in which Lowenkopf paused, looked down, and stroked his jaw sagely. Then he collapsed like the empty sleeve of a straw and was carried out, to his burning shame, in Homer's arms.

19

The rasp of tables and chairs on the marble floor. The squeal of the big oak door as it opened, and the slam as it shut. Uncomfortable squeaks from the hard courtroom chairs—Lowenkopf couldn't shut out any of the noises, whether he covered his ears with his hands or buried his head in his arms on the table. He buried his head *and* covered his ears. The decibels resembled the pounding of Niagara to a man at the top in a barrel. Lowenkopf felt the barrel swing and tip—he pressed the flaps of his ears closed. Better. But someone was shaking his arm.

"Good luck, Sergeant."

Lowenkopf peered up through swollen eyes. Madagascar. The captain pounded his back. "Don't fuck it up."

Dimly Lowenkopf was aware that the rest of the room was filling. In the last row on the defense's side of the aisle, Carla sat beside Weems. Lowenkopf inspected his fingernails on the desk. He was sure somewhere behind him Janice was choosing an entry point for the bullet with his picture on it. Next to him at the prosecutor's table sat the new young assistant district attorney, to whom Lowenkopf swore physical harm if he didn't stop reshuffling the same five sheets of paper. What on earth could he hope to learn from them now? If the young idiot didn't know his case yet, it was too late to read up on it.

"We've got him, Shell—remember that," the ADA reassured him, turning the pages face down on the table. Then he picked them up and read them over again.

What was his name? Lowenkopf tried to remember. Parsons? P-o-something. Better not ask any questions. Better sleep.

"There he is," Po whispered, a note of awe creeping into his young voice. His long lashes fluttered when he blinked.

Lowenkopf raised his head incrementally. Keppler was in fine form—a black tailored pinstripe suit, a red tie with small green curlicues, his famous checked scarlet socks. Beside Keppler perched Cecil Rowe in a gray suit and blue tie. His smile wasn't as broad as Keppler's, but then he wasn't being charged with murder.

The clerk was a frail woman with a high forehead. She looked at no one but the stenographer before the bench and the elderly bailiff leading the jurors to their seats. This was the clerk's moment: she dialed her phone and murmured something into it, then stood gazing fervently at a door behind the bench until it opened slightly. "All rise," she intoned as the judge, a distinguished black woman with a limp, entered. "C-c-court is in session. The Honorable Lan Ngoc Johnson presiding."

The judge sat lightly, on the edge of her seat, flicking her robe behind her. "Shall we get on with it?"

The prosecutor jumped up, scattering his papers. "The State is ready, your Honor." The State didn't look ready to Lowenkopf. The State shifted from leg to leg expectantly. Rowe looked ready—eased back in his chair, his features composed in an attentive, confident countenance. For an instant Lowenkopf fervently wished Rowe was his attorney; then Rowe coughed and he changed his mind. He hoped that cough was noticed by the jurors, a group who seemed disproportionately overweight and balding. There were three women in the front row, but the rear was held by a line of men whose suits imitated Rowe's. Po was appareled in mauve.

"It makes no difference," Lowenkopf swore. *"I'll nail him alone if I have to."*

The courtroom was hot. Lowenkopf undid his button under his tie but kept the knot in place. His head ached and the dry heat from the radiator made it worse. He searched the crowd for a likely aspirin and spotted Homer slipping in with a glance at Lowenkopf and a respectful eye on the bench. Lowenkopf lowered his head. Why had Homer come? The whole shameful past came rushing back to him. Their exit from the restaurant. The struggle for a taxi, and once inside the taxi, his sickness. The smell at the open window, the freezing night air and his lurching stomach, weakness in his limbs, in his bones. His straw-man impression in the elevator, the vaudeville routine for his keys at the door. Homer tugging his pants over his shoes on the bed, the left leg stuck at the angle where he found it in the morning. Why had Homer come? For moral support? He could keep his morals up himself. What he really needed was an aspirin.

Po-sner, that was his name. The ADA was in the middle of his opening argument, in what Lowenkopf dubbed the cigar-store-Indian delivery style—arms stiffly at his sides, head tilted back just enough for the jury to admire his nose hairs. Posner deftly accused the defendant of his crime but, unwilling to stop there, warned the jury against its own compassion and the judge against her innate sense of justice. Rowe was munching on an unlit cigar, listening with satisfaction. He shielded his mouth and whispered to Keppler, after which both of them rumbled with silent glee, leaning back over their bellies like the dominant males in a *National Geographic* gorilla documentary.

Posner sat down earnestly, scraping the table with his cufflink as he drew his briefcase towards him. Lowenkopf squeezed his eyes shut.

It looked like the coast of California—a high, craggy cliff over a calm bay at sunset. A woman's lithe figure crawled up the sheer side of the mountain, clinging effortlessly with fingers and toes, climbing without pause. The sun was crimson behind her. She advanced smoothly to the crest, lifted herself to the topmost crag, and stretched to her full height. With a single graceful motion she plunged towards the ocean and entered, an unrippled surface glistening behind her. A small head, plastered with black hair, broke the surface, swimming towards him. Jade-green eyes outflashed the sunlight on the water. Teri. Each sure stroke brought her impossibly closer. She stepped from the sea and approached, prismed droplets on her brow, beading on her lips like pearls. Fixed in her emerald gaze, her mouth parting, he heard her soft whisper: *Do you really believe I slipped in the bathtub?*

His elbow shook and he heard his name.

"Sergeant Lowenkopf? We're ready for your testimony now." The assistant district attorney was shaking him. The judge must have been standing on her seat. Lowenkopf walked to the witness box and took the oath.

Posner's questions were better than he had expected, breezing through most of the story—the tipoff by Eddie Pepper in the Riverdale Diner one night after Keppler had chewed him out; planning with Homer and the captain to make the most of Pepper's temporary disaffection; their attempts to turn one of Keppler's most trusted distributors, found two days later in three feet of water beneath the Whitestone Bridge. Posner didn't mention the endless surveillance and wiretaps, but went into great detail on the single dramatic encounter in which an intrepid Lowenkopf managed by chutzpah and good fortune to tape-record a sale by Keppler himself from beneath the negotiating table. Posner presented a cop with whom the jury could identify as they did before the television, a single man whose word in the end they would have to believe or deny.

"And how close were you to these dangerous drug dealers, Sergeant?"

"I was under the table, sir," Lowenkopf deadpanned.

"You mean down by their feet?" Posner feigned astonishment.

Lowenkopf nodded humbly. "I could have tied their shoelaces together, sir."

Posner rocked on his heels, deeply impressed. "That was very brave of you, Sergeant." He pivoted to face the jury, still nodding as if to say: Well, wasn't it? A fat lady in the first row nodded back at him.

Posner stopped and scowled as if something bothered him. "But you did see his face, didn't you, Sergeant?"

"Yes, sir." Lowenkopf enunciated carefully, as instructed. "I saw him come in and I saw him go out. I only saw his shoes and socks while he was seated, of course, but I saw him well enough before and after."

"And the man you saw in the restaurant, the man whose drug sale you overheard and tape-recorded, the man whose shoelaces you could have tied—"

"Is that man, sir. Immanuel Keppler." A murmur trundled through the courtroom. It was a duet they had worked out beforehand, and despite the throb in his head, Lowenkopf was rather pleased with their performance.

"Let the record show the witness indicates the defendant," the judge grumbled. "And easy on the histrionics, Mr. Prosecutor."

"Your Honor, at this time I would like to introduce the People's Exhibit A," Posner announced to the court, holding up a reel of audio tape. "A recording the witness made of the negotiation between William Farret and the defendant from under the table in the Blue Cross Café on that fateful evening. We will present expert testimony if necessary to demonstrate that this tape was not altered in any way, and the counsel for the defense has been provided with a copy for his own examination."

Rowe lifted himself out of his chair by his arms and addressed the judge from a position somewhere between his seat and his feet. "The defense has examined the tape, your Honor, and forgoes the need for expert testimony. It's a tape, all right."

There was a titter in the courtroom which the judge silenced with a scowl.

Posner seemed to lose a little steam. "I would like at this time to play the tape for the court, your Honor."

Rowe spoke before the judge could respond. "The defense has no objection, your Honor. My client is confident this tape will secure his acquittal."

Something about the sound of that made Lowenkopf uneasy. But Posner, determined to regain his momentum, started the tape without comment. It hissed for a moment and began with Keppler's voice.

KEPPLER: Let's have it.
FARRET: Here. Do you want to taste it?
KEPPLER: (sniffing): This is all I need.
FARRET: Happy?
KEPPLER: I'll make the most of it.

The tape ended with a sound of scuffling chairs. Posner snapped off the machine and asked Lowenkopf across the room, "Now Sergeant, would you tell us please, where did this tape recording come from? What was this we have just heard?"

"That was the tape I recorded, sir, from under the table, when Keppler met with Farret. What you heard was a drug buy. Farret offered Keppler a sample of his product, which Keppler tasted and bought. That's all there was to it."

Posner turned to the jury. His expression said: What more do you need? He thanked Lowenkopf gravely and sat down.

Rowe had never quite returned to his seat. Now he wobbled to the front of the courtroom, leaned on the witness box, and faced Lowenkopf squarely. For a long minute he was silent. He seemed to be considering something, thought better of it, and returned to the defense table, where he unbuttoned his jacket and sat on the table's edge, interlacing his fingers and tapping his thumbs together. Everyone in the room watched him breathlessly. He blew his nose and in three long paces was facing the judge.

"Your Honor," he said, shaking his head somberly, "this is quite a witness. In fact, Lowenkopf here is the prosecution's only witness. He's had a lot to say today. As I understand Mr. Posner's case, the whole ball of wax finally boils down to this: Lowenkopf claims my client is a criminal. The question the good people of the jury are going to have to decide is: how reliable a witness is this man? If Lowenkopf's story stands up, I'll vote for conviction myself. So all I've got to say to these good people can be said now. When I sit down again, my client's case will be over. So listen carefully," he admonished the jurors, "because we're going to decide this thing right now."

185

Lowenkopf didn't want Rowe deciding the case. He glanced at Posner, whose face ran red and green like a neon sign.

"Now, it seems to me," Rowe mused aloud, "that the testimony we just heard hangs on three points. The witness saw my client enter the room. He recorded the tape we heard a few minutes ago. And he was close enough to tie my client's shoelaces together. Were they untied, Mr. Lowenkopf?"

Lowenkopf shook his head. "Sergeant."

"Speak up, please," the judge instructed severely.

"No," repeated Lowenkopf for the record.

"No," Rowe orated with satisfaction, as if he had already forced the witness into a denial. "Your Honor," he announced suddenly, his voice rising precipitately in volume and intensity, "the defense would also like to play a tape for the court, not unlike the tape we have already heard. In fact, not unlike it at all."

Young Posner was on his feet. "Your Honor, this is the first I've heard of a second tape."

"I have a copy of the tape for Mr. Posner's expert to examine, your Honor," Rowe said quickly. "He can report on both tapes together, later on. Bailiff, would you run the second tape now, please?"

The bailiff looked at the judge, who shrugged. "Go ahead."

There was no hiss at the beginning of Rowe's tape recording. It ran for a moment in silence, until Lowenkopf heard his own voice and Carla's:

LOWENKOPF: Let's have it.
CARLA: Here. Do you want to taste it?
LOWENKOPF: This is all I need.
CARLA: Happy?
LOWENKOPF: I'll make the most of it.

The tape ran out. The courtroom audience erupted into noisy speculation, which ceased instantly as the judge raised her gavel. There was no need for her to bring it down. Lowenkopf stood slowly, turning from audience to jury to judge. "That was a recording of a script reading, your

Honor, which I did to help a friend in California. That friend is in the courtroom today, and will verify that." Lowenkopf searched the back row for Carla, but her place was empty. Weems sat in the next seat, laughing through his teeth like a handsome horse.

The judge was not smiling.

Rowe approached the bench. "My client and Mr. Farret are also ready to testify that the recording we have heard of their voices was a script reading, your Honor. In my opinion, they were a little more convincing, don't you think?"

Lowenkopf said, "That's ridiculous."

"It is, however, your own argument," Rowe reminded him, with a significant eye on the jury. "There is unfortunately no test to establish the subject of either conversation. You're a great believer in tests, aren't you, Lowenkopf?"

Lowenkopf replied cautiously, "When appropriate."

"And would you call testing food an appropriate use of police laboratory facilities?"

"It might be."

"But say for example a detective tested his own salami sandwich—would you call that appropriate?"

The judge leaned forward. "What did he test?"

"Your Honor"—Posner quivered valiantly—"I object to this whole line of questioning."

The judge didn't give Rowe a chance to respond. "Overruled. I want to hear this."

Rowe leaned towards the bench. He could barely suppress his mirth. "Your Honor, Sergeant Lowenkopf sent his own lunch to the police laboratory in Los Angeles for analysis."

"And what did they find?" the judge demanded.

"They found"—Rowe paused—"salami."

"In that case, the testing was appropriate, your Honor," Lowenkopf interjected, "because that sandwich was recovered with a piece of stolen property."

"Stolen property?" Rowe sounded as if it were the first he'd heard of it. "What was stolen, exactly?"

"A briefcase. My briefcase. Stolen on a street corner in the Bronx."

"Then why were you testing it in Los Angeles, Sergeant?"

"Because that's where I found it."

187

"That must have been some fancy detective work," Rowe commented, winking at the jury. "Where did it turn up?"

Lowenkopf hesitated. "In the back seat of a convertible."

"Whose convertible?"

"It belongs to a director named Warren Searle."

"But Searle wasn't driving it at the time, was he? Can you guess how the briefcase got on the back seat of his convertible?"

"Someone must have put it there."

"Someone must have," Rowe agreed amiably. "Isn't it true you were transporting several pieces of your own luggage in the back seat of the car at the time?"

Lowenkopf didn't hesitate. "Yes."

"So you could have carried it yourself from that Bronx street corner to that Los Angeles convertible."

"I could have, but I didn't."

"So you've testified. Well—let us be thorough. How else might that briefcase have traveled coast to coast within the space of . . . how long? Twenty hours?"

"Someone must have brought it on a plane."

"Why would anyone want to do that?"

"I don't know."

"Can you tell us why anyone would want to steal your briefcase?"

"No."

"What was in it?"

"My lunch."

"The aforementioned analyzed salami sandwich. Anything special in that sandwich?"

"No."

"Anything else in the briefcase?"

"No."

"So in other words, you have testified that someone went to the trouble of stealing your lunch, flying it three thousand miles to Los Angeles, and depositing it back in your hand?"

Lowenkopf wouldn't have put it exactly that way.

"Answer the question," the judge threatened.

"That's the gist of it, yes." Lowenkopf spoke with confidence but knew it was a setback and turned to his colleagues for encouragement. Posner was lost in his own briefcase. Greeley managed a smile, while his eyes glinted in loyal disappointment. Madagascar sank in his chair, his long brow furled. Detective Snyder, the blond Los Angeles cop, was sitting on the People's side, enjoying the show.

Rowe cleared his throat. "So. We will be thorough. The second argument in your testimony is that you claim to have seen my client leaving the room in which this drug deal is alleged to have taken place. Did you get a good look at the man who came in?"

"Yes."

"And do you have much of a memory for faces?"

"I'm a cop. I have to."

"Could you identify that man now?"

Lowenkopf stood up and pointed. "That's him. Keppler. But you must have been napping. I've already identified your client."

"I know that," replied Rowe with a hint of surprise. "But I didn't think you could do it again. You haven't had much luck with identifications lately, have you?"

"I don't know what you're talking about," Lowenkopf evaded.

"I'm talking about the late Mr. Eliot Hansen." Rowe turned to the jury. "Mr. Hansen was an acquaintance of Lowenkopf's in Los Angeles. I won't say 'friend' exactly. Perhaps the witness will tell us about him. Though I can see why he'd rather not." Before Lowenkopf could respond, Rowe was on him. "Isn't it true you jumped Mr. Hansen as soon as you reached the studio? Didn't you accuse him of stealing your briefcase on a plane thirty thousand feet in the air, when twenty witnesses will swear he was on the ground?"

How did Rowe know these things?

"I have the witnesses on call, Mr. Lowenkopf. I can have them in that chair in an hour."

"Your Honor," Posner objected, "what is the relevance of all this? Mr. Hansen has nothing to do with this."

"He had nothing to do with the briefcase either," Rowe commented critically. "But Sergeant Lowenkopf thought he recognized him. I'm merely exploring the limits of this witness's memory for faces, your Honor."

"I think we've heard enough about Mr. Hansen," the judge decided.

"That was a misunderstanding anyway," Lowenkopf added. "I saw his face once, quickly, from behind. I didn't know Hansen."

"But you did know Johnny Weems," Rowe insisted. "You watched him work for half an hour on the movie set. As a matter of fact, you discussed his size and coloring with a Miss Hollie, did you not?"

"I don't remember that."

"You don't remember. But the prosecution's entire case rests on your memory, Sergeant. Do you remember telling Officers Oquita and Snyder of the Los Angeles police force that you saw—correct me if I misquote you—that you saw Johnny Weems in the parking lot of the Oyster Pit restaurant on the beach the night Eliot Hansen was murdered? Sergeant Snyder is in the courtroom to help refresh your memory, should you need it." Rowe waved his hand and Snyder stood.

Lowenkopf blinked. "I may have said that."

"But Johnny Weems was several miles away that night, in the company of Warren Searle, a dear friend of the murdered man—or did you see him too in the parking lot that night?"

"No," Lowenkopf said stubbornly.

Rowe agreed. "Of course you didn't. Warren Searle asked you to investigate Hansen's murder in the first place. Warren Searle has provided an unshakable alibi. And yet you swore you saw a man who could not possibly have been where you swore you saw him."

"I know what I saw," Lowenkopf persisted. "I saw someone who looked like Johnny Weems. If it wasn't Weems, it was someone dressed to look like him."

"Then isn't it just possible it wasn't my client you saw from under the tablecloth, Lowenkopf? That it was someone dressed like him instead? Isn't it possible that it was just another of your misunderstandings, as with Hansen at the studio, or another disguise, as with Weems in the parking lot?"

Lowenkopf clung to his memory. "Not with Keppler. I was close enough to play checkers with the pattern on his socks."

The claim sounded ludicrous in Lowenkopf's own ears.

But Rowe seemed to give his objection more credence than the jury did. "Finally, we come now to your third point. My client's socks. The last of your solid evidence. Tell me, what kind of socks were they?"

Lowenkopf didn't hesitate. "Argyles. With red and black squares like a checkerboard." His credibility was hanging by a thread he wouldn't let unravel.

Rowe sidled up to the witness box. "Would you recognize those socks if you saw them again?"

Lowenkopf glanced beneath the defense table, but Keppler's feet were wrapped beneath his chair. "I'd know them anywhere."

Rowe raised his foot to the ledge of the witness box. To everyone's amazement, his socks were dark gray. "Then tell me—have you seen those red-and-black socks on anyone else recently?"

He had, but where? Suddenly it came to him. "As a matter of fact, I have."

"Oh?" said Rowe. "Where?"

It was beneath the hem of a desert robe. The Arab in his bathtub had them on. Lowenkopf paused. "I don't remember exactly."

"Come now," Rowe said, "the exactitude of your memory is the crux of the issue, Sergeant. You've clearly thought of someone. Share your thought."

Lowenkopf turned to the judge, who said, "Answer the question," kindly. He knew he was in trouble.

"It was in Los Angeles—"

Rowe pressed him. "Can you be a little more specific, please?"

"In my room."

"Where in your room, Sergeant Lowenkopf? On whose feet?"

"On an Arab."

"An Arab? What was he doing in your room?"

"I don't know what he was doing in my room. I found him there."

"You found him where, exactly?"

Lowenkopf hesitated. Out of the corner of his eye he saw Posner, who sat with his face in his hands. "He was lying in my bathtub."

The judge reached for her mallet, but the murmur never came. Everyone was waiting for the second clue to drop. Rowe spoke for all of them. "In his socks?"

Every eye in the room watched Lowenkopf. "Yes. He was fully dressed in my bathtub when I came in. I don't know how he got there, or why. He told me not to shoot him and ran out. It was the end of a long day."

It was the end of his testimony too. The murmur came, redoubled, twisting the sea of faces into eddies of private commentary. The judge waved her gavel, muttered, "What the hell," and didn't bother. The clerk approached the bench and they conferred for a moment. Madagascar was pounding his face with his hands. Greeley nodded absently, a thumbnail lodged between his lower front teeth. Keppler closed his eyes, a smiling Buddha. His two gorillas in the audience beamed. Snyder and Weems flashed their teeth. Lowenkopf looked at the jury. Two of the men in the back row were chatting up a woman in front. The only one who didn't seem to be enjoying himself was Rowe, who wore a stern, troubled expression.

"Your Honor," he said quietly, "I'd like to call a witness out of turn. If my esteemed colleague will indulge me in this, I think we can all be out before lunch."

Posner was doodling on one of his five papers. He didn't look up. "Why not?"

Rowe raised his palm as if swearing an oath. "Ladies and gentlemen, I believe this witness will set our minds at rest about Sergeant Lowenkopf's mental state these last few days. A witness personally disposed towards him, whose testimony will nonetheless reveal how this man sees the world around him. It isn't a pretty picture, I warn you." He turned to the audience and raised his voice. "I call Ms. Carla Hollie to the stand."

Sometime during the outburst Carla had returned to her seat. Lowenkopf watched as she made her way down the aisle in a dark gray suit with a white blouse ruffled at her throat, the image of responsible womanhood. He couldn't help noticing how lovely she looked. She passed him on the bottom step of the witness stand with a sympathetic look, and took the seat, still warm from his testimony. The expression on her face was unreadable. Pity? Vengeance?

Both? The bailiff helped Lowenkopf find his seat at the People's table.

It didn't take long. Rowe had his questions prepared. Yes, Carla had first seen Sergeant Lowenkopf running through the airline terminal after a stewardess no one else had seen. He ran into the ladies' room and tore open a stall on a squat lady in a flowered dress. Yes, he was after the same stewardess later at the studio when he tackled Eliot Hansen. Yes, Carla had seen Mr. Hansen in Gail Wranawski's office just before she left to pick up Lowenkopf at the airport. The briefcase Lowenkopf had accused Hansen of stealing had turned up in the back seat of their car. Why did Sergeant Lowenkopf take her to the Oyster Pit that night? To follow up on the case, she presumed. The Hansen investigation.

"But what was there to investigate if you had the brief-case?" Rowe asked incredulously.

"That's what I said," Carla responded indignantly. "But he wouldn't listen to reason."

Lowenkopf stopped watching her. He traced the pattern on the marble floor, thinking about Clem's lawn, about Ruth when he picked up Thom in front of their house on Sundays. He liked her in those frowsy housedresses. Holding Thom by the hand. He imagined himself in the picture. Why not? Stranger things have happened.

The gavel came down. Dismissed. Carla moved serenely through the crowd leaving the courthouse. Greeley watched her go and ran a hand through his hair. Madagascar rose painfully, with effort. His eyes were glowing embers.

Keppler gave him a gentlemanly nod. "Good day, Captain," he said. "Nice to see you again."

Madagascar tramped out. The sound of his shoes on the marble floor rang in Lowenkopf's head long after the captain had gone.

20

Homer set the shoulder of his London Fog to the roof door, and it opened without a squeak. Sunlight darted past him into the stairwell. He shaded his eyes and peered out. Lowenkopf, a few steps behind, imagined some Viking Greeley ancestor standing just so, scanning a conquered city. Homer patted his blond hair back into place and, with a wave of his hand, invited Lowenkopf to follow him onto the roof.

The snow had all but melted. Jagged lines of salt marked the tar beneath their feet, tracing the stages of evaporation; a few withered drifts huddled in the shade of a wall, and a thin napkin of ice clung to the center of the ledge, except where Eddie Pepper had jumped off. Or had been thrown— Lowenkopf resented that echo in his own thinking, reminding himself again what he had seen on that roof. Five days ago? Six? When had he left California?

The boy had *jumped*. Whoever he was. If that swing of his could be called a jump. Fallen? Not with that smile on his face. Of course, he had not expected to miss the fire escape. But how had he mangled his neck? On the railing? It was the last thing Lowenkopf wanted to think about now, the last place he wanted to be.

Homer breathed through his nose in the chill air. He stamped his rubbers on the buckling tar floor and headed straight for the snowless spot on the ledge.

"This was the site?" Without waiting for an answer, he pulled off his woolen gloves and stuffed them in the pockets of his raincoat. He placed his palm on the ice on the ledge, snapping it to clear a larger space. Then he threw the top half of his body over the wall, teetering for a moment on the ledge before the black toes of his rubbers found the roof.

Lowenkopf couldn't bear to watch him. Homer enjoyed detective work too much—it made Lowenkopf feel a little lazier, a little guiltier, than he would with another partner, as if he weren't as committed as he ought to be. He leaned over slightly. "See anything?"

Greeley couldn't quite touch the railing of the fire escape below them, so he inched further out on the ledge. His feet dangled in the air beside Lowenkopf.

"What are you doing down there?"

He pitched forward. Lowenkopf grabbed the hem of the London Fog and hauled his partner up. Greeley sat on the wall, rubbed his raw hands together, and sank them to the elbows in his coat pockets. He shivered. "Your theory is—what? That he jumped for the fire escape, lost his footing on the icy rail, and plunged to his death?"

Lowenkopf hadn't given much thought to the particulars. "Sounds reasonable, doesn't it?"

Greeley nodded without agreeing. "How far would you say it is to the fire escape?"

"Five or six feet."

"So much, you think? Look." He held his right arm straight up and chopped himself below the waist with his left.

"All right," Lowenkopf conceded, "four feet. So what?"

"The kid must have been a pretty rotten jumper. I wonder what made him risk it."

Lowenkopf hated when Homer spoke like this. If he had something to say, why didn't he just spit it out? Not that Homer was likely to spit anything anywhere. "Maybe his mother smacked him on the head for stealing from the cookie jar that morning and he wanted to get back at her. Maybe his girlfriend told him she was pregnant. Maybe he liked to sky-dive."

Greeley nodded absently at each suggestion. "The theory on the streets is that you strangled him and threw him over."

Lowenkopf sulked. "Maybe I did."

Greeley looked over the ledge. "That fire escape is a pretty big target to miss if your life depends on hitting it."

"Why don't you give it a try?"

Greeley wasn't listening. "There was no reason for him to jump from here. You were over by the door, weren't you? He could have moved a foot to his right and fallen into it blindfolded. When you remember the marks on his neck, there's a lot to recommend the strangle theory."

"Except it's wrong." Lowenkopf met Greeley's ingenuous face with glacial calm. "When I reached the roof he was sitting just where you are on the ledge. He swung his legs over the top, gave me a grin, and jumped. He might even have waved to me." Stupid, he thought, to add that. It was not in his report.

"And then what?" Greeley put his lips together and made a soft sucking sound.

Lowenkopf winced. *If he takes out his pipe, I'll punch him.* "And then nothing. That was the last I saw of him."

"Your theft report said you heard him hitting the railing."

"That's right."

"And a window opened."

"I heard a lot of windows opening. A man had just fallen to his death from the seventh floor—if you've got nothing better than laundry to do, it's worth a look."

"And then what?"

"Goddammit, Homer, I told you—then nothing. There was a crunch when he hit the pavement. Is that what you're fishing for?"

"No scream?"

Was there one? Lowenkopf couldn't remember. But there had to be. What kind of man drops to his death without a sound? Just what was the blond bastard driving at?

Greeley lit up, exhaling smoke and frost.

"All right." Lowenkopf was determined to take this slowly. "So he wasn't conscious when he bounced off the railing. But he was when he went over the ledge. So how did he pass out in the four feet between here and the fire escape?"

"Doesn't sound likely, does it?" Greeley inhaled heavily on his pipe and let the smoke find its own way out. Lowenkopf waited, gazing out over the housing project at the rooftops exposed to a bright, cheerless sky. All the buildings had been erected from identical plans, but each wore a different pattern of black tar and unmelted snow, rising and falling as the heat below had warped the underlying wood. Most sported antennae, twisted uncomfortably to accommodate many users, rusting in perpetuity. The snow piles were stained and peaked with soot from faulty chimneys. On one, a drift had piled against a door, sealing it, and a low curve of snow lay unspoiled in the protection of a wall. From the side of another the snow had been scraped. Two sections of a snowman lay melting side by side in the shadow of a stairwell, abandoned by the hands that had rolled them. Everywhere, the slow, pleasant sound of cold water echoed, dripping on bricks and the dull steel of protuberant water pipes. Lowenkopf pressed the ice on the ledge, and a trickle of water seeped out.

"Which did you hear first—the clang of the fire escape or the window?"

The question shattered the glaze of ice numbing his mind. Memory was painful, so Lowenkopf speculated. "He must've hit the fire escape before anyone came out to see what had happened."

"Your report said the window scraped first."

"Did it? Then I must have been wrong. For crying out loud, Homer, was I wrong about the whole thing? Tell me already and I'll believe you, but we can't keep going around like this."

Lowenkopf winced at the strain in his voice, sorely resentful of Homer's patient delivery. Greeley scanned his partner's face, then examined the toes of his own rubbers in precisely the same manner. "I think I know where we can find out."

There was a stink of turpentine in the sixth-floor hallway, and music, a Latin beat. Lowenkopf wiped the fog from his glasses and followed Greeley to a door at the end of the hall. Greeley pushed the buzzer. No one answered, but the music came from inside, and Lowenkopf thought he heard someone moving. He banged on the door, but received no reply. Greeley brought out his revolver, stepped to the side, and twisted the knob. It opened. They entered a short hallway, with an empty kitchen to the right and an empty living room in front of them. A carpet of paper led to the bedroom, from which the music blared. They moved cautiously to either side of the doorway, from which an old man with large ears suddenly stuck out his capped head.

"What do you want here? You better get out while you can. Before my helper gets back with the cops." The old man retreated to a paint can and snatched up a piece of wood pungent with turpentine and stained with ice-blue paint.

Lowenkopf kept his distance. "What do you need cops for?"

"What do I need them for? A party! What do you think? I need them to report a crime."

"We're police," Greeley intoned gravely, holding up his badge for the old man to squint at.

Lowenkopf grinned amiably. "Where's the crime?"

The old painter pointed with his stick to a spot low on the far wall.

Greeley stooped to investigate. "The telephone jack?" It was the old-fashioned kind that required connection by the telephone company.

"And what do you see coming out of it? No telephone! I'm always the first one in, and I didn't take it."

Lowenkopf joined his partner at the jack. "What makes you think there was one?"

"What kind of people don't put in a telephone?"

Greeley forced open the window and climbed out on the fire escape. "People who don't plan to use the apartment much—maybe not more than once. Doesn't look like it needs a paint job to me."

The painter was adamant. "Contract says a new job for every vacancy. Doesn't matter when we painted it last."

"When did you?"

"Coupla weeks ago."

Lowenkopf admired the trimwork. Ruth always hated his paint jobs. "Nice job. Probably get away with one coat this time. Can't be more than two weeks old."

"Three," the painter corrected.

"Three?"

Footsteps approached on the paper and Lowenkopf went to meet the painter's helper, a wiry young man with white teeth, followed into the apartment by a squat woman with her hair in a sloppy bun. She shuffled after the helper as if she were herding him towards the bedroom, while he turned, smiling at her, and kept his pace.

"What are you doing here? Having a party?" The woman turned to the old man without a break for air. "Why are you sending him for the cops? I don't need cops in my building today, I need painters. Stopping crime is not your job. When the cops come, will they help you paint?"

The old man shoved his helper into the next room. "He's a cop," he informed the landlady.

"Wow," said the helper, reappearing. "That was fast."

"When I want them, they come," the old man said complacently.

The landlady unbuttoned her coat and smoothed the front of her skirt. She wore a wool plaid dress with an orange collar and clean red rubber boots. "So? What now? Heat? I give them all the heat they can stand. Come with me outside, you'll see they keep the windows open, it gets so hot in my units."

"Not the heat," Lowenkopf assured her.

"What then? What do you want?"

He hadn't the least idea.

Right on cue, Greeley climbed in from the fire escape. "We have one or two questions we'd like you to answer, ma'am, about the tenants you rent to here."

"In my building?"

"In this apartment. Who were the people who just moved out?"

She shrugged. "I don't have my book with me."

"How long did they stay?"

"That, too, I need my book to answer."

"Really?" Greeley wondered. "Do many of your tenants rent for one or two weeks at a time?"

The landlady scowled at the painter in the cap, but he was busy with a roller, his back to her. "Now that you mention it, I seem to remember. These people were here for just two weeks."

"And how much of that time did they actually use the apartment?"

"I don't know. I never saw them. Is something wrong?"

Greeley shook his head, eyes averted. "A police matter."

The bastard! Lowenkopf watched him work. If that didn't get to her, nothing would.

The woman looked from one of them to the other of them to the other. Greeley tapped his foot on the tarp. Lowenkopf was about to cave in and say something to reassure her, when the woman brought out a purse from a pocket in her coat. It was a small patent-leather clutch with a dull pearl clasp, from which she drew out a card. "This was all he gave me," she said. "He said to call if anyone asked about him."

Greeley snatched it from her before Lowenkopf could read the name. The woman clutched her throat. "That does it," Greeley told her, his severity quickly evaporating. "You're off the hook. You too, Shelly." He turned to Lowenkopf and held up the card. It read "Cecil Rowe, Esquire. Attorney at Law."

They sat over Styrofoam cups at the counter of a luncheonette on Allerton Avenue. Lowenkopf bought the coffee. He chose the freshest, crumbliest doughnut from a plastic tray standing on the counter and had the girl set it on a plate in front of Greeley. It was a gesture of gratitude, but a vindictive one, since Homer was new at dunking. Lowenkopf chose a smooth plain for himself, dipped it smartly in his cup, and sank his teeth into it. Greeley's hands were still cold and he turned his cup slowly between them.

"Now I'll tell you what you want to know," he offered.

Lowenkopf didn't look up. The doughnut was good. "Go ahead."

"Ask. What do you want to know?"

"I didn't kill Waldo Pepper?"

"Not so far as I can tell." Greeley held his doughnut over his cup. A spray of powdered sugar fell in. "You didn't throw him off that roof, anyway."

Lowenkopf took off his glasses and rubbed his eyes. "So who did?"

"Nobody."

"Then I was right? He jumped?"

"No, he was thrown, all right. But not off that roof."

There was a pattern of silver checks beneath the laminated countertop. Lowenkopf studied it for a while. Suddenly it came together. "Off the fire escape?"

Greeley bit. "Uh-huh."

"You mean they had him waiting down there? Out cold? I came along and they pushed him off. So who was I chasing? Someone hired to get me there. By Keppler?"

Greeley nodded, holding up one hand until he had swallowed the dry sugar. "But why?"

Lowenkopf thought. "It kept Billy Ringo from testifying. To pay Eddie Pepper back for tipping us off."

"It also sent you to Hollywood."

"You think Keppler intended that? It's been a long time since I had anything to thank him for."

"He intended it, all right."

Lowenkopf swiveled on his stool and spread the idea like a napkin before him. "Why send me to Hollywood? To stop me from testifying. But I testified—not very well, I admit, but you're overestimating him if you think he arranged all that B-picture business from three thousand miles away. The briefcase that came and went thirty thousand feet above Milwaukee. The two Eliot Hansens. Do you really think he murdered Hansen just to confuse me?"

"This is a man who throws people face first from sixth-floor fire escapes."

"But Keppler's a killer of the old school. He doesn't play games with briefcases or dress his boys in stewardess drag."

"It worked."

"It's not Keppler's style. You might go undercover as a pimp, Homer, but you'd still be a Brooks Brothers pimp. When I think about all that Hollywood bugaboo, you know what it sounds like? Laurel-and-Hardy stuff. Slapstick comedy."

"Keystone Kops?"

Lowenkopf stopped smiling. "Like *The Taper Caper.*"

Greeley's doughnut came down hard on the lip of his cup. A half-inch piece fell in. He fished it out with his fingers and set it on his napkin belly-up. He extracted another napkin from the dispenser, wiped his fingers, and dropped it discreetly over the soggy brown lump. "The question, it seems to me, is this: who had that tape of you and Carla reading the lines of that script?"

But there was no one to answer. Two quarters still jingled on the countertop, but Lowenkopf was gone.

21

Warren Searle looked up at the bronze mass of Rodin's *Balzac* and crossed his arms. Above the great wrapped shoulders, the French novelist's glaring brows held sway over lanes and fountains and whispering visitors in the Sculpture Garden of the Museum of Modern Art. He had come with Gail Wranawski for one final reconnoiter before the next day's shoot. They had decided to go ahead with the film. Teri's part would be played by a friend of Johnny Weems's in the Auto Show at the Coliseum. Searle paced the length of a brook gurgling between the sculptures. Beyond the high stone wall, carbon monoxide wheezed from the uplifted exhaust pipe of a bus inching its way across Fifty-fourth Street.

Lowenkopf watched them through a glass door behind a bronze goat as Searle shifted his weight from hip to hip, imitating Rodin's great likeness of Balzac. Gail Wranawski stood between the French writer and the American director and compared stances. "You've almost got it now," she told Searle. Noticing Shelly, she called out, "Sergeant Lowenkopf! Are you here for your soul or are you looking for us?"

Searle wore a thick, elaborately knitted sweater and his hands were pale but limber, gesturing to Lowenkopf while he spoke directly to Gail. "Did you know that the French refused to pay Rodin for this when he had finished? They insisted that that preposterous cloak could conceal no human form. They refused to accept the proportions. What they didn't know was that Rodin had shaped the body, then wrapped the cloak around it." He recrossed his arms and mimicked the stance perfectly. "It does seem unlikely, though, doesn't it?"

Lowenkopf thought so. Searle turned to Gail with a patient, inquisitive face, which she seemed to interpret as a question. "I called Johnny a little while ago. Detective Lowenkopf was at the hotel, insisting he see you immediately. He wouldn't tell Johnny anything about it, but was quite certain we would want to be disturbed. Johnny told him where we were."

Searle regarded Lowenkopf. "Have you discovered something?"

"Yes and no," he said, "Tell me, Mr. Searle, when and where did you first meet Cecil Rowe?"

"Cecil Rowe?" Searle turned again to Gail, who was rummaging through her purse for a cigarette. Her penciled eyebrows arched. "I don't know a Cecil Rowe," Searle declared. "Does he know me?"

"He's paying for your movie," Lowenkopf said. "Do you know a Lester Cravit?"

"I know the name of Lester Cravit, though I've never met him personally. About six months ago I received his call. He said he was an attorney who had a client who was interested in backing my next picture—an admirer of an earlier film. As you might know, my last two attempts have not been tremendously successful at the box office, so I was quite taken by his offer. And, I will confess, I was flattered by it. The attorney's name was Lester Cravit, which has appeared with a minimum of complaint on a number of checks I have cashed—not at all unusual in my business, I might add, though I admit it seems unlikely in any other line. Then again, we have Rodin to remind us that what seems unlikely may be true."

Lowenkopf refused to be distracted. "Lester Cravit met with Eliot Hansen two weeks ago. Did you know that?"

Gail placed a cigarette in Searle's lips and one in her own. He unsnapped a lighter in the palm of his hand and lit both of them. "No"—he inhaled—"I didn't."

Point One, Lowenkopf.

"Someone else attended that meeting too. A lawyer named Cecil Rowe. Rowe's principal client is a Bronx businessman who calls himself Keppler most of the time. You don't know that name either, I suppose."

Searle exhaled. "Never heard of him."

"Then answer this," Lowenkopf said, his thumb and index finger like a gun on Searle's chest. "Where were you the night Eliot Hansen was murdered?"

"This is really too much," Searle complained to Gail. "I

couldn't use a line like that in a movie. And I've already answered that question. I was with Johnny, in my trailer, from ten o'clock, when we broke for the night, until midnight at least."

"I don't think so," Lowenkopf said. "Teri Kern gave me a receipt she found in Johnny's pocket from a restaurant midway between the beach and the studio. How do you suppose it got there?"

Searle shrugged. "I haven't the slightest idea."

"But you were together, you said. How could he have been eating with you and dining in Beverly Hills? What were you eating—each other?"

"There's no need for that," Gail interjected.

"Let him speak his mind," Searle said, "such as it is. So—you suspect me, Sergeant. But the bottom line, as the moneymen say, is this: what are you prepared to do about it? If you plan to arrest me, bring out your handcuffs, and my attorney can discuss it with your captain. If not, I think you've interrupted our visit here long enough. Now, which is it going to be?"

Lowenkopf brought out his handcuffs. "I've moved as cautiously as possible, Mr. Searle. Since you insist, I'll have to arrest you for the murder of Eliot Hansen."

A puff of frost escaped Gail's open mouth. "You can't do that."

"Watch me," Lowenkopf said, opening the bracelets with a deft flick of his thumb. Greeley would have been proud.

"Just a minute," Searle negotiated. His mouth was pursed thoughtfully, though his eyes showed strain. "Before you do anything we'll both regret. I see you're serious about this and I respect that, Officer. But you must understand the situation. The picture can carry on without a producer, with a substitute assistant director, and minus one actress, but it can't go on without me."

"Then the world will have to make do with one less Soapy Film."

Searle withdrew his wrist to avoid the cuffs. "This is ridiculous. You must have some vague policeman's idea of human motivation. Why on earth would I have murdered Eliot?"

Lowenkopf caught his wrist and snapped the first cuff shut. "Lovers' quarrel? You were lovers, weren't you?"

"Not for ages." Searle directed his answer towards Gail, who bit her lip and looked away.

"Perhaps you wanted to reconcile and he refused you. Perhaps it was a professional conflict—he was the executive producer of your next film, wasn't he?"

"Yes. The William-and-Mary project. But why would I kill him for that? He got me the job."

"McDonald told me Hansen was replacing you on that picture."

"That little bastard would say anything. It wasn't true."

Gail nodded deeply, vouching for him.

"When I saw Hansen at the studio, he was worried about your budget—you were running into expensive overtime, weren't you? Maybe he discovered something in his meeting with Rowe about your current financing that changed his mind."

For the first time, Searle faltered. "What could he have learned from Rowe?"

"Where the money for this picture came from. Keppler's no angel."

"Eliot wouldn't have cared about that."

"Maybe Rowe told him what you agreed to do for the money."

"What did I agree to do?"

"Set me up for Rowe at the grand jury. You gave me a special tour, so that everything I said would look ridiculous. All the resources you needed were close at hand—the actors, costumes, makeup. You put an actor with Hansen's face on my plane and another dressed in Arabian robes in my bathtub. There must be a thousand actors in your town who would do anything for a shot in your next movie." Lowenkopf neatly braceleted the second cuff. "And you gave Carla's tape to Cecil Rowe. That's what's going to nail you."

Searle raised his manacled hands. "Do you believe this?"

"Believe it." Lowenkopf took him by the arm. "Only a director could have managed it so neatly. All you had to do was lead me from place to place and count on me acting like a cop. But I'll tell you something you don't learn from cop films, Searle: real cops don't admire clever plotting. We just resent the time it costs."

Searle shook his head, a friendly warning. "They'll never buy it."

"They don't have to buy it. That's another thing about cops on the street: we may never really know your motive, and to tell you the truth, we don't give a damn. I don't know what Teri had to do with it, and I may never know. That bothers me. But you got Hansen and we got you. That's all. Miss Wranawski can follow us uptown, if she likes. But you'd be surprised how fast felons lose admirers."

"I'll call Sid," Gail said.

"Wait a minute," Searle directed, "I don't need a lawyer yet. You're jumping to conclusions here, Lowenkopf. All right, I admit I wasn't with Johnny from ten to twelve. I told that story to cover for him, not the other way around. Do you really think that bastard would cover for anybody? He was with someone he shouldn't have been with, and I needed him to finish the film. But that doesn't mean I murdered Eliot."

Gail asked, "Who was he with?"

"I can't answer that."

Lowenkopf rattled his bracelets.

"Robert Culpepper's wife," Searle confessed, grimacing at Johnny's taste.

Gail's purse dropped to her neatly booted feet. "Faith? I can't believe it."

Lowenkopf said, "Come on."

Gail stood in front of him, her hand on Lowenkopf's chest. "Didn't you hear what he just said? Johnny was with Faith Culpepper. Culpepper would have axed him from the William-and-Mary deal, and just about everything else in Hollywood. That's why Warren lied to you."

Searle unshouldered his burden. "I had to sit on it. If you discovered where Johnny was and who he was with, the whole town would have known. That's the way it is where I come from. Gail, am I right?"

"He's right," she confirmed. "No doubt about it."

"Let me get this straight: Miss Wranawski was sleeping with Culpepper while Culpepper's wife was sleeping with

Weems while Hansen was sleeping with his head in the fire. Who put *him* to bed? Maybe Searle here. In my business, we never know anything for sure. And you entered that business when you decided that making movies about murder wasn't enough. Right now there are checks from a killer's lawyer payable to this man—a killer acquitted by a grand jury as a result of my visit with you people. That's point one. Point two: his ex-lover was found dead on the beach two weeks after visiting the same lawyer who appeared in point one. Point three: the alibi Searle gave for the time of the murder has been found wanting."

Gail didn't let go. "Warren? Where were you really that night?"

"In my office."

"Alone?"

"Yes," Searle said miserably.

Gail stood her ground desperately. "There's got to be a mistake here. I've known Warren Searle for at least ten years, and he's not the kind of man to kill anyone. There's something to that, isn't there? A man doesn't just wake up one morning a murderer. It takes planning, and Warren hasn't got it in him."

"I'm a director," Searle objected, professional pride pricked.

Gail touched him tenderly. "I mean *premeditated* violence. Warren could have handled the intricacy, but not the gruesome details. It takes a certain kind of man to kill somebody."

Lowenkopf disagreed. "I've made this trip uptown with every sort of person you can imagine. People entrusted with everything. Psychiatrists. Surgeons. TV repairmen. Even a nun—though she turned out to be innocent. Her mother superior did it."

"Not Warren," Gail insisted.

Lowenkopf pushed her gently aside. "He looks good for it to me." Lunchers in the restaurant were starting to notice.

Searle played his last, desperate card. "You don't understand," he said softly. "I loved Eliot Hansen. I still love him."

Gail's face went white.

Lowenkopf nodded vigorously. "We get lots of lovers. I'd say one in three. Maybe more. Love's our best-selling motive."

"I wasn't his lover," Searle corrected. "But I loved him. Can you understand that? Do you know what it means?"

They were both staring at him. Lowenkopf hated these scenes of horrified resistance. He clenched his teeth to get through them and they dragged interminably. His jaw started to ache and a sharp pain nagged his neck. "Why don't we talk about it on the ride uptown?"

Gail poked his stomach unkindly with a gloved finger. "You've got to feel it in here."

"He doesn't know what love means," Searle told her, defeated.

Lowenkopf snorted and pushed Searle ahead, rubbing his stomach where Gail had poked him. He knew what love meant.

He tried to tell Carla in a coffee shop near her hotel, in the last booth before the rest rooms. But there was a jukebox on the wall between them with tape over its coin slot. When he told her what Searle had asked him, she was flipping the dial and skimming the song titles. When he told her he loved her, she was fixing her hair, while looking in a black circle of glass set between the speakers as a centerpiece.

"What did you say?" Golden curls shimmered in a halo around her.

"I said I loved you," he repeated. The repetition took something out of it.

"I mean before that," she said. "You arrested them *both?*"

"Who?"

"Warren and Gail. Who were you talking about?"

"I was talking about us."

"Before us."

He tried to remember. "No, Gail's not arrested. There's nothing on her. Culpepper's testimony guaranteed her alibi. Especially now, with Searle's dope on Culpepper's wife. The cuckolded husband feels vindicated in his adultery, and doesn't mind telling anyone who'll listen."

"Then you've just arrested Warren."

"That's right."

"Good."

"Why good?"

"You wanted to get your murderer, didn't you? Now you've got him. So it's all over, isn't it?"

Lowenkopf nodded. "But there's something I want to continue. Where we left off on the beach."

She pressed a button on the jukebox. "Shelly, I know what you're going to say, and you really shouldn't."

"I don't think you do."

"Then tell me."

He paused. "What did you think I was going to say?"

"That it looked like we really had something good starting. That it's a long time between looking-goods, and we'd better grab one when it comes."

"There's more."

"That you think if we really tried again, if we pretended that nothing happened with Teri or Homer, we could really make a go of it."

"Not exactly," he said. She waited. "Couldn't we?"

"No," Carla told him. "I couldn't. I don't know how you feel about what I did with Homer, but I'm an old-fashioned girl at heart. When you kissed me like that on the beach, it meant something to me. When I saw you with Teri, it blew me away. I could forgive you, I guess, but I'd never forget that. We could never be the same."

Lowenkopf sank in his booth. "Carla, I was stupid. I admit that. We've both been stupid, but mine was worse because I was first. But that can't be the end. I'm not a young man—I mean, I'm not too young to enjoy life, but I've learned something I don't think you know yet. It's not so easy to start again. I feel something for you I didn't expect to feel again after my wife left me. If you think it's easy for me to say that, you're wrong. I think I can offer you something you're not going to find between the assistant director and the cameraman. Before you came to Hollywood, before you learned what you can and can't hope for, what did you really want? A man who really loves you, wasn't that it? Well, I do. I'm crazy about you."

Her eyes were glued to her hands, spread on the table between them, with bright red nails flaking at the edges. She rubbed an invisible smudge off her left pinkie cuticle. He waited. "Goddammit," she said. Her eyes flickered on his cheek, looked as if they were about to meet his, and widened in what he hoped was emotion. "What the hell is *he* doing here?"

Lowenkopf turned and over his shoulder saw a vague shape in a fur collar slow its forward progress at the sight of his face. Keppler. Behind him, two figures dawdled in the entrance. The skinny kid wore rabbit-lined gloves and had one eyelid half-closed. He drew a cigarette from the pocket of his blue flannel shirt and offered it to the waitress, who snubbed him. He grinned after her, and lit the cigarette with a pearl lighter. Against the wall, Janice lifted the telephone receiver from its cradle and let it dangle free. Keppler considered Carla and Shelly for a minute, then lumbered down the line of booths towards them.

"Lowenkopf," he wheezed. "What a coincidence."

Carla didn't believe it for an instant. Keppler gave her a crooked smile and sat down next to her. Lowenkopf tensed, one hand on Carla's arm and the other on the edge of the table near his open coat.

Keppler beamed at each of them. A little space showed between his teeth. "This is comfortable."

Lowenkopf said brusquely, "What do you want?"

"Cuppa black coffee," Keppler growled in the direction of the counter, but the waitress who stood behind it was reluctant to take the order. The night manager, a slender woman in her middle forties, closed the cash register and set a cup and saucer on the table. Carla shriveled in her corner. Lowenkopf stretched his legs beneath the table and closed them. Keppler ripped open six packets of sugar and poured them all into his cup without stirring. He lifted it and sucked noisily at the lip, holding the saucer beneath to catch spills. "I hate coffee," he said.

"So do I," said Carla emphatically, "but what else can you drink in this weather?" She looked despondently through the front windows at the rainy night. "I wish I were in California," she said.

Keppler nodded, his cup and saucer clattering. "Marvelous state. The fifth-largest economy in the world. When do you intend to go back?"

"In the morning."

It was the first Lowenkopf had heard of it. A shot ran through his belly. In the slow warmth that followed it, he discovered a powerful urge to empty his bladder. He felt Keppler's scrutiny like a heat lamp.

"What do you fly?" Keppler wondered.

"They're all the same to me," Carla said.

Small talk with criminals was never Lowenkopf's forte. He leaned forward and squeezed his knees. The two men in the entranceway jumped at his sudden movement. Janice's hand slipped into his overcoat pocket. Lowenkopf rocked with his knees pressed together, conveying a universal message.

Carla scowled. "Why don't you excuse yourself, Shelly? Mr. Keppler won't mind."

Lowenkopf turned to Keppler, who stared at him and continued to stare until he stood and disappeared behind the door labeled "Knights." Then Keppler leaned across the table and muttered, "You weren't to see him again."

"This is the last time," Carla promised. "He called me. I couldn't refuse to meet him without arousing suspicion. I've told him there's no future for us. He'll see me to my hotel and that will be the end of it."

"I don't like arrangements altered," Keppler mused.

"Nothing will be altered. It all went without a hitch, didn't it? I picked him up at the airport and delivered him in knots to the grand jury. My agent received the William-and-Mary contract this morning."

"You'll sign it this time?"

"Yes."

"Then what is it you want? Money?"

"I'll take a bonus, if you're offering one. But I've got what I want. I don't like altering arrangements either."

"Then what am I doing down here?"

Carla looked into the black glass circle on the jukebox on the wall and fluffed her hair. "I haven't the least idea."

"She's turning this way. Perfect." Greeley adjusted the contrast on the monitor hooked to the video camera he was pointing through the grimy wall of the men's room. Lowenkopf waited outside the stall. Greeley's neat oxford shoe stepped on a cable and slipped beneath the next stall before he caught his balance.

He didn't want to, but asked anyway. "What's she saying, Homer?"

"Everything she has to. The audio's perfect. I never saw a camera with such sharp resolution in low light. Where did you see this camera?"

"Johnny Weems has one in his bedroom."

"I'm impressed. You're traveling in the right circles at last, Shelly. You should see what we're getting here. Gorgeous."

Lowenkopf pressed the tile wall. "For a good time . . ." The rest was under his palm. "Don't miss the two at the door, Homer. The skinny one killed Teri Kern."

Greeley's head emerged from the stall. "Why don't you take a look?"

Lowenkopf leaned on the stall door and Greeley angled the monitor. Behind him, reels of videotape turned. On the screen, Lowenkopf's future was passing before his eyes.

Carla sat up and turned to Keppler. "I didn't ask you here. What are you doing, following us? If he puts two and two together, it will blow the whole plan."

Keppler pulled a crumpled note from his coat pocket and dropped it on the table in front of Carla. She refrained from touching it, so he spread it out. "What is this, then?"

She stared at it blankly, then picked it up. From the angle of the camera, Lowenkopf couldn't read it. But he knew what it said. *Meet me tonight or Lowenkopf will know everything.* A time and the coffeehouse address. *Carla.*

"I didn't send that," Carla swore. In her indignation, she forgot to whisper. Keppler must have made a signal off-camera, because Janice ambled towards them and plopped down in the booth behind his boss.

"Are you sure?" Keppler rasped.

She began speaking fast. "If I did, you can keep the part. Wait, you don't understand—to an actress that's as good as an oath. Why would I go through the whole charade and throw it all away just when it's time to collect?"

"I don't know why you would."

"I wouldn't. I mean, I didn't, I swear I didn't. Believe me—I'm not this good an actress."

Keppler examined a spot between her eyes. "Then *he* did. But why?" He turned towards the men's room, then around the coffee shop. His eyes finally came to rest on the black circle of glass. "Ah-h-h."

"That's it." Greeley grabbed his walkie-talkie from the floor behind the toilet and snarled into it, "The front door's open, boys. Come on in." He tugged Lowenkopf's sleeve. "Come on, partner. The rat's in our trap. Let's get him."

Lowenkopf wasn't in the mood. Under his palm the graffiti continued: ". . . phone home." He put his finger to the stall door and felt the graffiti scratched there. "Fuck Me: 55-something-4902." Below that, "Niger" and, faintly in the corner, "Richard loves Lois."

"Go ahead, Homer. You don't need me. He's not going to bother standing up."

"This is your bust, Shelly. Your man and your plan and you've earned the coup de grace."

Lowenkopf spun his partner around and pushed him out the door. "Go get him, Homer."

When he heard the siren wail outside, he shut the door, sat down on a toilet, and put his head between his hands. The wall shook for a moment. There was a scuffle at the door. He heard Greeley's voice once, sharp: "That's all." Then he moved his hands up over his ears.

He felt a tap on his shoulder. Isabelle stood over him, smoothing the front of her narrow skirt. His sister was a bit nervous in the men's room. "It's over. I thought Tiffany was going to wet herself, but everything went like butter. You guys can work pretty smooth when you have to."

"That's Homer," he said.

"Nice-looking guy." She spit on a square of toilet paper and tried rubbing a particularly sexist remark off the wall. "He said you should come out now if you want to ride with them to the precinct house."

Lowenkopf shook his head.

She dropped the wad of paper neatly in the next toilet and kicked the knob on the wall. As she leaned forward, her hand brushed his shoulder. "It's a shame. She's a nice-looking girl."

He placed his hand over hers.

She looked at it uncomfortably for a moment, then pulled her hand away. "Got to run. Tiff is still shaking, and she's the only one on tonight. Like you asked."

He nodded. "Thanks."

"Glad to do my civic duty. But I've still got to sell some coffee tonight. Don't worry, I'll put the Dolly Doughnut Special in the window. That always brings 'em in."

Lowenkopf sat for another minute on the edge of the toilet seat, then wrapped up his cables and video machines in a large suitcase, which he rolled out the door. As he passed the counter, the waitress was telling the story of the arrest to a pair of taxi drivers dunking doughnuts. He sat down at the last stool and had a Dolly plain.

The one place Lowenkopf could be sure he knew what love meant was Thom's house in Pelham. He had visiting rights only on the weekends. So when he drove up later that night, he parked around the corner and walked along the far side of the street, but when he reached the driveway, he left the path to the front door and squeezed behind the bushes by the side of the house. Sharp twigs pricked his legs as he edged along, moving with a determination tempered only by the need for secrecy.

There was a light in the front window but the living room was empty. Lowenkopf crept further back along the alley, past the side door, and knelt below the closed kitchen window. The screen was still on it, rusting through the winter. He raised his head and peered through the mesh. Inside, Clem was beating Thom ruthlessly at checkers, Thom's three short boardmen surrounded by Clem's legion of kings. Lowenkopf felt a powerful urge to defend his son's position. Listlessly, indifferently, Thom lost one man after another, while Clem reveled in each capture.

It was Lowenkopf's classic stance—witness to an injustice he was powerless to remedy. He rose from his crouch, leaning against the wet timbers of the house. Clem was too caught up in his victory to notice. Thom watched his stepfather set up the board again and dutifully made the first move in another game.

"What the hell are you doing here?" The shock almost drove him through the window. It was Ruth, an empty garbage pail in one hand. She wore a sweatshirt he recognized and a kerchief around her head. She set down the garbage pail and yanked off the kerchief, her honey-colored hair cascading down.

Lowenkopf admired it in spite of himself. "I needed to see the kid," he said.

She glanced through the window at Clem, exulting in his new triumphs, and Thom, watching him with large brown eyes. "He looks pretty good, doesn't he?"

Thom looked up and seemed to focus on the window, sensing his father's presence. Ruth's breath at his shoulder had a singular effect on Lowenkopf. He could smell the familiar scent of her laundry detergent clinging to that sweatshirt he remembered. He breathed it in deeply and said to his wife, "He looks great."

They might have shared a moment had she not said, "Well, you've seen him. Now get lost before Clem spots you. Go home and sleep. You look like the walking dead."

The thought of his apartment, silent and untidy, repelled him. "I've got to stop by the precinct first."

It took him three days to get there. He wobbled in at eleven on the third day, two hours after calling in sick, looking thin and disconnected. His glasses were crooked and he needed a shave. A delicate pattern of creases ran from the elbow of his jacket to the shoulder, where a dark stain hung from his armpit. His pants bagged badly—the same suit, Greeley noticed, he had been wearing in the coffee shop.

Madagascar stood in the doorway of his office. "Well, if it isn't Sherlock Holmes."

Lowenkopf fell in his chair with a rusty twang and put two feet on the desk. His left sock had vanished in his shoe.

Greeley was filling his pipe with cherry-scented tobacco.

"What've we got?" Lowenkopf croaked.

"Not much today," Greeley said amiably. "I'm expecting

a tip from a man on the docks about some Kosher pork chops moving from Brooklyn to Hunt's Point. He said he'd be in touch through this." He held up the personals column from the *Village Voice*. "A letter came for you. Sorry we had to open it, but it was marked 'Urgent' and I thought it might be."

"Aren't you going to tell him what it says?" Madagascar prodded.

Greeley shook his head. "He'll read it."

Lowenkopf accepted the envelope and tossed it on his desk, but the hotel mark in a corner of the envelope caught his eye. "One of ours?"

Greeley folded his newspaper under his arm and headed for the men's room. "One of yours."

The middle of the envelope said "Lowunkopf, NYPD." Above it was scratched in an unsteady hand: *Please deliver ASAP. An innocent man is in jail whose freedom depends on you.*

There were four sheets inside, smelling of powder. The boys in the crime lab had had it already. No date.

Sergeant Lowunkopf, it began, *You were close to the truth but disastrously off the mark. Warren Searle is innocent. He could no more have arranged with your friend Keppler to dupe you than he could have murdered Eliot Hansen. A man with fingernails like his doesn't smash his ex-lover over the head with a piece of wood. Please, let him out of his cell. It's cruel to keep him there. I don't know you well, but I know you're not cruel.*

Lowenkopf needed coffee. His throat was dry.

You have to understand. After Warren's last three pictures, no one in town would let him walk their dog. That's Hollywood. A man makes The Taper Caper, *full of human warmth and a big moneymaker, but three films later they write him off as a loser. You saw him yourself on the set. Do you know what it takes to keep your eyes uncrossed when you've got to deal with Johnny Weems every day? With Eliot sprinkling fairy dust on cast and crew? Warren has patience for them all—I don't know how but thank God he does, because there isn't a less temperamental man alive.*

This was not what Lowenkopf wanted to read.

But that isn't what you want to read. Listen: Keppler put up the money for The Next to Die. *Lester Cravit doesn't know who he is. Or he didn't when we made the arrangement. Cravit's like a lot of lawyers—happy to sit on your money and eat celery. But Warren never had anything to do with it. Never. He got a call from Cravit one day with an offer to finance his film, and why should he have looked a gift horse in the mouth? Lots of movies are paid for with unreported income from cash businesses, hardware stores in Brooklyn and the garment district of Manhattan. These moneymen are called angels only because you pray for one.*

"I pray" had been written and crossed out.

Cecil was on the Coast representing one of the unions in a contract negotiation. I met him through Culpepper and we went out once or twice. He looked like East Coast Money, so I talked up the movie business. He listened with half an ear and I thought I'd lost him, when all of a sudden he offers to back a project I thought looked good—that was to get me—if the director was willing to make an arrangement. I had Warren in mind all along, of course, but I didn't like the sound of this arrangement. Warren's a bit delicate in some areas. But Rowe was willing to deal with me.

All I had to do was gaslight a New York cop—keep you chasing imaginary people and so on. He couldn't have chosen better than a casting director. I snapped my fingers and there were actors willing to play the sheik in your bathtub and Eliot Hansen on your phone. I set you up and like a charm you fell for it—I'll never forget the expression on Eliot's face when you attacked him on the lot. I made all the preparations ten days before your arrival, when Eliot was in New York.

At that time I didn't know what the whole thing was for. Eliot told me. One thing you should know about him—he was a prick. We knew each other for a long time—he was Warren's lover when Warren and I went to school together— but I've never been able to stomach Eliot for more than half an hour at a time. Warren used to make us sit through horrible lunches together, the three of us. It's a testament to Warren's loyalty that he kept me with him picture after picture despite Eliot's cattiness.

The irony is that Eliot, who actually crawled into bed with Warren, was jealous of me, who couldn't. He tried to make Warren throw me over a few times, even after their split.

That's what he was trying to do with the information he picked up from Cravit in New York. He would have gone straight to Warren, but he couldn't be sure Warren would hate me for it, so he took a more devious approach. He tried to force me to jump ship by threatening to expose me to Warren. He figured I'd rather have Warren's respect than the job. He was right—but then he knew more about the arrangement than I did. Eliot laid it all out—who Rowe worked for, why they wanted you misled, everything. He was always good at digging things up. He tried to blackmail me. I told him I had to think about it. He agreed to meet me near his restaurant on the beach. That was the day you arrived.

Greeley announced his return with a jangle of pocket change. He waited for Lowenkopf to acknowledge him. Lowenkopf didn't look up.

Greeley folded his newspaper twice the long way. "Did you ever read these personals? Listen to this: 'Woof-woof, you slack-jawed coyote, come home. Mama's on the range, hungry and alone. Oo-o-oh.' What kind of love note is that?"

I decided to kill him. After your scene on the lot that day, I knew you'd be trailing Eliot, so I needed a disguise. It's a closely held secret, but Johnny Weems is going bald. In public, he wears a wig. He's got a few of them, slightly different shades of red. I knew one of his wigs was in his trailer on the lot. I also knew he'd never report its disappearance. I wore loose running clothes to hide my shape—not that I've got the biggest boobs in the world to start with. When you put the lettering on the jacket together with the wig and fingered Johnny for the murder, it gave Warren something to use on his temperamental star. At least I gave him that!

The exclamation point ran into the next line of script.

An alibi was simple. I got Robert Culpepper to ask me out and take me to a very public hotel. I made a lot of noise going in, and slipped him a Mickey as soon as I saw his shorts. One thing you can trust in a man is his vanity. When I got back, I crawled into bed and told him it had been great for me. Which do you think he chose to remember—that he'd fallen asleep or that he'd been wonderful?

But what is this—gossip—to you? You want to hear about Eliot. When I parked my rented car in the lot, I headed straight for the beach. Eliot used to walk there after dinner. As I drew near, I saw him by the fire, talking to two men. I assumed they were two of his waiters come to play footsie in the sand. But the two others swam out to a boat offshore. I crossed the sand and felt it was going to be an easier interview than I had anticipated.

When I approached, he was throwing bits of wood into the fire. He asked what I had decided to do—he didn't even look up at me! I told him I hadn't known why Rowe wanted you framed. He said, "That's bad luck, isn't it?" He was a pig.

There was a pile of firewood behind me. The top piece had a nail sticking out of it. I picked it up and sat down. I said, "Eliot, you know why I did what I did—because Warren wouldn't do it for himself."

"That's just why he's not going to forgive you for it," he said. Then he called me some filthy names. He was on his knees, poking the fire. He reached forward to drop a twig into the flames—called me another vile name—I let my piece of wood fall on his head. It felt wonderful. He fell straight into the pit.

I dropped the wood and ran. I was exhilarated—I don't know why. It was like slaying a dragon. I could smell . . . there was a rush of clear air on the beach—you must have felt it. You were there too.

Lowenkopf swallowed, with difficulty.

You have been led, or misled, since your first moment in Hollywood. But Eliot's death wasn't part of Keppler's plan. It gave you something real to investigate. You were supposed to be chasing only shadows. When Keppler found out that Hansen had been killed, he knew who had done it and was angry. He didn't want the murder investigation discovering me and then his plan. He sent someone to finish me off, to tie up loose ends. Only I wasn't in my hotel room when he arrived. Teri was. Keppler didn't know about Hansen until you told Lester Cravit, who told Cecil, who told Keppler at the zoo. So you and I killed Teri together.

There were two false starts, blackened out. Then darker, more pressure on the pen.

That scared me. I'm scared now. There's more going on that I can explain. Someone else must be involved in Keppler's plan too. The paragraph broke. Beneath that was written: *Check out Carla Hollie. I've never known her to give it away before, and her sudden attraction to your partner was very convenient for Teri's murderer.*

At the next desk, Greeley laughed softly.

Please tell Warren I'm sorry for what I did—for the murder—for the way everything worked out. The film is going to be wonderful—Warren's the best in the business. The best. I'm sorry—I don't know what to say—Warren, you know, you know, I'd never do anything to hurt you—I . . .

The rest was blocked out, scribbled over. Underneath, in capital letters was written: LOWUNKOPF, PLEASE DON'T EVER LET HIM READ THIS. PLEASE. It was signed at the bottom of the page, "Abigail Wranawski." A for Abigail.

Lowenkopf creased the pages and returned them to their envelope. Greeley was watching him, a thumb keeping his place in the ads, ready to read another aloud. Lowenkopf said, "Did you bring her in?"

Greeley shook his head. "Midtown picked her up. The maid found her yesterday in the bathtub with her veins opened. The letter was taped to the mirror on the medicine cabinet."

"Where's Searle?"

"They released him last night."

"Did he see this?"

"I didn't show it to him."

"It's going to have to come out, though, isn't it? To get Rowe and the others?"

"I should think so."

Lowenkopf sank in his chair. "You know, Homer," he said, "I called in sick this morning. I was right."

Greeley nodded without lifting his eyes from the page. "It's a shame, all right. Let me read you something."

He never got his chance. The chair was still squeaking, but Lowenkopf wasn't in it. He heard Greeley's dry chuckle fade behind him, and through the glass saw Madagascar readjust his pillow and bite down hard on his Turkish cigarette. Lowenkopf needed air, and a dark place.

The hallway was dark. There was a rain of typing, the sweet smell of alcohol, black shoes scuffling dirty tile. A woman in a brief leather skirt wept at the window. On a hard bench, a boy sat beneath the flashing white cuffs of an